# Promise Me Tomorrow

# PROMISE ME TOMORROW

## LINDA INGMANSON

**FIVE STAR**

*A part of Gale, Cengage Learning*

GALE
CENGAGE Learning™

Detroit • New York • San Francisco • New Haven, Conn • Waterville, Maine • London

Set in 11 pt. Plantin.
Printed on permanent paper.

**LIBRARY OF CONGRESS CATALOGING-IN-PUBLICATION DATA**

Ingmanson, Linda.
    Promise me tomorrow / by Linda Ingmanson. — 1st ed.
        p. cm.
    ISBN-13: 978-1-59414-651-0 (alk. paper)
    ISBN-10: 1-59414-651-9 (alk. paper)
    1. First loves—Fiction. 2. Homecoming—Fiction. I. Title.
PS3609.N466P76 2008
813'.6—dc22                                                    2007041355

First Edition. First Printing: March 2008.

Published in 2008 in conjunction with Tekno Books.

Printed in the United States of America
1 2 3 4 5 6 7 12 11 10 09 08

To my husband, for putting up with me.
I love you, sweetie.

# CHAPTER ONE

Only one person had the power to leave Abby McGuire speechless, and she thought she'd seen the last of him six years ago.

But no. There he stood, hard and dark as the waking edge of a bad dream.

"Ashton Wheeler." Abby nixed the awe in her voice with a frown—which helped to close her hanging jaw. She folded her arms across her chest for good measure and stiffened her spine. If she held his stare, maybe he wouldn't notice how her knees had begun to shake.

She'd breezed into the Cranberry police department expecting to see . . . well, anyone but Ash standing behind his brother's desk. She would ask what the heck he was doing here, except she couldn't stand it if her voice trembled again.

One side of his mouth tightened a fraction. Those criminally sensual lips curved just enough to rivet her eyes on them. Could be a smile. Could be a grimace. Was he as shocked to see her as she was to see him? Cool gray eyes assessed her. Nothing shocked Ash. How could she forget?

"No one's called me Ashton since . . ." His deep voice curled around her like smoke. Ash had that way of speaking, low and slow, as if every word were fashioned for her ears alone. Then he sloped a smile, and her traitorous heart twisted. "Abby. It's been a long time."

Not long enough for her racing pulse. After so much time, she would've thought—hoped—she would be free of Ash's spell.

She wasn't the same naive twenty-one year old who had believed her love alone would hold him. She slipped her fingers into the pocket of her white shorts, seeking the smooth comfort of the worry stone she kept there. Somewhere down the hall of the cramped police department, a phone jingled. A cracked, tan air conditioner gurgled against the late June heat and churned out a chilly stream that raised goosebumps on her bare legs and brought her back to reality.

She squared her shoulders. "I'm here to see Pete." Ash's brother, golden-haired, blue-eyed, angelic-by-comparison Officer Pete. Abby held up the envelope that had been warming under her arm. "My aunt got this letter about the new sign in front of her store. They say it violates town ordinances and has to come down."

"Can't fight city hall," he said with an ironic grin, but he reached to take the letter.

Abby pulled it back. "I'd rather show it to Pete. He's got friends on the town council. He promised he'd talk to them for me."

Ash shoved his hands into the pockets of his stone-washed, button-fly jeans. Though why her gaze was wandering low enough to notice he wore button-fly was beyond her.

"He's out on a call. Are you sure I can't help?"

"Not unless you're working here now."

He held out his hand again. "It's your lucky day. I just started."

"You're kidding." Ash, back in the hometown he'd once professed to hate? And why wasn't he in uniform? "What happened to Los Angeles? I thought—"

"I'm taking a break." He wiggled his fingers, beckoning the letter into his broad palm. After a heartbeat's hesitation, she laid it there.

He pulled the white sheet of paper from the torn envelope

and bent his head to read it. The overhead lights painted softly gleaming patterns on his dark hair. He wore it so short now, an almost military cut. Eight years ago, it had been past his shoulders, a pirate's flag that bannered out behind him as he pushed his old dirt bike to ungodly speeds. He'd trimmed it when he started college, but there had still been enough for her to sink her fingers into. Thick, resilient hair, the kind women envied. It had been soft against her cheek, against her breast—

"Just how big is this sign?" He glanced up. Startled, Abby blinked.

"Not so very big." She stretched her arms awkwardly, which in any case were too short to adequately demonstrate the size of the shiny new sign on the rooftop of Lucy's Deli. Exasperated, she let her arms drop. "Aunt Lucy had it all checked out and approved before she installed it, I'm sure." Well, pretty sure. "It's almost like someone in town has it out for her."

"Who?"

"I don't know, but lately everything's gone screwy. Last week, someone spray painted graffiti on the side wall. Then a rock came through the front window."

"Was anyone hurt?"

"No, it happened at night." Abby let out a tense breath. "No witnesses, of course."

"Most likely this letter and the vandalism aren't related."

She scowled at him.

"Abby," he said, a warning in his tone, familiar even after all the years of separation.

She shrugged off her irritation. "What other explanation could there be?"

He folded the letter and shook his head. "Is Lucy working today?"

"No. I left my friend Miranda in charge." Lucy was at the doctor's. Abby dropped her gaze, afraid he'd see the concern in

9

her eyes. "Just tell Pete to stop by later, will you?"

"I'm here. I'll come with you."

"You?"

"I won't bite," he said with a grin that promised otherwise.

Goosebumps flashed over her skin. Ash always had been walking temptation. Guess he hadn't lost his touch, not with her at least. Abby dug her nails into her palms. The door was right there. She could walk away. But his perceptive gray eyes held hers, and curiosity jangled like an unanswered phone. Sure, that was all it was, this adrenaline coursing through her. Curiosity. Right?

"What could you do?" she said. "I mean, Pete could handle it."

"Somehow I don't think you're on the top of his list."

As she'd suspected. Pete had been taking his sweet time about things. That was the reason she'd come in person today.

"Let me check out the sign," Ash said as if reading her mind, "take a look at the damage done by that rock. I'll report back to Peter and put a fire under him tonight."

Well, having Ash, who could be pushy as a bull, in her corner might actually help matters. Wanting to stare her fill at him or get to the bottom of his unexpected return, of course, had nothing at all to do with her decision.

"I . . . I guess that would be okay." After all, what had happened between them was long over. They should be able to deal with each other as two neutral adults.

"Did you walk or drive?" he asked, coming around the desk.

Abby took an involuntary step back. "I walked." She'd forgotten how tall he was, and broad, and imposing. Seemed like she'd forgotten a lot of things.

Just as she turned for the door, Pete came in. His eyes narrowed. His gaze darted between her and Ash. "Abby, can I help you?"

The differences between the two brothers struck her then. Ash, lean and muscular; Pete, already a little soft around the middle, and the fast-food bag in his hand promising to help him down that road. Most of all, the energy in the room sparked and leapt between Ash and Pete. If Abby had been shocked to see Ash, Pete seemed none too happy to have his brother home.

She smiled to ease the sudden tension in the air. "Ash was going to walk over to the store with me, to take a look at something."

"At what?" Pete plopped his lunch on his desk. The salty aroma of a burger and fries spread like an oil slick.

"Aunt Lucy's new sign. Your pals at city hall say it's too big." She wanted to show him the letter but realized Ash still held it and didn't look as if he was going to surrender it any time soon. Ash laid the flat of his palm against her lower back. His gentle, insistent pressure nudged her toward the exit.

"You're not a cop here," Pete said to his brother, displeasure clear in his tone.

"I'll take care of her, Peter."

"You have no—" Pete's last protest was cut off when Ash closed the door behind them.

Abby turned to face him. "You did say you were working here, didn't you?"

He lifted a shoulder. "Okay, so I'm filing and answering phones. It's temporary. Still want me to come with you?"

Of course, it had been his suggestion, not hers, that he walk with her, but with her body still humming from the touch of his hand and her curiosity burning like an itch, Abby said, "I don't see why not." When really, she saw a million reasons why not to let Ash Wheeler get involved. She had to be nuts.

He stepped past her and held open the outer door. They walked out into the late afternoon sunshine. Ash fell into comfortable step beside her.

"How long have you been back?" she asked.

"Only a few days." His gaze swept over her, as tangible as a silk scarf drawn across her skin. "You look the same."

"You look . . ." Not the same. Harder. Heavier through the chest, more muscled in the arms. His jaw seemed more prone to tense, his stride more purposeful. Like a seasoned warrior instead of the young rebel she'd once known.

"Older?" he filled in helpfully when the silence gathered.

"Different. Your hair—" She tamped down the urge to lift her fingers to his temple. "Where'd it go?"

He pushed his palm over the dark brush of hair. "I donated it to science."

That startled a laugh out of her. "I wouldn't put it past you."

"Yours is even longer."

His softly spoken appreciation made her aware of the dark gold waves bouncing against her shoulder blades as she walked. Self-consciously, she reached behind her head and drew it over her opposite shoulder. As if that would protect her from the impact of his gaze. Walking with Ash, feeling his arm brush against hers—accidentally?—raised all sorts of memories and raw emotions she was in no shape to deal with. Thank goodness her aunt's store was only a few blocks away, on the right side of Main Street under the sheltering bower of a hundred-year-old oak.

"There," she said on an exhale, and pointed to the green and gold sign on the roof. "That doesn't look so big, does it? No bigger than the Supermart's."

It seemed to take an effort on Ash's part to draw his gaze away from her. He tipped his head as if measuring. "It's, uh, eye-catching."

Abby frowned. Okay, so maybe, on closer inspection, the sign did look a little . . . overblown.

"Does it really matter? For heaven's sake, Lucy grew up here,

12

everyone in town loves her, and her store is a town landmark. Shouldn't someone cut her a little slack?"

"Ash Wheeler! Ye gods, is that really you?"

Aunt Lucy, gripping the railing, came step by careful step down the store's front stairs. Her gingerly pace belied the excitement sparkling in her bright blue eyes.

Abby wanted to groan. Her stubborn aunt was supposed to be at her doctor's appointment. What could have happened this time? She moved to take hold of her aunt's frail arm. "What happened to your appointment with Dr. Herbert?" she whispered so Ash wouldn't overhear.

Before Lucy could answer, Miranda came out of the store with her new baby, Mae, snuggled in her arms. Her eyes went round when she spied Ash. For the last couple of years, Miranda had been on Abby's case to start dating, and Abby could just about hear the wheels turning in that pretty brunette head. The only person more given to preaching than a reformed smoker was a happily married woman who couldn't believe her buddies shouldn't be similarly blessed, whether they wanted that blessing or not.

When her friend reached them on the sidewalk, Abby made hasty introductions. "Thanks for watching the store," she said to Miranda.

"No problem. There weren't any customers." Miranda bounced Mae and swapped smiles with Ash. Mae reached out to him with sticky fingers. Abby rolled her eyes. Was there anything female not attracted to the man? Cupping Miranda's elbow, she pulled her down the sidewalk a few feet.

"When did Lucy get back?"

"Oh, not five minutes after you left." Her brows furrowed. "Should I have called you?"

"No, it's okay." Abby always seemed to be the last to know things. Why should anything change now?

The grin flirted back to Miranda's lips. "Call me later." She wiggled her eyebrows and whispered, "Your friend seems nice."

"Don't let appearances fool you." She kissed Mae on the top of her fragrant, downy head. Miranda walked to her car.

Abby turned, ready to confront Lucy, but Ash had gone to greet her aunt. The sight of six-foot-something Ash bending down to hug the tiny, elderly woman coaxed a reluctant smile from Abby.

Lucy's gnarled fingers patted Ash on the shoulders when he straightened. "My goodness, boy, you've put some meat on those bones. I always said you were too skinny. Doesn't he look good, Abby?"

"He looks . . . healthy," she conceded.

Ash turned his gaze on her, and Abby stiffened. A question hovered in his eyes, one she wouldn't answer. Had he felt Lucy's thinness when he hugged her? Her aunt's uncertain health was a secret. Knowing how gossip spread in the small town, Lucy had asked Abby to keep it under her hat. Protecting Lucy, protecting the little deli that she counted on for her future, was Abby's top priority.

Yet something in Ash's gray eyes tugged at Abby to share her burden. She was getting desperate for help. Even Pete seemed to be dragging his heels. But she couldn't let herself open up to Ash any more than was necessary. She'd made that mistake six years ago, and he'd broken her heart.

She'd never make that mistake again.


Ash helped Lucy back up the stairs. Abby followed at his heels. Her tense silence pressed at him. She was as prickly as ever, and, he had to admit, more beautiful. Her cocoa eyes assessed him warily, but with a woman's curiosity that hummed like an electric current through his body. Her hair had deepened to the golden brown of hot buttered toast. She'd grown into the sleek curves of a body that had matured well ahead of her innocence.

He'd been her first lover. Now . . . Had she had others? Of course, she must have. He was surprised at how easily the question rose in his mind, and even more surprised at how the thought disturbed him. He had no right to be angry with anyone but himself. Certainly not with Abby. Even now he couldn't look into her eyes and not remember her pain when he'd told her he was leaving and swore to never come home to Cranberry.

The memory sobered him. He took his hand from Lucy's shoulder. The old gal didn't look too good. The pall of age hung on her like fog, even though her eyes were just as bright as he remembered. Sad to think of time catching up with her. Somehow, he'd always thought of this place, this graceful old woman, as being eternal. Maybe that's why they said you couldn't go home again. It hurt too much to see the things and people you love disappearing down the river of time.

"How've you been, Lucy?"

"Oh, well enough." She turned to him and smiled. "Come on in. Nothing's changed a whit since you left."

"I believe it. Nothing in Cranberry ever changes."

Abby, who'd never been good at hiding her emotions, brushed by him, her soft lips pressed in a line. He caught her by the wrist while Lucy went on ahead through the door.

"What's the matter with Lucy?" he whispered.

Those fine brown eyes sparked defensively. "She's getting on, that's all."

"Abby—"

"Coming, you two?" Lucy called out through the door.

He glanced up to see her beaming at them. Her thoughts were clear on her gentle features: Abby and Ash, together again, and it made her happy. Inside his chest, Ash's heart felt as hard as the stone that had smashed through the deli's storefront window. Whatever feelings he and Abby once had for each other

15

were long dead. He wasn't even sure now he was capable of feeling tender emotions again. Not after what he'd been through in Los Angeles.

He dropped Abby's arm and went into the store.

At once, familiar smells wrapped around him: the tang of dill pickles from the big, iron-bound wooden barrel in front of the deli; the spicy scent of salami and sausage; the mustiness rising from the plank fir floor warmed by golden sunlight streaming through the side windows. A basket of lollipops in rainbow hues sat by the antique brass cash register. His fingers itched to pilfer a couple sweets as he'd done a thousand times as a child.

Lucy had never said anything, and he'd even managed to believe he was getting away with something. But she'd known. She'd also known he was a lonely, troubled kid bucking the rules of a tough dad, living in the shadow of his brother, who could do no wrong in his parents' eyes.

He tipped his gaze to Lucy, who nodded as if she knew every thought going through his mind. She smiled and the years lifted away. He was twelve again, skipping school on an early summer day, coming by to bug Auntie for an odd job to earn a buck. She never turned him away or turned him in, just quietly urged him to do the right thing.

In the end, he had, and lost everything because of it. Including Abby, who swept by him now on her way to the counter, her back straight and proud, her hips swaying with a charming blend of sensuality and defiance. As if to say, "Look at what you could have had."

"Abby," Lucy said, patting her niece on the shoulder, "make Ash a nice sandwich."

He managed a smile for her and took a seat on one of the tall stools. "Thanks, Lucy."

Her brows drawn, Abby went behind the counter and began to slap the sandwich together. Seedless rye, roast beef, hot mustard, red onions. Damn, she remembered! She hadn't even had to ask.

She plopped the sandwich onto a plate and slid it over to him. "What are you smiling at?"

"Nothing." Then he couldn't resist. "You remembered how I like it."

A hot blush raced over her cheeks. Oh, man, he hadn't meant . . . But red was a nice color on her. He chuckled. "I meant the sandwich."

"Oh." She swiped her hands together then pressed her palms to her cheeks. "I knew that."

He sank his teeth into the sandwich. A whole new flavor of memories rushed over his palate. He closed his eyes and savored paradise. "Abby, you still got it."

She put a hand on her hip. "Really? And how would you know?"

"I guess I wouldn't. Although I have a good imagination."

Whatever color had dimmed from her face flamed back. She tossed her hair over her shoulder and turned away, giving him an unintended but delightful view of her curvy rear. He'd have to be dead not to respond to her. This was Abby. His Abby. He'd slid his hands down those long, bare thighs, tasted her summer-warm skin. His body heated like a racehorse champing at the bit, longing to pick up where they'd left off.

A soft hand on his shoulder startled him. Lucy asked, "Are you living home again, Ash?"

He shook his head, more to clear his thoughts than to deny the answer. "Only temporarily. I'm visiting for a few days before I take off again."

"What a shame. I was hoping you'd decided to come home."

"You know me, Auntie. I don't like to put down roots."

Lucy glanced at Abby as if in sympathy, which made Ash cringe.

17

"You always were the restless sort," Lucy said, her pale blue eyes meeting his. "You have to follow your heart. I understand. But tell me, what made you leave California?"

"Uh, things just didn't work out."

"Your father said you were doing wonderfully well as a police officer in the city. He was so proud when you got that commendation."

Ash hid a grimace around a mouthful of sandwich. "Being a cop there was good while it lasted, but I'm thinking of trying my luck somewhere else."

Lucy squeezed his shoulder. "There's always a place for you here. You're always welcome. Isn't that right, Abby?"

Not in her life, not anymore. Abby stopped staring at Ash. "Auntie, can I talk to you for a minute? I think we're running out of hot mustard."

"But I'm sure I ordered some." The tiny lady bustled toward the end of the counter, muttering about deliverymen and their unreliable schedules. Abby herded her into the back room.

Closing the door behind them, Abby relaxed the bunched muscles in her shoulders. Leaving Ash behind felt like stepping from blazing sunlight into cool shade. She shook off her tension with a sigh and focused on her aunt. "Auntie, you're supposed to be at Dr. Herbert's. It took a month to get an appointment."

Lucy gazed up at her with mock-innocent eyes. "Was that today, dear?"

"You know it was. You promised you'd go."

"But who would run the store?"

"Don't try that old line on me." Abby set her hands on her hips. "Miranda was ready to cover for an hour or two. I knew I should've driven you myself."

"I've really been feeling much better lately."

"You don't look better." Abby pursed her lips at her aunt's

18

crestfallen expression. "I'm sorry, but I'm worried."

"Don't be." She tidied her silver-blue hair with prim fingers. "I've made it this far, I'm tough. They'll have to shoot me twice to get rid of me."

It was an old joke that had seemed a lot funnier when Lucy was well. "I'll have to reschedule that appointment."

"Oh, don't bother. I'll do it when I get home. I could've sworn it was for next Tuesday . . ." Lucy trailed off and turned to the stocked shelves. "Now where was that mustard?"

"Auntie, will you at least please go home and get some rest?"

"What would I do there? I'd just be bored. Unless—" Lucy turned back to her, hands poised in the air, eyes bright. "You'd like to have some time alone with Ash. Of course, dear."

Abby almost choked. "No. That's not it—"

"It is good to have him home again, isn't it?"

"Ash Wheeler doesn't have a home. He's just drifting through."

"Every man wants a home and family."

"My father didn't."

Lucy sighed. "If he wasn't so driven to save the world, I'm sure my brother-in-law would be just as much a homebody as I am." Her smile eased the sting of a touchy subject. "I can tell Ash is happy to see you again. You two were always so close."

"That was a long time ago." The nostalgic tone of Lucy's words alarmed Abby. "Don't get your hopes up. Ash proved what kind of man he is, and I'm smart enough to learn from my mistakes. I don't want anything to do with him."

The mistake himself poked his head around the door at exactly that moment. Abby's stomach flopped and sank. Had he overheard? Oh, what did it matter?

"Customers," he said. His cool gray eyes held hers a moment too long.

He had heard. She just knew it.

19

"You go on," Lucy said. "I'll find that spicy mustard."

The mustard had just been a ploy to get her aunt out of Ash's hearing, but maybe it was better if she let her putter around back here while Abby took care of business.

She brushed by Ash without a glance. Already the man was in her way, underfoot. Didn't he have police business to attend to? The young couple at the counter wanted sandwiches, which she made on automatic pilot. Without glancing up, she felt Ash's gaze on her. What did he want? An explanation?

She wrapped the grinders in brown deli paper and taped them shut. "Anything else?" she asked the teenaged boy who was waiting. Waiting, and mooning at his little girlfriend. He was apparently in too much of a romantic haze to hear Abby. He whispered something in his girlfriend's ear. She giggled. They were so cute, so innocent, it was . . . depressing.

Had she and Ash looked that way once?

Feeling absurdly old, Abby tallied back their change then watched the pair walk, hand in hand, into the sunshine. The bell over the door jingled in their wake.

Ash leaned a forearm on the counter and gazed up at her. "Young love."

"They'll learn."

She kept her back to him while she gathered up the long, sharp bread knife and cutting board. When she turned and nearly bumped into the wall of his chest, she gasped. He caught the falling knife neatly before it sliced off her toe. He handed it back to her, handle first.

"Have dinner with me tonight," he murmured.

He'd ask her such a question when she had a knife in her hand? "No. Thank you."

"As friends," he said, moving out of her way.

"I don't think it would be a good idea."

Crossing his arms, he canted back against the counter. "I'm

only in town for another week. I want to see you."

She lifted her hands and tipped her head. "Here I am. Now you've seen me."

"Can't we catch up on old times?"

"Old times are best forgotten."

"I heard what you told your aunt," he said, his voice low. "We should talk."

Abby forced a final smile. "Good luck with your new job, wherever it is, whatever it is. Have a nice day." Here's your hat, what's your hurry, don't let the door hit you on the way out. Please, Ash, leave, she silently begged, before she did something dumb like say yes.

Disappointment darkened his face. "Okay." He pushed upright with a fluid motion. "Can't blame a guy for trying. Look, I'll check out this sign business—"

She'd forgotten all about it. She rubbed her fingers over her forehead. "Let Pete handle it."

"I can—"

From the back, there came a crash and a bang. Abby gasped and spun toward the sound.

"Lucy?" Oh, God, no. Pulse rocketing, Abby raced toward the room. Ash was quicker. He swung through the door ahead of her.

Abby's world froze when he went down on one knee beside her aunt, sprawled unconscious on the dusty floor.

# CHAPTER TWO

Ash turned to Abby and told her to call 911. His voice sounded miles away. Instead of doing as he'd said, she ran to Lucy. The indignity . . . The aberrant impression struck her first, to see her aunt with her always-tidy floral-print dress in disarray, her usually cheerful face still and gray, looking much older than her sixty-eight years.

Oh, God. Abby touched Lucy's arm and murmured her name. A shape shifted at the edge of her vision: Ash, a dark blur, rising as if in slow motion, going for the phone.

*It's my fault, my fault,* Abby chanted silently. She should have driven Lucy to Dr. Herbert's. Swamped with helplessness, she stroked Lucy's thin hair back from her forehead, held her limp hand, tried to rub some life back into it. Then Ash came beside her. He pushed away some fallen cans and an overturned stool and tried to rouse Lucy.

"Her pulse feels strong," he said, "and she doesn't seem to be having trouble breathing. I think she might have taken a tumble off the stool and pulled the boxes down on top of her. An ambulance is on the way."

His calm voice penetrated Abby's panic. Thank God for his police training. If only she could be so calm. Clutching Lucy's hand to her chest, she nodded and bit back tears.

The ambulance parked at the curb and the back doors swung open. While the paramedics strapped Lucy onto the gurney, Ash filled them in on what he knew and coaxed Lucy's medical history from Abby. As she listed the medications her aunt took and her health issues, Ash's dark brows drew down. So much for Lucy's privacy.

They followed the medics outside and watched the ambulance pull from the curb, sirens wailing. Only then did Abby realize Ash's arm was looped around her waist, supporting her, as he must have been doing from the moment the paramedics showed up. Weak-kneed, she bowed her head to hide her quivering chin.

"I'll drive you to the hospital," he said.

She nodded, all the fight drained out of her. "I'll have to put a sign in the window." She risked glancing at him. God, she'd really fallen apart. If Ash hadn't been there . . . She masked her emotions with a strangled laugh. "Lucy won't like that the store is closed for the day."

One side of his mouth curved as he slid his hand to her hip. "She'll be okay, Abby. It's probably only a mild concussion."

"Only . . ." Abby sniffled and turned from the comforting strength of his grip. She didn't deserve it. "We can take my car. It's the red Saturn around back. The key is under the driver's mat."

The tension in Ash's jaw eased, and Abby realized he'd expected her to refuse his help and say she'd drive alone. And of course, that would be best. Maybe she should. But even as she locked up the store and left the "Closed" sign in the window, Abby keenly felt his absence.

Despite every lick of common sense crying for caution, she said a silent prayer of thanks that he'd been beside her.

"How long has Lucy been having problems?" Ash asked.

Against her protests, he'd dragged her out of the waiting room and down to the hospital cafeteria. They sat at a nondescript table, eating white bread sandwiches off of paper plates. Abby looked like hell. He could only imagine the strength

23

of will she exerted to keep from bursting into tears. He'd tried to get her to talk, but nothing had penetrated her sorrow.

He reached across the table and covered her hand with his. Her fist tightened, small and uncertain as a child's in his grip. "We have a few minutes," he murmured. When she glanced at him, he leveled his gaze at her, forbidding her to drop her chin and avoid him. "Eat, Abby. If nothing else, it'll give you something to do other than watch the clock."

"I can't help it." She lifted half the sandwich, put it down again. "Why couldn't they let me stay with her?"

Around them, the hospital cafeteria hummed with steady business. Outside, the sky was darkening. Ash didn't want to admit it, but it did seem as if the doctors had been with Lucy a long time. The initial examination made the doctor suspect she might have broken her hip. That would mean surgery. Ash felt the sting of helplessness and wished there was more he could do to ease Abby's mind.

He sat back in the flimsy plastic chair. "I think I recognized one of the docs from when I fell off my dirt bike years ago and needed stitches. Lucy is in good hands. Besides, look at the bright side. At least we were there when she fell. She got help right away."

Abby moved her head in an automatic nod. He knew she was numb, agreeing with him without really hearing what he'd said. He'd seen the same reaction from most people after a crisis. He struggled to maintain his professional distance, go into cop-mode. In reality, he wanted to hold her close, stroke her hair. But that was dangerous ground. He took a sip of his hot, black coffee.

"Peter must be wondering where the hell I've gone," he said to change the topic. "He must have heard the ambulance on the dispatch. I can hear him now. 'What did Ash do this time? Not back in town two days and already he's doing damage.' "

She glanced at him with sad humor. "Obviously you two haven't made peace yet."

"It doesn't matter. I won't be around long enough to cause trouble for him."

"Where will you go this time?"

"Miami. My ex-partner and I are setting up our own security business. He's down there already, scoping out prospects."

"When I saw you at the police station, I was shocked enough to think you might be back to stay."

He shook his head. "What is there for me in Cranberry?"

"You could be a cop like your brother."

"I'll never be like my brother."

The poignant understanding in her eyes made him clench his back teeth. He brushed it off with a stiff wave of his fingers. "You know what I mean. I can't see myself spending day after day not doing much more than directing traffic or hauling in truant kids."

"Oh, things have really picked up since you left." Abby pulled a lifeless mayo-soaked lettuce leaf from her sandwich and plopped it onto her plate. "Last year we had quite the dispute when the Martin's cows kept roaming into the high school football field. Then the Martins couldn't afford to keep their dairy going and they had to sell. A new development is going up on the property. There's no room for family businesses in this town anymore."

She took a vicious bite out of her egg salad, her small, white teeth leaving a tidy half-moon gap in the bread. Ash had to smile. Nothing got Abby going like the big guy stepping on the little guy. There was more of her activist parents in her than she'd like to admit.

"Come on, Abby, tell me how you really feel," he teased.

"It's not funny." She pressed her lips together. "It's proof of how the town is changing. Now we have a chain convenience store in the north end, and they tore down the Cranberry Cinema without even telling anyone."

"Well, that does stink." He nudged her foot under the table with the toe of his shoe. "You and I sure had some memorable moments there. Remember the balcony?"

Her lashes fluttered. "That was a long time ago."

"I remember it like it was yesterday." He slouched back in the chair as warm recollections of her sweet kisses teased at the edges of his mind. She'd been so damned cute when she was a teenager. Now she was sexy as hell. He stretched his legs under the table and bracketed her sneakered feet. "So why aren't you married?"

"Maybe I am."

"Won't your husband be concerned when you're not at the store?"

"All right, then, detective. I could ask you the same thing."

"Go ahead," he replied, knowing she wouldn't because it would mean she cared.

They stared at each other for a moment, the tension shining like a silken strand between them. Ash absorbed the vision of her: wide, expressive mouth held in a stubborn, kissable line; short, straight nose; clean skin that glowed with fresh-scrubbed good health and a small, square jaw that heralded the vibrant spirit that lay beneath Abby's deceptively lush and lovely exterior. Any man foolish enough to think Abby was a pretty pushover would sure have his work cut out for him.

Something stirred deep within him. It was more than desire, though he couldn't deny that provocative sensation. No, it was some intangible, invisible force that smoked over his nerves when he looked at her, that made his pulse thicken when she turned those liquid eyes on him.

He mentally shook himself. Hard. Bad case of nostalgia. Yeah. That's all it was.

She tilted her head and rested her chin on her folded fingers, her elbow on the table. "I never thought I'd see you back in Cranberry."

"Funny, neither did I."

"Why didn't you keep in touch, Ash?" Her voice was soft, but he heard the underlying hurt. "Six years. It's a long time to go without dropping a letter, picking up the phone."

He ran the pad of his finger around the rim of his coffee cup. "Yeah, I know." What was the point of apologizing? Anything he could say would be inadequate. "I thought a clean break would be better for both of us."

Straightening the paper napkin on her lap, she nodded. Her gaze dropped demurely. "I was married. For a little while."

"What?" Shock lightninged through him, followed by a rumble of anger. "Who to?"

"A guy I met in school." She gazed at him through her lashes. "About a year after you left."

"No one told—Pete. He must have known." And Ash was going to throttle him next time he saw him. Already his hands were curling into fists.

"Sure, I guess the whole town knew, not that we had a big wedding or anything. But why would they tell you? What difference would it have made?"

A dozen answers clamored in his mind, but behind them all came the dull thud of the truth: it wouldn't have made any difference. He wouldn't have come back.

"You're not married anymore though?" He tried hard not to sound too aggrieved.

"We lasted eight months, until he was transferred to North Carolina."

For once, the thick roots she'd set into her hometown soil had worked in his favor.

Ash suppressed a groan of irrational relief. "He should have known you wouldn't leave Cranberry."

"I might have, if . . ." She tilted her head and left her thought unfinished. "We're still friends. He calls every so often."

The way Ash never had. Hmm. Then another thought jarred him. "No kids?"

"Four," she said. "Two boys and two girls."

"What?" He sat bolt upright in the flimsy chair. "He left you with—" Whoa, wait a minute. His overheated brain did the math. He sagged back, one arm dangling. "Oh, man, Abby. You really had me going there. Don't scare me like that."

The ghost of a smile drifted over her lips. "Remember Elspeth and Lancelot?"

Their imaginary children, from the days when he and Abby used to spend hours gazing up at the summer stars, laying out a future that went down the drain with everything else.

"Those were godawful names," he said. "What were we thinking?"

"We were lousy parents. Lancelot got beaten up at recess all the time."

"Yeah, but Elspeth was a peach. She looked like you." He smiled into her eyes. His fingertips tapped the sides of his coffee cup. This was dangerous; this was bad, resurrecting faded dreams. "We weren't much more than kids ourselves."

"Yeah." A moment of bittersweet understanding passed between them. The brightness in her eyes faded as the same thought crossing his mind must have crossed hers. The reminiscing had to stop. Abby flicked her hair back over her shoulder and cleared her throat, and the moment passed.

"The marriage part," he said, unable to let it all rest just yet. "Was that . . . ?"

"True? Yes. I was, to Brian Allen Scott. And we did get divorced when he went to live in North Carolina. It was a friendly parting. We both knew we'd made a mistake." She turned to gaze out the window. "Besides, I would miss the New England seasons, and Cranberry, and Lucy. I couldn't leave. This is my home. It's where I belong."

"I know." And it's where she would stay, long after he left her again.

"Ms. McGuire?"

The man's voice broke the stillness of the waiting room. Relief and anxiety collided in Abby like two great waves and propelled her to her feet. "Yes, Dr. Herbert. How's my aunt, is she . . . ?"

Dr. Herbert ran a hand over his thinning gray hair. "Your aunt is resting. Her vital signs are strong. It wasn't a heart attack, Abby."

She hadn't even realized she'd sagged until she felt Ash's firm grip circling her waist. They'd been back in the waiting room for at least half an hour, and she'd been about to prowl down the hallway and find the good doctor herself.

With Ash by her side, she listened to the doctor's report. The news wasn't all good. Lucy's left hip was fractured. They'd scheduled surgery for the following day.

"Afterward," Dr. Herbert said, "she'll need some kind of home care. We can arrange for a visiting nurse, but it would be best if a friend or family member could stay with her."

"That's not a problem." Abby rubbed her bare arms. "I can stay with her."

"Another thing you might want to do is prepare her home for her. Make sure the essentials are within easy reach. Do her grocery shopping for her, that sort of thing. Even though her prognosis is good, she'll be out of commission for quite a while. The more help you can give her, the easier her recovery will be."

Abby nodded to every request. There wasn't anything she

wouldn't do for her aunt. "Can we see her?"

Dr. Herbert directed them upstairs to recovery. While they walked to the elevators, Ash kept his hand on her back.

"You can let go of me now." Abby leaned forward to punch the button for the recovery floor. "I'm not going to keel over." Or get too attached to the warmth of Ash's body close beside her, if she knew what was good for her.

As soon as he leaned away, a chill settled on her shoulders. Her shorts and yellow t-shirt with the Cranberry Country Fair logo printed in maroon across the front seemed inadequate against the air conditioning.

"You look the way you must feel," he murmured, "like a wrung out dishrag."

"It's been a long day."

"At least I got to take you out to dinner."

She grimaced at his small attempt at humor. "If this was your idea of a good time, let's not do it again real soon."

"It wasn't your fault, Abby."

Wasn't it? His softly spoken words triggered tears behind her eyelids. She gripped the handrail. How she wanted to believe him, to trust him. Instead, she lifted her chin and watched the floor numbers blink by.

At last, the door shushed open and they stepped into a brightly lit area.

When the nurse led them to Lucy's room, Abby suffered her third shock of the day. Lucy lay unconscious beneath a white sheet. Tubes and IVs hung on steel poles. Beeping machines glowed with green LED numbers. A stinging antiseptic smell cut the air. Not until Ash pulled a rolling stool around for her to sit on did she realize she'd been standing, staring, with her hand clutched over her heart. Her knees gave out and she sank onto the stool.

"Oh, God," she whispered.

To his credit, Ash said nothing. He stood behind her, hands resting on her shoulders. After a few moments of uncharacteristic silence, Abby glanced up. His cheeks were hollow with worry. His eyes ticked from Lucy to the monitors, as if he was trying to figure them out.

"Ash?"

He blinked. "Sorry. It's hard to see her this way."

His tone rasped. Of course. Lucy—his "Auntie" from the olden, golden days of his youth—she'd been like a second mom to him. Abby understood. She turned on the stool and slipped her fingers over his. "If you hadn't been there today—"

"You would've done fine," he said. "You would've come through for her."

"She wasn't even supposed to have been at the deli today. I should have—" Her voice hitched.

"Hey, now." He tightened his hands on her hunched shoulders. He leaned down closer to her ear. "She's going to be okay. The doctor said so. I've known a few people who went through the same operation and they're all doing great, feeling better than ever. Lucy'll be up and about in no time."

"I hope so. I . . ." She bent her head and pressed her fingers to her upper lip. "Can I have a minute?"

"Yeah. Sure." Feeling like an awkward intruder, Ash glanced self-consciously at his watch. "I'd better go check in with Peter. By now he probably really is worried."

"All right."

Ah, God, it was enough to break his heart, that soft voice, the slumped shoulders. He reached out and stroked a hand over her hair. Warm silk slid beneath his palm. Abby. If he could turn back time . . . But that was a pointless wish.

He shuffled back a step, and the space between them yawned. She didn't take her gaze from Lucy's face as he left the room.

★ ★ ★ ★ ★

Since use of cell phones was banned in the hospital, Ash sought out the pay phone in the waiting room. His brother picked up after one ring.

"Hey, Peter." In as few words as possible, Ash told him what had happened. "I'll drive Abby home. Tell Meredith not to keep dinner for me."

"Lucy going to be okay?"

"Sure. She's going to need some help from us for a while, though."

"Us?"

Ash pinched the bridge of his nose. How easily he'd linked himself to Abby. "Abby, you, me . . . whoever can lend a hand."

"What about the store? Guess that'll have to shut down for a while, eh?"

"I'm sure Abby can handle it."

"And take care of her aunt at the same time? That's a full-time job right there."

"Don't be such a negative Nellie, Peter." His brother's offended huff on the other end brought some satisfaction, even though he made a logical point. How would Abby handle it all? "She said some weird stuff has been happening at the deli. Rock through the window, graffiti. What do you know about it?"

"Just some local kids roughhousing is my guess. Abby got pretty bent about the rock. She came in raising hell."

Good for Abby, Ash thought, irked by Peter's dismissive tone. "Tell your crew to keep an eye on the place, anyhow. Abby doesn't need anything else to happen while she's worrying over Lucy."

"Roger that."

Over and out, Ash finished in his head as he hung up. His brother always sounded like he was talking into a handset, even

32

when off duty. Like their father, Peter lived his job twenty-four/seven.

He rubbed the back of his neck as the first wave of fatigue poured over him. It wasn't as if there was anything wrong with the way Peter lived or worked. He was a dedicated lawman, stringently moral, punctual, upstanding. All the things Ash had not been in his youth. Peter could do that living in a black-and-white world. Ash couldn't operate that way. Life, he'd learned, was full of gray spaces, split decisions and risks.

The smells and sounds of the hospital closed in on him, sent his mind reeling back to the darkest night of his life. He'd left his injured partner in the hands of the paramedics and followed the ambulance carrying the kid he'd shot. Blood had dried black on Ash's knuckles and beneath his nails. His muscles had been so tight that he trembled. The pulsing red lights and keening siren strobed into his mind. The brass had wanted him to get whatever information out of the suspect that he could, but he knew when they rolled the body into the ER under a soggy red sheet that it was too late.

He'd killed a sixteen-year-old boy.

"Excuse me, are you done with the phone?"

A short woman with thick braids and dark eyes gazed up at him. "Mister, are you—"

Ash started. He'd been staring down at his open palms. Embarrassed, he jammed them into his pockets. "Yeah, I'm finished."

He stalked away. He needed to get out of this place, but he had nowhere to go, no place to call home.

# CHAPTER THREE

Abby stood with her purse hooked over her shoulder when he returned to Lucy's room. "How is she?" he asked. Dumb question. Lucy looked much the same, unconscious and tiny.

Abby closed her fingers around her aunt's hand. "I wish I could stay until she wakes up, but the nurse suggested I go home. There's no telling when Lucy will wake."

"We can come back tomorrow."

"I will. First thing in the morning."

The nurse stood by the door, waiting for them to leave. With his hand on the back of her arm, Ash coaxed Abby into the hallway. From there, they took the elevator again to the lobby.

"How are you holding up?" he asked as they walked through the lobby to the wide, automatic emergency room doors.

"I'm tired," she admitted.

"I'll drive you home. Where are you living now? At Lucy's?"

"No, in the Greenwood apartments across from the high school."

"I know the place." Dark circles looped beneath her downcast eyes. She probably wouldn't sleep, despite her obvious exhaustion.

"And where are you living now?" she asked.

"On my brother's couch," he replied with a slanted grin. "Not exactly five-star accommodations, but it'll do for the time being."

Their footsteps echoed in the cement parking garage as they

walked to her car. He held the passenger door open for her. Without an argument, she slid into the seat.

When he folded in behind the wheel, she glanced at him. "I'll drop you off at your brother's, then. Otherwise you'll have no way to get back."

"It's a small town. I got legs." He smiled, hoping to flirt her into a better mood. "Trying to dump me already?"

"We're not together, Ash. I can hardly dump you."

"Point taken." And how. Ouch. "Still, I'd like to be around for you as much as I can."

"But you're leaving soon. Isn't that what you said?"

"I have a week. I won't be leaving until after the fourth." Down in Florida, his ex-partner Ryan Cutler was counting on him to arrive on the fifth. Ryan had taken a bullet in the leg on that terrible night in L.A. and still walked with a cane. He could handle the phone and office work, but Ash would field the more physical end of things, like meeting with clients and training employees. He already had plane tickets and an apartment lined up.

But then, almost of its own accord, his gaze turned to Abby and his pulse began that slow, rolling rhythm again. It took all he had not to reach out to her, to smooth that sleek fall of golden hair from her face, to feel the satin warmth of her cheek against the back of his hand. The discipline, the control, the taming of emotion he'd perfected over half a decade in law enforcement, seemed to skid away when she was there, an arm's length away, beautiful, alive, breathing softly in the night air.

Ash caught himself up short. Nostalgia, hell. Not this intoxication of lust and yearning. He realized with a start that snapped his gaze forward again that he'd have to be careful. Careful not to confuse the Abby he knew, the girl he'd left behind, with the woman beside him now.

He wasn't the same man he'd been. And Abby wasn't the

same woman. He couldn't be certain if he was attracted to her or to his memory of her. To the innocence they'd both lost. It wouldn't be right to get involved with her again. Not fair to either of them.

He curled his hands around the steering wheel and tightened his grip. "For as long as I'm here," he clarified, his voice steady with resolve, "I'm yours."

Hers? If she hadn't been so weary, Abby would have scoffed. Ash would never belong to anyone.

They traveled in silence, Ash at the wheel as he drove them back to Cranberry. Passing lights silvered the silhouette of his strong jaw and straight nose and gleamed in his clear gray eyes. She couldn't help it. When she looked at him, a twist of longing rose up inside her, a dangerous, unwanted temptation that prodded at her bruised soul.

He hadn't been in her company more than a few hours, and already he was turning her world upside down.

Abby slumped back in her seat as the unreality of the day washed over her. Lucy was in the hospital, and Ash Wheeler, the very last man she'd ever expected to see again, had come to her rescue like a white knight.

"Do you need to get anything at the store before you go home?" he asked.

She slapped her palm to her forehead. "Oh, God, the deli! I left everything out, all the lights on. Yes, I'd better stop by there first. And Lucy's dog, I'll have to take care of him, too." She was so tired, but there was much to be taken care of. What was that poem? Miles to go before I sleep.

"How about for yourself? Milk, bread? A jug of moonshine?"

She heard a smile in his voice.

"Tempting, but no." The familiar buildings of Cranberry came into view, lifting some of her anxiety. "It'll take me a while to settle everything."

"It'll go faster with two of us." His tone left no room for argument. "Speaking of the deli, do you have any other employees you can trust to handle the place while you're busy with Lucy?"

"Miranda, but just for an hour here and there. Other than that, I've got Candy, a teenage girl who works part time after school and on the weekends."

"On the basis of her name alone, she doesn't sound qualified. I'll fill in for you."

"You don't know anything about running a deli."

"I can be taught. Besides, how hard can it be to throw a few sandwiches together?"

"There's a lot more to it than that. And what about your desk job at the station?"

"Oh, yeah, I sure would miss filing. The excitement of sorting out the Mc's from the Mac's, the thrill of answering the phone."

"Hate to tell you, but deli work isn't much more glamorous." She massaged the back of her neck. "I'll have to go in extra early tomorrow and see what orders Lucy has out, and the quarterly taxes are due."

"Don't worry." Ash brought the car to a stop in front of Lucy's Deli. "We'll get through this."

There was that "we" again. She shook her head in wary disbelief. "There is no 'we.' Let's get that straight right now. I appreciate your help and I admit, if nothing else comes through, I might have to take you up on your offer to help at the store, but, please—"

He switched off the ignition and slung an arm over the steering wheel. "Abby . . ."

The intimate sound of her name spoken in his smoky voice raised goosebumps on her bare thighs. How many restless nights had she spent alone in her bed wondering if she'd ever hear that voice again? Longed for it, yearned for it. Now she wished he had stayed a dream. The undeniable reality of him was too much to bear.

Before he could say anything else, she opened the car door and jogged up the steps to the front door of the deli. She fished for her keys in her purse. Normally, she and Lucy closed up around five o'clock. It had to be close to eight now.

Ash came up beside her. "Find your keys?"

"I know they're in here somewhere." Why were her fingers trembling? He stood close, too close. She half expected to feel the rough hair of his forearm brush against her as he reached over to find the keys himself.

A car rumbled up behind them. Beneath his breath, Ash muttered, "Here comes the cavalry."

Cool air slipped between them as Ash stepped away. Abby glanced over and saw that Peter had pulled his blue and white police cruiser next to her car and was getting out. Ash went down to talk to him just as she found her keys. She opened the door.

And let out a heavy breath. With the exception of the lights being on, nothing in the store looked out of place. She could almost pretend nothing had happened. She set her purse on the counter and wrung out a sponge in the sink to clean the counters. Going through the routine was a comfort. The knives and other utensils could wait until morning. She slid those into a pan of soapy water then turned to close out the cash register. As she pivoted, she noticed the door to the storeroom stood ajar. Her eyes locked on it. All her fears for Lucy flooded back. She gripped the edge of the counter.

Inheriting the deli had been some long-off dream. Funny, she'd never considered just *how* she would inherit. In her daydreams, Lucy would retire in comfort, and Abby would take over. Until today, it had never occurred to her that she might inherit it because something bad had happened to her aunt, an accident, or worse.

Her stomach rolled. That old, familiar fear of being alone shrouded her mind. Her fingers sought the cool smoothness of the worry stone in her pocket and rolled it round and round.

As a child, she'd often been left alone with sitters or friends while her parents traveled the globe. They were missionaries sometimes, activists others, whatever role would carry them into controversy. Abby would catch bits of conversation about them, how they'd been arrested during a protest, or how they'd been successful stopping rainforest destruction. Even though her mother had often told her on bended knee that they'd send for Abby when they could, it had been too unpredictable a life for a child.

Her aunt Lucy had taken her in, finally. Insisted on it. Abby could still recall the night when her mother and Lucy had struck the deal. She'd been only six. She had overheard Lucy demanding that her parents let her stay with her permanently, that it wasn't right to shuffle Abby around the way they did. And her mother, beautiful and strong, with the courage to fight for the poor and downtrodden all over the world, hadn't fought for her own daughter. She'd given her up with soft-spoken promises of how someday they'd come back and they'd be a family again.

Of course, that had never happened.

The only person she'd been able to count on was Lucy. And Ash, she'd thought, when she was young, and naive. But he'd left her, too.

She drew in a shuddering breath. She had to pull herself together. There was no getting around it, but no point in dwelling on it, either. She'd have to soldier on until . . . until whatever happened, happened. Gathering her tattered courage, she reached for the storeroom door.

"Abby?"

Ash's voice made her leap. She realized her jaw was clamped tight. In fact, her whole body was rigid. She slipped her damp palm off the doorknob and took a breath. "I'm back here."

"Do you need help with anything?" He stepped into the pool of light thrown by the overhead bulb and studied her face. The shadows cast over his cheekbones and dark brows sent his handsome features into stark relief. Her stomach did another kind of flip. If she took a step forward, one tiny step, and laid her cheek on his shoulder, he would wrap her in his arms. She knew he wouldn't push her away. Fine trembling coursed over her skin; nerves and adrenaline, and a pulsing need.

Abby forced her gaze away. It was the stress of the day that left her vulnerable and wanting. Wanting comfort in his arms.

Touching her tongue to her lower lip, she made herself turn toward the open door. "I'm about finished. Just have to pick up these cans."

He bent to help her. "What about this stool? It looks like it's broken." He picked up the wooden stool they often used to get cans down from the higher shelves. "This might have caused Lucy's fall."

"Broken?" Abby reached for it when he handed it to her, glad to have something else to focus on. "It can't be, not our old, faithful stool. It's been here for decades. Rumor has it some civil war hero had made it for one of Lucy's great-grandmas." But, sure enough, the nails holding one leg were loose. She wiggled the leg, then peered at the vent over the door. "Oh my gosh."

"What?"

Abby didn't know whether to laugh or cry. She pointed at the vent. "Remember when we were kids we used to climb up on boxes and listen through there? We could hear what anyone was saying at any table because of the way sound carried."

"Sure." He waggled his eyebrows. "We always got all the

40

good gossip around town."

"I think Lucy might have been eavesdropping."

"On us?"

"I wouldn't put it past her. Would you?"

"Nope. Not for a minute."

"Where do you think I learned about that vent, anyhow?" She turned the stool over. Years ago, it might have been blue with a yellow sunflower hand-painted in the center. Much use had worn away the cheerful image, and the wood was chipped and faded. "I should throw this out, I guess, but it's been here so long."

"Give it to me. I'll put a couple of new nails in it."

"You're a man of many talents," she said with a teasing grin. But it gave her an unexpected sense of relief to see the old relic in his capable hands. He could be trusted because . . . Well, because the store, and Lucy, were almost as important to him as they were to her. No matter what he said or wanted to believe, Ash had ties to this town. For a slip of breath, she wished she was one. Then, just as quickly, she dismissed the thought. Foolish thinking, the product of an overtired mind.

Ash set the stool on a utility table along the wall. "Guess we don't have to wonder why she was eavesdropping."

"Well . . . no." The last thing she wanted was to get into a conversation about Lucy's attempted matchmaking. "She's, uh . . . Well, she's always liked you." Oh, that was lame.

He put a big can of chickpeas alongside the beans she was setting down, and the backs of their hands brushed. Abby jerked. The storeroom seemed ludicrously small with Ash right there at her side, his heat flowing around her. She took a step to the right and dusted off her hands—as if she could dash away the awareness dancing over her skin.

"What did Pete have to say?" she asked to change the subject. "He didn't hang around long. I thought he might come in for a cup of coffee."

His expression tightened to a frown, but she sensed it wasn't directed at her. "He asked about Lucy and he said he'd keep an extra close eye on the deli while she's laid up."

"That would be good. Kind of aggravating when a store three blocks from the police station is vandalized."

"Be gentle on him, it's probably the biggest crime wave in Cranberry history."

"Nothing like Los Angeles, I'm sure."

"No. The city . . ." His gaze turned inward as he rolled a big can of peaches between his palms. "It's like a whole other world from this place. Harder. Colder. For all the people there, it's still lonely. You wouldn't have liked it." He set the last can down with a thud that put an end to the conversation.

She wondered at his rueful tone. Los Angeles had changed him. Something must have happened there to drive him home. For a moment, she regretted losing the closeness they'd once had, the precious trust that had allowed them to share fears and hopes. A poignant regret welled inside her, one she didn't want to feel.

She stood back, forcing a note of briskness into her voice. "Well, things are in shape here. Next stop, Lucy's house. Her dog must be about ready to explode. No one's let him out since before lunch."

"Don't tell me she still has Pawpaw?"

She brushed past him into the store to collect her purse. "Believe it or not, she does."

Big, tough Ash gave a comical shudder. "I still have the scars from when that little stinker nearly took my leg off."

"Oh, Ash, what's he weigh, all of five or six pounds? You big baby."

"Promise you'll protect me?"

"I'll do my best to restrain the killer poodle." She waited by the door while he went around to all the doors and windows, checking the locks.

As he made his rounds, there was no doubt in her mind that he must be, or must have been, she corrected herself, an excellent police officer. He moved silently, efficiently, focused on his task. In his dark jeans and darker shirt, he appeared a black shadow cruising the perimeter of the store.

Abby leaned a shoulder against the doorway and tracked him with her gaze. Why had he quit the force? When he'd left, he'd been so determined to be a cop that when it came down to Abby or Los Angeles, Abby had lost out. He'd left for a noble purpose, of course. To save the world. It seemed like people were always leaving her for noble purposes.

Marriage between them probably wouldn't have worked out, anyhow, or at least that's what she'd told herself to get over the hurt. If there had been a baby . . . Unconsciously, her hand drifted to settle over her midriff. Well, Ash was good with kids. That wouldn't have been an issue. But would he have been happy doing what he called "the right thing"? Would she? He had always valued his freedom, and she'd never wanted anything more than stability.

The irony now was that she understood his point of view. Her brief marriage had proven to her that she wasn't cut out for it. She and Brian had been good friends, but unhappy spouses. They'd both known their marriage was a mistake. A mistake she wouldn't make again.

She preferred being plain Abby McGuire. Independent, with no one to answer to but herself. Just like Lucy. After all, Lucy'd never married or had a family. Instead of having children of her own, Lucy had taken local kids under her wing, kids whose parents were too busy with their own lives to pay them much attention. Young ruffians like Ash, who might've taken a turn for the worse without some gentle guidance. Even Abby, though she'd more or less been dumped on her aunt by her own too-busy parents.

No, love and marriage were not meant for Abby, although there had been a time when she'd believed enough in what she felt for Ash to dream of having it all.

Ash clanked the bolt on a windowpane. Metal pinged against metal, pulling her out of her thoughts. "This hardware is ancient," he said. "And flimsy. Grab me a piece of wood out of that pile, will you?"

Abby walked over and handed him one of the heavier slats they sold as kindling. He fitted it at an angle across the top of the window. Anyone breaking in would now have to shatter the glass. He thumped it into place with his fist.

"It'll have to do until I can fix these locks tomorrow," he said.

"Tomorrow?"

"What kind of alarm system do you have here?"

"Alarm system?" She knew she sounded like a dopey parrot, but he was moving too fast. "We don't have one. Why would we need it?"

He sent her a sidelong glance. "Only in Cranberry."

She chafed under his cynical gaze. "The fact that we don't have to lock doors or bolt windows is one of the things I like best about this town."

"Yeah, but someone already threw a rock through the window, and spray-painted you a new logo on the side of the building. The town is changing. You have to stay one step ahead."

"These locks have done a good enough job keeping the burglars out." She hitched her purse on her shoulder. "If some of them are wearing out, I'll have Jamie from the hardware store come and replace them."

"I'll do it for free. And I'll be here tomorrow, anyhow."

Had she really agreed to let him work at the deli? She

couldn't remember much of anything beyond worry and confusion. How did she get herself into these situations? Then again, maybe he was right. Extra security could mean a little extra peace of mind.

"All right," she said on a sigh. "If it'll make you happy."

"Thank you, dear, that's very generous of you."

He sounded so beleaguered, Abby surprised herself with a laugh. "I'll bet you're wondering how you got dragged into this mess. One minute minding your own business sorting files, the next racing to the hospital and then playing security guard."

He rubbed the back of his neck. "Yeah, whatever happened to my idea of getting together over a nice quiet dinner? Somehow this isn't how I pictured our reunion."

She turned and started walking to the door. "Did you picture one at all? I mean—" Biting her lip, she struggled over asking a question to which she really didn't want to know the answer. "If we hadn't bumped into each other, would you have . . . ?"

"Tracked you down?" He stopped beside her, close enough that the clean, subtle scent of him became elemental in the air she breathed. His easy smile faded. "No."

Well, that was honest. And painful. Keeping her expression neutral, she nodded and looked away.

His fingers curled around her chin, gentle and startling at the same time. He turned her face up to his. "The only reason I wouldn't have is because I was afraid this would happen."

"What? What would happen?" Her pulse became a hot rush in her ears.

"That we'd . . ." He stopped. His brows tightened and his jaw shifted. His gray eyes mirrored the same confusion and longing that wound through Abby, and his lips curved in a frown. Those lips. His kisses couldn't possibly be as good as she remembered. Time had a way of making everything seem better than it really had been. Didn't it?

He stroked the pad of his thumb over her cheek before he dropped his hand back to his side without another word.

Flustered, her face on fire, Abby took an unsteady step away from him. What had she expected? She didn't want to dredge up these unsettling emotions again, and clearly, neither did he. Whatever had happened between them was long over. Ash understood that. She understood it, too, but somehow, when he touched her, looked at her, all sound reason flew right out of her head.

She moved through the door when he pushed it open for her. He waited with his hands in his pockets while she locked the deadbolt.

"I'll drop you off at Pete's," she said, relieved to hear her voice was only a little shaky. She dropped her keys into her purse and zipped it shut.

He rocked back on his heels. "I said I'd go with you to Lucy's. I don't mind."

She presented a smile. A polite, business-like smile, the kind she summoned when telling an especially stubborn salesman good day. "There's no need for that. I can manage on my own. After all, I've been doing just that for years. Come on, I'll give you a ride to your brother's house."

She managed not to break into a run to get to the driver's seat of her car before he could beat her to it. Her door was swinging shut when he grabbed the top of it. "I think I'll walk over to the station instead," he said. "Peter's shift is over in an hour, and I want to talk to him. What time should I be here tomorrow?"

She took a deep breath. "Look, Ash, that was a nice offer, but really, I'll handle the store."

"What about when you want to visit Lucy? Who'll run it then?"

He would have to muddle her logic. "I'll call Miranda. She

might be able to cover for an hour or two." She gave a breezy shrug to show just how easy this impossible task would be. With the new baby, Miranda didn't have much flexibility in her schedule. Still, once she heard about Lucy, she would surely chip in. "At two-thirty, Candy will come in and help me finish out the day."

"Candy, eh?" He crossed his arms over the top of the door and narrowed his eyes. "Does she know about the vent?"

"The vent?" She frowned. "I doubt it."

"Or where Lucy hides the petty cash?"

"No, I guess I never showed her that."

"Because you don't trust her."

"And you're saying I can trust you?" As soon as she spoke them, she wished she could call back her incredulous words. Fortunately, he spared her the embarrassment.

He straightened away from the door. "I'll be here at six." He crossed his muscular arms across his solid chest and gave her an implacable I-Am-The-Law stare that would make any criminal throw up his hands in surrender.

Abby wasn't willing to surrender just yet, but unfortunately, everything he said made sense. Practical sense, the kind she'd been lacking the last few hours. Besides, if there was one thing she knew about Ash Wheeler, it was that there was no point in trying to budge him from something once he'd made up his mind.

She blew a puff of air up at her bangs to toss them out of her eyes. "Okay, okay. Maybe you can help out during the morning rush." She focused on turning the key in the ignition, because the sight of his self-satisfied grin would have her kicking herself. "But make it five-thirty." She glanced up, careful to keep her expression bland and business-like. "And don't plan on staying later than two. I can't afford to pay both you and Candy."

"Will work for food," he said, snapping his fingers then swinging a double thumbs-up.

As he shut her door and stepped to curb, triumph and something else lit his eyes. Something too close to anticipation for Abby's comfort. Lucy had always said she attracted trouble like a lightning rod. Darned if it didn't look like trouble was about to strike twice.

# CHAPTER FOUR

Ash found Peter sitting at his desk at the police station. The glass window rattled in the old wood frame as he clapped the door closed behind him. "Why didn't you tell me Abby was married?"

Peter took his own sweet time finishing his report before he said, "She's not any more, is she? Thought she divorced the guy."

"Yeah, she's divorced." Seeing his brother wasn't about to be rushed, Ash tugged a plastic chair over from the wall and dropped into it.

"I suppose it didn't occur to anyone to tell you," Peter murmured after a leisurely moment. He peered up long enough to tap the eraser of his pencil against his lower lip. His pale blue eyes narrowed. "Weren't you going with that Julie girl any how? Julie or Jenna or something?"

Ash had to calculate back to the right timeframe. "Janet," he said at last. "Julie was last year."

"Got a thing for J's," Peter observed.

No, got a thing for A's, Ash grumbled to himself. One in particular. He stretched out his legs and scowled at the scuffed toes of his black sneakers.

The phones were quiet and only a skeleton crew manned the station. The office, originally his father's, now passed on to Peter, smelled of cold coffee and Lysol. Although their father was still acting chief of police, Peter had taken over many of his du-

49

ties, including long days spent behind the desk.

Ash took a deep breath, made himself relax. He had the jitters for some reason. Despite the past stressful hours, energy pumped through him. He felt like he could jog ten miles without breaking a sweat. He glanced at the clock, calculating the time until morning.

Peter handed him a scrawled note. "Your friend Ryan called the house. He wants you to get in touch. Sounds like he's got a potential customer already."

"Thanks." Ash took the piece of paper and stared at it. Ryan was proving to be a sound businessman as well as a good friend. As if that weren't enough to get excited over, Ash would soon be living in sunny Florida. Fantastic weather, gorgeous girls, plenty of earning potential. Then why did he have this odd urge to crumple the note and toss it? Unsettled, he riffled it against his fingertips. "It was nice of Meredith to make sure I got it so promptly."

"She's very concerned about your future employment," Peter said dryly.

"More concerned about the future of her new sofa." Meredith never missed a chance to remind him that he was sleeping on a hunk of furniture that cost more than she estimated his hide was worth. She was clearly counting the days until Ash was gone and she could have her sofa professionally dry-cleaned and back the way she wanted it, primped and pristine.

Peter's chair creaked as he leaned back and linked his hands behind his head. "I think you're growing on her. She sounded genuinely concerned that you'd be missing dinner."

"And what was she serving? No, let me guess. Liver and onions."

"You got it. Your favorite."

Ash laughed. His mellow brother might be hen-pecked by his high maintenance wife, but at least he had a sense of humor about it. "Yours, too, as I recall."

"I've learned to pretend I like it. The last thing I want to do is give Merry more ammunition against me."

Peter grinned, and Ash shook his head. He dropped his hand with the note onto his lap. "So who was this man Abby married? Did you know him?"

"No, not well, anyhow. Saw him around. Looked like a nice enough kid, clean cut. Think he worked at the college. It was a while back. After you left, Abby kept in touch with the family for a while, but eventually it dwindled down to saying hello when we met by chance. We didn't know her husband except by name." Peter propped his feet up on the corner of his desk. The buttons on his tan uniform strained over the belly Meredith's Southern cooking had built. "Why's it so important to you?"

"We were friends, and I was concerned for her, especially after what happened today with Lucy. Abby doesn't have much family."

"So you thought you might contact her ex for moral support?"

"No!" Ash's sharp reply betrayed him. Though nothing overt changed in Peter's expression, his brow raised an almost imperceptible degree. "I mean . . ." Ash clutched at excuses and found none worth voicing. How could he explain to Peter what he hadn't quite yet gotten a handle on himself? "I want to help her, make sure she's back on her feet before I leave."

Peter's old chair groaned as he leaned back a little more and gazed up at the yellowed ceiling tiles. "It'll be nice to have a brother with a place in Florida. Merry and I will have somewhere to stay. You don't mind the kids stampeding through your house for a couple weeks every summer, do you?"

Ash had to grin. Despite the times he and Peter had butted heads, he found he'd missed his older brother's dry wit. "I'll be sure to pick up a fancy sofa for your wife."

51

"And for me, a big hammock on the deck, under a swaying palm." Peter stretched his arms over his head and yawned as if he could just imagine it.

Only a day ago, Ash's head had been filled with the same inviting image. He loved hot weather and saltwater fishing and all the other bonuses living in the Sunshine State could offer. Now the prospect of moving to Florida seemed like a knife hanging over his head. He needed more time. More time with Abby. For Abby, he meant—to help her out, of course.

Which reminded him. "Since we're on the topic of jobs, I'm going to need a hiatus from my paper pushing here. I offered to cover for Abby at the deli while she takes care of Lucy."

"All right, I think we can spare you. I know you were only doing it to get out of the house and away from my wife." Peter picked lint off his tan pants. "Abby always was a nice girl. Much as I hate to see Lucy laid up, it might be the best thing for Abby if she moves on from that store. I don't know how much longer it will be in business, anyhow. There's been some grumbling that it's an eyesore in the center of town."

"Eyesore? It might need a coat of paint and some sprucing, but it's been there forever."

"Maybe that's the problem. Some new, young families have moved into town. You know, the kind of people who buy the house because of the quaint countryside but then want the cows gone once they find out they smell. It's all image with them."

Concerned by this new twist, Ash tucked Ryan's note into his shirt pocket. "Did you find out who threw the rock through the deli window?"

Peter swung his feet back to the floor and straightened. "Just kids with too much time on their hands."

"What are their names? This town is tiny, you've got to have some clue."

Closing his manila report folder, Peter shook his head. "I've talked to the parents. It's being handled. Don't worry about it."

Ash's well-honed instincts buzzed. Why the reluctance to share the information? "Maybe I'd like to talk to them, too."

"In what capacity? You're not on the force." Peter stood and slipped the folder into a tall file cabinet. "Speaking of which, Dad's practically got your uniform tailored and pressed. He's asked me to try to talk you into staying."

"I've told him I'm committed to this new business."

"He's retiring, you know." Peter reached for his blue windbreaker hanging over the file cabinet.

"What? Why?"

"He turned sixty-three in June. He's done more than his time and he's ready."

Ash couldn't imagine the Cranberry PD without Chief Peter Wheeler, Sr. at the helm. "When?"

"In the fall. The town council will elect a new chief. Likely me." Crow's feet etched the corners of Peter's eyes and deeper lines bracketed his down-turned mouth. "In Dad's ideal world, you'd come on board as an officer. It's what he always envisioned for both of us."

The weight of his brother's tone made Ash look at him with new eyes. He'd never detected even the slightest hint that maybe Peter would've liked to be something other than a Cranberry police officer. He'd always toed the line with uncomplaining fidelity. Yet when his brother lifted his gaze, Ash was almost certain he saw an echo of regret.

"Don't you want the promotion?" he asked.

"Sure I do." Peter looked down to zipper his jacket. "It'll make Dad happy, and you know Merry will be thrilled."

"What about you, though? What do you want?"

Peter glanced behind him to the wall hung with two decades' worth of dusty photos of Peter Sr. shaking hands with various political bigwigs, and gilt-scripted citations for his professional achievements.

"To do the right thing," Peter said. "Just like Dad taught us."

He came around the desk to clap Ash on the shoulder. "Think about it before you make any final decision, okay? It would mean a lot to the old man, and to tell you the truth, I'm kind of glad to have you back, too. It's good to have the family together again."

Huh. Ash rubbed his palms on his thighs. Peter's declaration was about the closest thing to brotherly love he'd ever expressed. "Sure," he managed after a moment, getting up. "I'll give it some thought, I promise."

He followed Peter out to the car. His mind tossed. If he didn't know better, he would've sworn the dust kicked up by his footsteps was twining around his ankles like roots to bind him to Cranberry's soil.

Pawpaw exploded into a barrage of yips that startled Abby about a foot out of her seat. It was only five-thirty in the morning at the deli, and her nerves were in no way ready for the sudden barrage of noise. The poodle's tiny, beige body bounced on all four legs and his tail stood straight up as he rushed the opening front door.

"Pawpaw!" She launched herself from the desk chair and raced to grab the pooch before he could dash out the door and into the road.

Ash was quicker. Stepping in, he reached down and scooped up the snarling dog in one big hand, then held him at arm's length. "Nice to see you, too, buddy." He grinned.

Abby rushed past him to shut the door. "Good catch!"

Ash studied the elderly poodle, who grumbled like an antique engine trying to turn over. "I am so grateful you're not a pit bull, old dog." He flipped a sorrowful glance to Abby. "He still doesn't like me. All dogs like me. I don't get it."

She leaned back against the door and shook her head. "Pawpaw doesn't like any men. I don't understand it either, but it's always been that way. Here—" She took the little dog, who shook with rage, and cuddled him against her chest. "I'll have to tie him up in the back room, I guess."

"He's going to be going nuts all day with customers coming in and out."

That had been her worry, too. Stroking Pawpaw's lamb-curl fur, she sighed. "I just didn't know what else to do with him. He was so lonely by himself at Lucy's house. By the time I got there last night, he was a nervous wreck, but I can't keep him at my apartment."

He reached a tentative finger toward the poodle's muzzle. Pawpaw curled his lip to reveal tiny teeth. Ash held his finger just out of snapping range and murmured to the dog, "I'd take you home with me, boy, but I value my jugular, yes I do, you silly puppy." His words dissolved into syrupy baby talk as he fussed over the poodle and seduced him with his voice until Pawpaw's grumbles subsided and he finally allowed Ash to skritch the top of his head.

Abby knew there was a silly grin on her face, but she couldn't help it. The sight of rugged, tough Ash goo-gooing his way into the dog's icy soul warmed her the way even the early morning sunshine couldn't. When he'd been a teenager knocking blocks in school, only she had known about his secret soft spot for four-legged creatures. She was glad he hadn't lost it. "You've always had a way with animals," she whispered, not wanting to disturb the spell Ash was weaving.

He didn't break eye contact with the dog, who submitted to an ear-rub, but the corner of his mouth edged up. "As soon as you put him down, he'll forget all about it and go for me, I guarantee it."

"I don't know. He looks like he might fall asleep."

"Like a baby." Ash glanced at her, a smile in his eyes, and Abby melted. He was inches away, the golden sunlight glowing on his freshly razored cheek, the spice of his aftershave rising to her on a wave of warmth. Whoever invented those aftershaves knew what women liked, yet somehow, this scent, soapy and subtle, seemed unique to Ash. Abby found herself breathing more deeply to draw it to her senses. He wore a simple gray t-shirt that brought out the silver in his eyes, and jeans that had been washed and worn till they hung on him like an old friend.

"Ash—" She hesitated, pressing her lips together. "Thanks for coming in this morning. You really didn't have to."

"And miss all this excitement?"

"Can we start over?" she whispered, not wanting to disturb Pawpaw, who relaxed in her arms. "Good morning."

"Good morning, beautiful," he murmured in his sexy, bedroom undertone.

A wave of awareness broke over her shoulders. Before Ash could say anything else to fluster her, she raised one eyebrow and turned. Between what she'd discovered in the company books this morning and now this, she was plenty flustered already. "I'll put him in the office for now. Maybe later I can find a way to tie him up out back."

His footsteps on the wooden floor followed her. "I could ask Peter if they could watch him for a few days. Does he like kids?"

"Sure, for breakfast, lunch and dinner." She set Pawpaw on his blue plaid doggie bed. He circled a few times and settled down for a nap. She crossed her arms beneath her breasts and allowed herself a sigh of relief. "Maybe this won't be so bad."

By her side, Ash said, "Probably for the best. Meredith doesn't like dogs, and she doesn't like me too much either, since I've commandeered her couch. I don't think it would endear me to her."

"You haven't charmed her over to your side yet?"

"I don't seem to have the same effect on her as I do on nasty little poodles. She still tries to bite me when I pat her on the head."

Abby laughed. "Where's her sense of humor?"

"If she has one, I haven't seen it." He shook his head as if it amazed him. "At least the kids are okay."

"They've got three now, right? Little Pete, Missy and Clay?"

"That's right. Missy would love a dog, any dog, even old Pawpaw, but Meredith would never allow it. She thinks animals are dirty."

"That's too bad. I can't imagine growing up without pets. Lucy was always so indulgent with all the stray cats I brought home."

"And birds with broken wings. Remember that owl?"

"Yes, the ingrate, it practically scratched my eyes out. Guess that wing wasn't so broken after all. I still have a scar." She lifted her hand and turned it so he could see the quarter-inch scar between her first and second knuckles. She caught her breath when he captured her hand and raised it into a stream of light.

He stroked his thumb over the tiny mark. Subtle sensation vibrated from her scalp to her toes as if angel wings brushed her. His hand was broad and strong, his fingers warm. Her own hand looked small and delicate lying in his. She remembered all the time they'd spent hand in hand so long ago. The mar on her knuckle couldn't compare to the scar on her heart. It would be smart to remember that. Abby drew her hand away and clenched it by her side.

"I called the hospital this morning." She steered the conversation onto safer ground. "I spoke to Lucy. She's doing well— resting comfortably, as they say. Doesn't seem concerned at all about having an operation."

Ash hooked his thumbs in his worn leather belt. "Lucy's got some kind of faith that sees her through. She always said things happen for a reason."

"That's true. Though whatever the cosmic reason is for this, I can't imagine." Abby managed a small shrug. "I wish I had her courage."

"You can be as scared as you need to be. Just keep moving, one step at a time, and you'll get through it."

She rubbed her arms and nodded.

"When have they scheduled her operation?" he asked.

"Early this afternoon. I'd like to leave here by ten. Then Candy will be in at two thirty."

He must have heard the worry in her tone, because he put a hand on her shoulder and squeezed. "Everything will be fine." He caught her gaze and held it. "Everything."

He made it sound so easy. Abby slipped from beneath his touch and moved behind the counter. "We should get things ready for the morning rush. I've got the coffee started. The newspapers need to be unbound and sorted. Can you do that?"

He flicked a utility knife out of his back pocket. "I didn't run my paper route for three years for nothing, you know."

"There, see? I knew you had some skills to bring to the job." She reached to a cupboard to get sugar packets and creamers ready. A quick wave of her hand over the hot grill told her it was ready for eggs. They didn't do nearly as much cooking at Lucy's as she would've liked, but egg and cheese on a hard roll was one of their most requested morning sandwiches. "Mr. Darcy will be the first one in. He likes his *New York Times* ready for him at the table in the far corner over there. Make sure there's a *USA Today* put aside for Pattie Greenfield."

The plastic straps binding the stacks of papers popped as Ash sliced through them with his knife. She indulged in the view of his strong back and shoulders, bone and sleek muscle shifting beneath the thin, soft-looking fabric of his shirt, before she made herself focus on arranging Danishes and muffins on a covered tray.

She really had to stop sneaking looks like that or she'd never get anything accomplished. Still, she battled a sense of disbelief. Half the night she'd wrestled with the idea that Ash was back in town. The other half, she'd slipped and spun through restless dreams. Morning found her in a light sweat, moaning, with the warm sheets tangled around her like Ash's arms.

Just then, Ash glanced up at her. Their eyes met. An electric jolt splashed through her. For a moment, she stood paralyzed in the focused beam of his perceptive gaze.

"You okay?" The sound of his voice slid over her like a caress.

Feeling an increasingly familiar rush of heat spill over her cheeks and throat, Abby stammered, "Yes. Sorry. Just thinking."

His lips curved up at one side and his lashes lowered before he turned. As if he knew exactly what she'd been thinking.

Good grief. She had to keep her mind on work. Abby busied herself with the morning routine she knew so well. Yes, if she could keep her mind on work, everything would be fine.

Ash crouched to fill the wire newspaper rack, and for a while they worked in companionable silence. When a delivery truck came, bringing the day's supply of fresh milk, Ash stepped in to handle it. He was so efficient and helpful that the load of stress Abby bore eased from her shoulders. She didn't even realize she was humming under her breath as she laid out supplies until Ash pulled a stool up to the counter.

"I finished setting up the tables and chairs." His rangy body settled on the high, padded seat. "That coffee smells great. Can you spare a cup for a poor, underpaid newsboy? And those bagels look good, too." He trailed off with a hopeful, raised eyebrow.

"Oh, sure, eating us out of house and home already," she said with mock seriousness, but she grabbed one of her own ceramic mugs from under the dish rack and poured him a cup. She smeared a sesame bagel with half an inch of cream cheese then dug around for the strawberry jam she remembered he liked. He ate at the counter, taking wolfish bites out of the bagel and gulping hot, black coffee.

She parked a hand on her hip. "Slow down, there's more where that came from. Doesn't Merry feed you?"

"I wasn't about to bother her at three-thirty in the morning, and God help the man who messes up her kitchen making his own meals. I figured it was safer to eat here."

She wiped her hands on a dishrag. "Three-thirty? No wonder you were able to get here on time."

"I jogged." He made a circular motion with the hand holding the remains of his bagel. "For about an hour. All around town."

That explained his most excellent physique. Now that her mind was on it, her eyes burned to rake the length of his hard, lean body, but she stoically kept them on his face—which wasn't a bad view, either. "See anyone you know?"

He sucked a bit of jam from the end of his thumb. "Nah. Besides, I don't think anyone but you and Lucy would remember me. I hope not, anyhow." His throaty chuckle made Abby grin.

"You were a little hellion," she admitted.

"Little?"

"Okay, a big hellion." And she doubted anyone living in town at that time would soon forget the young rebel Ash on his blood-red dirt bike roaring down Main Street, blatantly playing hooky, smoking in the school stairwells, making old ladies wag their fingers—and young ladies sigh and swoon. At least Abby had gotten him to quit smoking. "This town's been too quiet since you left."

"Really? I thought you liked it that way."

She had, as a matter of fact, until recently. Tossing the dishrag over her shoulder, Abby took his empty plate and dunked it into the soapy water. "It must be very different from Los Angeles."

"Totally. Los Angeles is a beautiful city, as cities go, but it's non-stop action, people moving all the time. It's not like here, where everyone knows your name. There, you're just another face in the crowd."

"And you prefer that?"

He finished his coffee before he answered. "I did," he said, in a thoughtful tone that made her wonder if he was questioning his own comfort zones the way she found herself uncomfortably reevaluating hers.

# CHAPTER FIVE

Had she remembered to tell Ash where she kept the spare plates? Or the extra pickles?

Darn it. Abby bit her lip and focused narrowly on the road. It was too late now. She was pulling into the hospital parking lot, and Ash was on his own to run the deli. They'd had a good morning. The beautiful sunshine must have coaxed people out of bed and into town. Without his help, she would never have been able to handle everything. Any time she'd become frazzled juggling people's inquiries after Lucy's health or making coffee and sandwiches, Ash had swooped in to take a plate or serve up a bagel. He'd been efficient and polite and, most of all, calm. Thank goodness one of them had been. Abby felt as if it was her first day on the job, not his.

He'd be fine while she was gone. Sure he would. And his help afforded her this time to see her aunt.

She parked in a space near the hospital's front entrance and took a minute to fix herself in the rear-view mirror before she stepped out. She tugged the elastic from her ponytail, then felt around in the glove box for a comb. None there, of course; not when she needed it. She finger-combed her hair over her shoulders, then pinched some color into her cheeks. Her reflected mouth slanted down. What a godawful mess she looked, with no make-up and purple circles beneath her eyes. She just wanted to appear unstressed, at least, for Lucy. She didn't want her aunt worrying about her.

But when she went into the hospital and walked past the nurses' station to Lucy's room, she realized her concerns were unnecessary. Lying in bed but looking relaxed, her aunt turned and beamed when she walked in. "Abby!"

Lucy's shoulders had a bird-like fragility to them when Abby hugged her. The scent of lavender wafted from her silver hair. Tears Abby should have anticipated began to well in her eyes.

"You didn't have to come today," Lucy said, patting Abby's hand.

"Oh, what else did I have to do?" Abby sniffled and grinned. "Nice outfit." She plucked at the sleeve of Lucy's green and white checked hospital gown, teasing her way out of her tears. What a relief to see Lucy looking almost normal. The last image she'd had, which was burned into her mind, was of her aunt looking like death beneath a white sheet. She turned the cold memory away with a smile.

Lucy preened and smoothed her hands down the front of the gown. "Everyone will be wanting one of these. They're all the rage. You've always looked good in green, dear, maybe I can filch one for you before they give me the boot."

Abby pulled up a chair and sat. She didn't want to ask about the operation to come, or the prognosis; that was all too depressing. "It's a beautiful day," she said instead. "The parrot tulips you planted around the fountain last September are starting to come up. Everyone at the store this morning was asking for you."

"The store? I thought you might not open today. It would've been all right if you hadn't."

"Oh, sure, now you tell me," Abby answered with a wry grin.

"Well, really, Abby, after last night, we were all exhausted. I wouldn't have expected you to get up early and handle the place by yourself. After all, it's not the end of the world if George Darcy doesn't get his paper first thing, much as he might think it is." She smiled, but Abby could see she was turning something over in her mind. Her silvered brows dipped down. "I do worry that you work too much sometimes. You're too young to be chained to that deli seven days a week."

"But I love it," she said, and she did, and a spark of alarm shot through her that Lucy was speaking this way when she'd never done so before. "It's . . . it's part of the town. It's like the heart of Cranberry. Where else would the kids stop after school for a snack, or the old timers hang out on Sunday mornings?"

"They'd find somewhere else to take up space." She began to chuckle, but it turned into a raspy cough that had Abby grabbing for a glass of water. It took Lucy a minute or two to get the coughing under control. Two spots of red had blossomed on her cheeks, and her eyes were half-closed while she tried to catch her breath.

"Should I get a nurse?" Abby wished to God she could do more.

With the back of her hand against her mouth, Lucy shook her head. "Abby," she said, the edge of her voice ragged, "if . . . this operation doesn't go as we hoped—"

"No." Abby couldn't bear to even think about it.

"Now, listen, dear. There are a few things you need to know."

For her aunt's sake, Abby forced herself to sit still and listen even while her stomach clenched in a tight, achy ball. Lucy took a shaky breath, but the coughing fit seemed over. "I never wanted you to know, but the deli has been running at a loss for the last few years. I took out another loan for the sign and the landscaping, but I don't know if I can recoup the cost."

"Don't worry about that now, Auntie." Besides, after perusing the books this morning, she did know—all too well.

"I don't want you to be stuck with the bill. If I . . . If anything should . . ." Lucy paused and curled her hand into a loose fist over her blanket. "I want you to sell the deli. The property alone is worth enough to cover the debts, and it will give you a nice little nest egg to get started."

"But what else would I do? That's all I know. It's all I've ever wanted."

"For the last few years, perhaps. It wasn't always that way."

Abby knew in her heart to what—or to whom—she was referring. Ash, of course. Now was not the time to get into a debate with Lucy about him, though, not with her own feelings in such a tumult. She gave a distracted nod. "The deli will be there, waiting for you when you're better. Everyone misses you and wants you back, so think positive, okay?"

"You know I will. Most likely, this will all be much ado about nothing." The smile she shared with Abby did little to ease the sudden gloom threading the air. "There's something else I'd like you to do."

"Is it about Pawpaw? Because he's all taken care of. I brought him into the deli with me this morning and he's keeping Ash company now."

"At his brother's house?"

"No, at the—" Abby realized in her rush to change the topic, she'd stumbled right back into it. "At the store," she admitted. "Ash is covering for me."

A genuine brightness lifted Lucy's expression. "Is he? How wonderful. He always was a helpful boy."

Abby couldn't help but roll her eyes, thinking of Ash as a "helpful boy." There was nothing boyish about his dark features or powerful physique. Although maybe, at times, when he grinned, he had a certain playful charm . . .

Realizing her aunt watched her, Abby tamed her dreamy expression and cleared her throat. "It's just for today. I guess I'll put an ad in the paper and get some help until you're back on your feet."

"That's a good idea, dear. But it wasn't Pawpaw I was think-

65

ing about. It's your mother. I'd like you to call her and tell her what's happening."

Oh, no. Abby hadn't spoken to her mother in almost two years. Lucy was always the one to make the long-distance calls. "I don't even know where she is right now."

"I do," Lucy said, dashing any hopes Abby had of squeezing out of the predicament. "In the top right drawer of my work desk, there's a purple sticky note with a phone number on it. The people there will know how to get in touch with your parents."

"I could bring you the number. I'm sure she'd love to hear from you—"

"And she'd love to hear from you even more."

Abby hesitated. "She won't come home, you know. Even for this."

"I don't expect her to. But she is my sister. She should be kept up to date."

When had her aunt ever asked her for anything? Straightening her spine against the back of the chair, Abby nodded. "All right. I'll take care of it tonight."

Nothing else had to be said. Lucy knew how difficult this phone call would be, but she also trusted Abby to make it, and Abby wouldn't let her down. Because, unlike some others, she would never turn her back on someone who loved her.

When Lucy's cool fingers touched the back of her hand, Abby glanced up. Her aunt tipped her head. "People come in and out of our lives for a reason, dear. Don't be too hard on your parents. When the time is right, they'll be with you again. Just like Ash is here now, when you need him most."

"Oh, Auntie." Well, let Lucy believe what she wanted if it helped her through this difficult time. "Maybe you're right. You always see things more clearly than I do."

Lucy rested her gray-haloed head on the pillow. "It's a

comfort to know he's taking care of you while I'm here."

"Uh, Candy . . ." Ash gripped the end of Pawpaw's leash in one hand and a pink plastic watering can in the other and did his level best to ignore the girl gazing up at him. "Isn't there something you should be doing? Inside?"

Candy—aptly named with her candy-apple red hair that looked like a Halloween leftover—flashed her braces in a dimpled smile and giggled. God help him, Candy had developed the world's fastest crush. For the past hour or so since she'd arrived for work, she'd clung to him like toilet paper on the heel of his shoe. What was it with these little teenage girls? Didn't they have men in these parts?

When Candy didn't take the hint, he twisted the leash from his wrist and held it out to her. "Maybe you could take the dog for a walk?"

She giggled again. "Okay, Mr. Wheeler."

Pawpaw darted at a squirrel rustling in the bushes. Ash counted his lucky stars that Candy took it as her cue to exit, with dog, stage right.

This was the girl Abby was going to leave in charge of the deli? She needed help even more than he'd realized. Even though there were basically only two rushes during the day— breakfast and lunch—a steady trickle of customers had kept him hopping. During this brief break in the action, he thought he'd catch up on some of the outside work. After flicking a cautious glance toward Candy, he got back to his task of watering the pansies.

Familiar laughter shook him from his thoughts. Arms crossed, leaning against the brick face of the deli, Peter shook his head. "What have you gotten yourself into this time?"

Ash scowled and hefted the watering can his way. "Laugh all you want. It's honest work."

"If I laughed all I wanted, I'd be rolling on the ground." Pete pushed away from the wall and strolled over. "That apron is you." He eyed the grease-stained white apron sashed around Ash's waist. "And the pink watering can. Nice touch."

"You can borrow it any time. I'm sure Meredith would be impressed."

"Funny you should say that, because she's why I'm here. She's invited Dad over for dinner tonight. You'll be there, right?"

"Of course. I live with you, remember?"

"Yeah. I just thought, with you and Abby—"

Ash turned a narrow glance on him. "Me and Abby what?"

His brother nudged his dark glasses up the bridge of his nose. "Eh, never mind." Beneath his shielded eyes, his mouth curved. "What a woman. She's got you domesticated already."

"Abby's at the hospital while Lucy is in surgery," Ash grumbled. Muddy water splashed out of the lip of the window box he'd been saturating. He stepped back and muttered a rude word under his breath.

"Little tense, bro?"

Peter had that special way of being extra irritating sometimes. "It's my first day. Give me a break." He put down the watering can and swiped his wet hands on the apron. Soggy soil puddled on the sidewalk and dripped toward the curb. Purple and white pansies sagged in the mild breeze. Good going, killing Abby's flowers.

"Getting back on the force might be the easy way out, you know." Peter flashed a smooth grin and set his cover back on his head. Unlike Ash, who was now a dirty, greasy mess, Peter looked sharp as ever in his tan uniform and dark shades. "Six o'clock. Don't be late."

"Yeah, yeah." Watching his brother's retreating back, Ash squelched the urge to toss a mud ball at him. It would serve him right.

Ash bent to scoop up the dirt and poke it back into the window box. Abby had called once, late in the morning, to check in and let him know that Lucy had been taken into the operating room. He could tell she was trying to sound strong and casual, but her voice didn't fool him. There was too much at stake. Not just Lucy's well being, but Abby's future, too.

All afternoon he'd rolled ideas around in his head, thinking of alternative ways for her to run the store, make a living, be happy. It was a guy thing, he guessed. He saw a problem; he wanted to fix it. He wanted to fix what was wrong between him and Abby. That was the real problem.

Grimacing, Ash shook the last of the dirt off his fingers and swiped his hands on the apron. It couldn't be done, not in the week he had. And even if it could, it would be undone again when he left.

What a liar he'd been when he'd told her he hadn't intended to find her. He'd been on the lookout for her since he rolled into town. He'd still been debating whether to approach her or not. Then she walked right into the PD. Fate? Luck? Who knew, but he was in the thick of it now.

Just as he finished with the window box, a small herd of high schoolers thundered into the deli—with no one inside to help them, of course.

"Candy!" He glanced around. The girl had disappeared. Probably around back now with the dog. Ash kicked the watering can into the shade beneath the window box then strode inside. The kids crowded the counter. A couple poked through the candy and gum, and one pulled a soda from the cooler. Their sticky fingers seemed to be everywhere. As he shouldered through them to get behind the counter, he glanced from face to face. Were any of these the kids who had smashed the window?

"Who's first?" His gaze landed on a blond boy who'd grabbed a bag of chips.

"Huh?" The kid gave him a blank stare.

Ash scowled. "What can I get you guys?"

"Uh, nothing, man, we're just, like, browsing, ya know?"

Just over the boy's shoulder, Ash saw another kid, dark haired, wearing a hooded sweatshirt too warm for this weather, drawing his hand from his pocket. The kid had lifted something, he was sure of it.

Ten teenagers milled around the store. Grabbing one and causing a scene would be more trouble than it was worth. The dark-haired kid couldn't have taken more than a couple of candy bars.

Ash came around the counter and confronted Blondie, since he seemed to be the ringleader. As expected, the kid backed a step when Ash approached. The others fell silent, expectant.

"Come back when you know what you want," Ash said. He kept his voice low but authoritative. From experience, he knew that sometimes a murmur could be more intimidating than a shout.

"Th-the old lady." Blondie seemed to trip over his own tongue. "She used to let us hang out here."

Lucy, of course, the softie. "She's not in," Ash said. "I'm in charge now. If you want to buy something, fine, but only two in the store at a time from now on. Understand?" Ash pointed at the potato chips. "That's a buck five, with tax."

The little group grew tense, all waiting to see what Blondie would do. Just as the kid's shoulders hunched and he started digging into his pocket for change, the back door burst open and in rushed Pawpaw. Yipping and snarling, he zigged through the teenagers. Candy dashed through the door, slipped and fell. The blue leash skidded across the floor.

Pawpaw made a go for a skinny brunette's ankle. The girl screamed and threw her soda can. It missed the poodle but hit the floor hard enough to crack open.

"Pawpaw! Dammit!" Ash grabbed for the dog.

"Hold still," he yelled. Pinned in the corner, the girl screamed, her hands up around her ears. Blondie tried to tackle the dog and knocked over a display case of snacks. Wing Dings and beef jerky spilled in a cellophane crescendo. A couple of cheering boys scooped them up and bolted for the exit. Candy started bawling.

Half-crouched, arms spread, Blondie blocked Pawpaw long enough for Ash to get a hand around the damned mutt and wrap his fist over his muzzle. Not before the stinking poodle lanced him with his little needle teeth. Grinding down a curse, Ash strode to the store room and tossed Pawpaw inside. He slammed the door shut. That stupid fur ball—

"Ash!" Abby's exclamation nailed him to the floor. "What is going on?"

He balled up his fist and thumped it against the door. Timing was everything.

# CHAPTER SIX

A bomb had gone off in her store.

Abby swept an unbelieving gaze over the spreading puddle of cola, Candy huddled and sobbing at the edge of it, and then to a blond teenage boy and his trembling girlfriend who tried to sneak out without drawing any more attention to themselves. A small mountain of crushed snack cakes piled in front of the counter. And the beef jerkies were scattered in the aisles . . .

Ash held up his hand. "Abby—"

"You can explain. Right?" Her fists tightened in dismay.

Candy raised her tear-streaked face. "It was my fault. Paw-paw slipped his collar and I thought if I scared him in through the back door, I could catch him." She held up the leash, from which the poodle's frayed nylon collar hung like a noose. "I'm sorry."

Abby rushed over and bent to help her up. "It's okay, Candy. It's not your fault."

Ash snatched up some paper napkins and held them out to Candy, who honked her nose into them. "Oh, Mr. Wheeler, I ruined everything."

He waved her off. "Don't worry about it, that dog's got a mind of his own."

A thin line of red looped the underside of his wrist. Blood? Abby reached out and seized his hand before his arm dropped. "And you're hurt!"

"Hurt?" He stared at his hand. Surely he couldn't be unaware of his injury. Just seeing the puncture wounds dripping crimson polka dots onto the plank floor was enough to make Abby's stomach flip.

"What the heck happened here?" She let him go.

He wrapped the corner of his apron around his hand. "Take care of Candy. I'll clean up this mess."

Her mind awhirl with questions, Abby put her arm around the girl's shoulders and told her to take the rest of the day off. Ash went to get the push broom from storage and Pawpaw, yapping, shoved his white muzzle through the opening. Pushing the dog back with the toe of his sneaker, Ash closed him in again.

"God, that mutt!" He kicked the bottom of the door and shoved his hands over his hair. "You know, I'm a patient man, but enough already."

That resolved the mystery about his wound. Pawpaw must have bitten him.

"All right, all right." Abby dragged out a stool for him to sit. "Give me your hand." When he resisted, she locked her fingers around his wrist and pulled down his bloody knuckles. About five or six punctures in a narrow horseshoe pattern marked the back of his hand and his palm. Adrenaline shivered through her. "He got you good. Let me get the first aid kit."

With his unwounded hand, he touched her under the chin until she glanced up into his serious gray eyes. "First," he said, "tell me about Lucy."

A tremor of exhaustion moved over her. She shifted her head, and his hand dropped away. "The operation went well. She's in recovery now, and in a few days, she can come home."

"That's good news. It was a long surgery."

She nodded. His touch made her thoughts tumble, made the skin of her throat feel naked to the cool air. It had still shocked her, seeing him when she came in the door. She'd been thinking about him on the ride home. Oh, why not admit it, she'd thought about him all afternoon while she sat in the waiting room. She'd stared, unfocused, at a novel she'd brought to keep her company during Lucy's operation and wished he was there beside her. Wished she had his shoulder to lean on. Wished she knew an easy way to tell him to go away so her heart wouldn't wing up into her throat whenever she met his granite-gray gaze.

Maybe it was a good thing she'd come back to chaos; it kept her mind off her true emotions.

She turned his hand over in hers. "Did anyone get hurt? Besides you, I mean."

"Nah. Although I think you might have lost Pawpaw's intended victim as a customer. Did any of those kids look familiar to you?"

"Any? How many were there? I only saw two. They're regulars, Charlie and—" She gripped his wrist before he could wrap his hand in the apron again. "Hey, don't do that, you'll get it dirty all over again."

"S'okay." He made a halfhearted effort to pull away.

"Oh, no you don't. I'm going to bandage this up, and then maybe we should walk you over to the doctor's." She glanced up and gasped. Blood streaked one side of his head. "Did you bump your head, too, or is that from your hand?"

"Huh?" Scowling, he touched the spot. "It's from my hand. Don't worry, Nurse Abby."

"Come on." He let her tow him to the sink, where she doused his hand in a stream of icy water. "The bleeding's almost stopped. I'm surprised old Pawpaw could penetrate that rhinoceros hide of yours."

That got a twitch of a smile out of him, albeit a guilty one. She felt a little guilty, too, from the way she'd reacted. Abby shook her head. "Okay, talk. I think I'm calm enough now to listen." She bent and got the first aid kit from under the cabinet.

"You know what the problem is? It's that crazy dog."

"I left you in charge. When I came up the walk, the first thing I saw was the window box half overflowing onto the sidewalk. The front door was wide open, letting all the hot air in, and then—"

"Okay, it was my fault. You're right."

"No." Her grip tightened on the scraped red and white tin of the old first aid kid before she clunked it down on the counter beside the sink. "It's mine. I shouldn't have expected you to handle the store by yourself."

"The day went fine. It was just the last few minutes that went haywire, I swear."

"Don't swear, Ash."

"Or what? You'll wash out my mouth with soap?"

Without thinking, she glanced at his fine, chiseled lips. She used to threaten to do just that, until he'd learned to curb his language around her. Now she could think of better uses for that mouth. Unsettled by his nearness and the intimate turn of her thoughts, she dropped her attention back to the bandages.

"Things will run smoother tomorrow," he said.

"I can handle it alone."

He groaned dramatically. "So you steal me away from my dream job of filing reports and now you crush my hopes of becoming a professional sandwich maker?"

She couldn't stop a grin. "Sorry, but when you're an entrepreneur, you have to be ruthless."

Beneath the intense pressure of his gaze, Abby, who actually had not a clue about how to wrap up a wound and hadn't opened the rusty first aid kit in years, criss-crossed the gauze around his broad palm and scarred fingers until the bite marks were covered. Then a few more layers just to be sure nothing bled through. And one more for good luck. All the while, she felt his attention on her, and his warm breath tickling the top of her head where he leaned in closer as if to catch her with a kiss

75

when she lifted her chin.

"Your hands are shaking," he murmured.

"I'm fine."

"You're always tending to someone else," he observed in that dark voice of his. "Pawpaw or Lucy or your friends."

"I like doing it."

"Do you ever stop to take care of yourself?"

"Sure. Do I look uncared for?"

She tried to make a joke of it but made the mistake of peeking up and saw his narrowed and too-observant eyes assessing her.

"You're as white as a sheet, you look wiped out. I'm worried about you."

"Ash." The softly spoken reproach did nothing for the zing of awareness that sped over her skin. Taping down the tail of the gauze, she stepped back. Her face felt hot. She turned away, but not before she noticed Ash puzzling over his mummy-wrappings.

"My dad's heading over to the house tonight for dinner," he said. "Why don't you come with me? Take a break from all this?"

She snapped the first aid kit shut. "To your brother's?"

"Merry's idea, so I can only imagine what she's got planned. Rescue me?"

Abby smiled wryly. "I can't. I've got parent problems of my own."

"Why, what's up?"

"Lucy wants me to call my folks."

"How long has it been?"

"Twenty-seven months." She scooped a loose tumble of hair away from her forehead with her thumb and ring finger. "Lucy told me she has a phone number for them at her house, but she wasn't sure exactly what part of the world they're in. I guess I'll find out soon enough. God knows, they certainly haven't been in touch. It should be . . . interesting."

From behind the store room door came an impatient yip that startled them both. "Oh, Pawpaw." Abby groaned and turned toward the sound. "What am I going to do with him now?"

"I'll take him, or try, at least."

"You can't. Meredith would have a fit."

"The heck with her." He stood and gave his fingers an experimental stretch. "It's about time Pawpaw and I bonded. Two old bachelors on a borrowed couch. We'll stay up late and watch movies together, have a few beers."

He painted an appealing picture, but Abby shook her head. "I appreciate it, but I think I'll stay at Lucy's tonight. I'll need to stock her refrigerator and get her house ready for when she comes home."

The bell over the door jingled, and Miranda breezed in to cover for the last hours of the day.

"Your reinforcements are here," Miranda chirped, setting Mae's baby seat on the counter. "How goes the battle, you two?"

Ash displayed his bandaged hand. "I've taken some shrapnel, but I'll live."

"Oh, no! Abby, you should go easier on the hired help."

He offered that ready, sloping grin of his. "The things I put up with for free food."

Miranda laughed, totally charmed, while Abby felt like a gray rain cloud lurking behind Ash's shoulder.

Bright-eyed and rosy cheeked, Mae kicked in her cushy seat. Miranda unbuckled her and lifted her out. "Abby, how's Lucy?"

"Good. She came through the operation fine and she'll be home in a few days."

"A few days? My gosh, that's not long at all. Well don't you worry, I've cleared my schedule and I can work as much as you need."

"And I'll be here, too." Ash gave Abby a reassuring smile.

Behind his back, Miranda raised her eyebrows and mouthed, "He's cute," then winked.

Abby cringed. "Miranda . . ."

But when Ash turned around, her friend grinned innocently. Thank God Miranda's cell phone took that moment to interrupt with a chime. She shoveled around in her purse for a moment, then held Mae out to Ash. "Here, hold this a minute, will you?"

Before he could object, the baby was in his arms, cradling his face with her chubby hands and gazing at him with drooling adoration while Miranda strolled away to chat on the phone.

He looked so helpless, Abby had to chuckle.

"What do I with do with it?" His words came out funny because Mae was squeezing his cheeks together and grinning toothlessly.

" 'It' is a girl, and her name is Mae. Here, like this." Abby mimed holding a baby against her shoulder, one hand on the back, one hand on the bottom. Brows drawn, Ash manipulated the little bundle until Mae was busily gnawing on his t-shirt around his collarbone.

"Is it hungry?" He took a tentative sniff of Mae's wisp of hair and made a face. "It's trying to eat me."

"She's teething." Abby caught one side of her lower lip to hold down her laughter. "Haven't you ever held a baby before?"

"Not unless I was pulling it out of a burning car or something," he said in heroic fashion.

She patted Mae's back. "How does Uncle Ash taste, baby? Like window box dirt?"

He gave her a smirk then followed her lead, rubbing his hand over Mae's pink-shirted back. His big hand spanned little Mae's shoulders. His fingers brushed against Abby's. Briefly, he curled his pinky around hers. Their gazes met over Mae's tuft of hair.

Abby's smile faded.

She slid her hand away and touched a bent knuckle to the baby's ear. She used to daydream about the children she and Ash might have.

A sweet fantasy she hadn't indulged in for years drifted through her mind, of a sturdy little boy hand in hand with Ash, going off fishing with his daddy on a summer's day. Somehow, she'd been sure they would have a boy. Their first child, at least.

She'd managed to stuff those feelings into a dark closet in the back of her mind, but Ash's touch unlocked the door. All the more reason to guard her heart, before he pocketed it and stole away from her life again.

"Don't you make a cute family!" Miranda came back to take Mae. "You're a natural with babies, Ash. I'm surprised Abby hasn't told me more about you." As soon as Mae lost contact with Ash's broad chest, she began to wail, which sent Miranda skittering to her diaper bag for a bottle.

Clearly alarmed, Ash held up his hands. "I didn't make her cry, did I?"

"No," Abby said. "She's hungry. You were only an appetizer. Your shoulder's all wet."

"Ugh." He lifted the sopping t-shirt from his neck. "Laundry night, anyhow." He glanced at her and his expression grew serious. "Miranda's here now, and I don't have anywhere to go until later. We'll close up the store. Go home and get some sleep."

Oh, so tempting. She could almost feel the mattress yielding to her exhausted weight. "I have to get groceries for Lucy, and set up her house so it'll be easy for her to get around."

"She won't be home for days. It can wait. Or at least wait until later when I can help you."

Before she could protest that she didn't need his help, he curled his bandaged mitt around the back of her neck and drew her close. He pressed a kiss to her forehead, soft and tender—and all too brief. He must have thought the same as she, because he slid his arms around her and pulled her against the wall of his chest.

"Ash—" Abby bit the edge of her lip. Her breathy moan had sounded more like encouragement than protest. But oh God, he was so solid and warm. With a shudder she felt to her toes, she surrendered—just for a moment, she promised herself—into his embrace. She settled her hands on the waist of his jeans. His strong fingers massaged the back of her neck behind the heavy fall of her hair. His heart thumped steadily beneath her ear. His chin settled on top of her head.

"Go home, honey." His murmur reverberated through her, and all the exhaustion she'd been fighting swept through her like a sleeping potion. "I'll take care of everything."

She'd get rid of him tomorrow. She would. But for now, Abby decided, she'd take him up on his offer. It was too tempting to pass up. Just as, heaven help her, Ash was becoming too tempting to ignore.

# CHAPTER SEVEN

Staring into the hay field that bordered his brother's property, Ash rubbed the warm spot on his chest where Abby's cheek had lain earlier that afternoon. He'd put on a clean, baby drool-free shirt as soon as he'd gotten back to his . . . couch. But the glow on his skin remained.

If only he had a place to stay, an apartment or a hotel room. Somewhere Abby could go where she wouldn't be reminded that she had responsibilities. She needed rest. He only hoped she'd done as he'd told her and slept. Knowing Abby, though, she was probably grocery shopping, or re-siding the house, or repaving the sidewalk.

"Hey." His father, coming up beside him, handed him a tall, water-beaded bottle of beer. "How'd your first day at the deli go?"

"Like I was born to the job." Tipping back the bottle, Ash took a long drink. The cool beer helped ease the heat of the day, which slid down with the sunset. Peepers chirped in the swampland beyond the field, and scattered handfuls of black birds winged back to their nests. Behind, in the house, the muffled clink of plates and the good smells of dinner wafted on a mild breeze. "It's so quiet here. I'd forgotten."

His dad leaned on the white porch railing that lapped the farmhouse and picked at the peeling paint. "Yup. No traffic jams, no drive-bys. Not one murder in a hundred years. Real boring."

81

"Yeah, I don't know how you deal with it. Me, I might be importing some criminals by now, just to have something to do. The only real threat," he said, lifting his white-wrapped hand, "is Lucy's old poodle."

Pete, Sr., turned and propped a hip on the edge of the railing. He was the prototype of Peter, Jr., for sure. Broad-jawed and sandy haired, only a little gray at the temples. His father still looked like he could wrestle a two-ton bull and live to brag about it the next day. "Cranberry's a good town. A solid community." There was more than a little pride in his voice. "Nice place to settle, raise a family." He took a sip of his beer.

"Don't tell me you're getting married again, Pop?"

"Now that wouldn't happen in a hundred years, either." His brown eyes twinkled. "But I am planning on a change. I guess Pete told you I'm going to retire."

"He mentioned it."

"I thought I'd make the announcement at the town picnic on the fourth. Most everyone will be there. You're invited, too."

It would be his last night in Cranberry. Maybe he could sweet talk Abby into going with him. A blanket on the grass under the stars, a bottle of wine, fireworks exploding overhead . . . And Abby relaxed and laughing beside him, the lights reflecting in her beautiful eyes. Easy to picture; maybe not so easy to make happen, but it was worth a shot. He nodded. "Sure, Pop. Count me in."

His father's broad cheeks relaxed into a teasing smile. "So how is that McGuire girl, anyhow?"

"Abby." Brother Peter must have ratted him out.

"I always liked her." His father picked the peeling paint from the railing. "Nice, settled girl."

"She's doing well. Did you know she was married?"

"Married?"

"Divorced now." Peter walked up behind them.

Ash paused, beer half-raised to his mouth, and narrowed his eyes at his brother. "Any progress on her vandalism complaint?"

"Some. I don't think those kids will be bothering her again."

"Talked to their parents," Pete Sr. said sagely. "That still counts for something around here."

"I'll let her know," Ash muttered. Not for a minute did he believe his brother. He wouldn't even look Ash in the eye. "Who were they, anyhow? Locals?"

"Yeah," his father said with a resigned shrug. "Kids these days don't appreciate the quiet life. Like you never did." He laughed and poked his beer bottle at Ash. "Now you're a city slicker. I can see it. You're restless. You always were your mother's son."

Ignoring the irritation of his father's words, Ash said, "What did the kids look like? I had a few teenagers at the store today. I was pretty sure one shoplifted some candy."

His father looked back at Peter, who swigged his beer. "Don't worry about it. It's under control."

"This isn't L.A., son," his father said, rolling back his shoulders. " 'Round here, we let family handle the youngsters."

Peter smiled, though it didn't reach his eyes. "Pop, why don't you go in and see if Merry needs help with the grill. You always do the best job with the steaks."

"I can't deny it." Pete Sr. shook his head. "It's all in the charcoal. Bet you don't have many cookouts in the city, eh, son? Nothing but tofu and bean sprouts out there. We'll put some meat on your bones tonight." He laughed and patted his round belly, then swung open the screen door and went into the house.

Peter stared at Ash. Anger simmered in his cool blue gaze. "What do you want us to do, clap them in leg irons and send them off to juvie hall?"

"Give me their names," Ash replied. This was between him and his brother now.

"There's no point."

"At least give me a description so I can keep watch for them. It's no big deal."

"The problem's been resolved."

Ash ground his teeth. Shut out, as usual. It had always been Peter and his father in collusion, and Ash the rebel on the outside. He was still on the fringes.

"Make sure it stays resolved," he said to his brother, sick of it all.

Peter stepped closer, beer clutched in his fist against his chest. "Or what? You're going to take care of it the way you took care of that problem in L.A.?"

Shit. His jaw clenched. "You know I was cleared."

"Stay out of it, Ash. We handle things one way around here. Your hot temper might have been called heroic in L.A., but in my town, we do things different."

Shock froze Ash. Could Peter actually think he'd shot that boy in a fit of rage?

"You have no idea." He pushed upright and stalked Peter, circling him on the porch. "The worst thing you have to deal with is a few rocks thrown through windows. I was in a war zone. Gangs. Drugs. Murders every day, not just every hundred years. I did damned well not to snap."

Peter held his stare so long that Ash wondered if he was looking for signs of insanity. Well, let him look.

Peter wiped his lower lip with the edge of his finger. "You couldn't even shoot a squirrel when you were younger."

In his mind's eye, Ash saw time like a tunnel, the end zooming out away from him, a light like a pinprick getting farther away. The past was gone. He turned his face to the open field. Truth was, he still couldn't, didn't want to, kill anything. He was too angry with his brother to explain. It wouldn't make any difference, anyhow.

Peter set his own empty bottle on the porch railing. His eyes were cool and wary. "You've been gone a long time. Let's take this slow. Okay?"

Ash leaned his forearms on the railing and let his head sag. It felt full of rocks grinding together anyhow. "It doesn't matter, Peter. I'll be gone a long time again, believe me. The sooner the better."

"I didn't mean it that way, Ash. I just had to let you know where I stand."

The parting pat on the back his brother gave him did nothing to ease Ash's mood. Nothing ever really changed in Cranberry. Colors faded, dust settled, but suspicion and judgment remained vivid and rigid as ever. If he had a brain in his head, he'd pick up and leave now. Peter could explain it to Pop. Let him tell him whatever he wanted.

Instead, Ash finished his beer and hung on the railing, letting the warm breeze riffle through his hair. The breeze smelled sweet, of long grass ripening and a flower garden swelling with life. Like Abby, when she'd come into his arms and let him hold her, her hair velvet against his throat. She was everything good in this world, when he'd thought there wasn't anything left worth having.

He couldn't leave. Yet. But he couldn't stay either.

A little more time. Just a little. With her.


"So you and that gorgeous man used to date?"

Abby hunkered down on the balls of her feet and steadied the big piece of plywood against Lucy's top porch step. "Yes, Miranda, but it was a long time ago. How does this look?"

Miranda tipped her head and touched a finger to her lower lip. "I don't know. It still looks crooked to me."

"It does to me, too, darn it." Groaning, Abby straightened to her feet. Taking a rare day off from the deli, she'd hoped to get

85

so much done today, but this little project alone had taken several precious hours. "This wheelchair ramp seemed like such a good idea. Why can't I get it right? All I can picture is this board tipping like a see-saw, and Auntie landing in the philoden- drons."

"Why not call Ash?"

"It's his day off, and mine, too. Besides, I can do this myself."

"So what happened?"

Abby bent to pick up the hammer. "I must not have put enough nails in the base."

"Not with the ramp." Miranda hopped down from her perch on the back of Abby's car. "I meant with Ash Wheeler."

"I know what you meant. I was ignoring you."

Miranda chuckled. It was an evil chuckle, and Abby knew her friend well enough to tread with caution. "Miranda, don't get any ideas."

Miranda gave a dramatic pout. "Mae likes him, and she's a wonderful judge of character." She walked over to check the baby, who lay in her seat beneath a shady pink dogwood. Seeing that Mae was still asleep, Miranda strolled over to Abby. "You can't blame me for being curious."

Abby hammered another nail into the handrail. "We dated, that's all. High school crush." She gave the bar a shake. "I don't know why you won't believe me."

"Because anyone can see there's more to it. The man adores you."

Oh, sure. Why did he have to decide now that he adored her? Timing was everything. Of course, Miranda had always been a romantic. Whatever she saw in Ash, Abby needed to ignore, just as she ignored the spark of hope her friend's words set off in her heart. If she let herself begin to believe that Ash still cared for her, she would just be setting herself up for a fall.

She waved the hammer toward the ramp. "Do me a favor and try it out?"

With a frustrated sigh, Miranda shook her head. She strutted up the ramp. At the top, she turned, hands out, then sashayed down again, hips swinging like a model on a catwalk.

Abby hooted. "Finally!" She hooked the hammer into a loop of her painter's jeans and cocked a finger at Miranda. "I told you I could do it. Who needs men?"

Miranda's attention wandered over her shoulder, and an ominous grin curved her lips. "I don't know, but there's one headed this way now."

The throaty rumble of a motorcycle cut through the quiet morning. The fine hairs stood on the back of Abby's neck. She turned. Even though the rider wore a battered red helmet, there was no disguising the lean, muscular body. The man seemed to throw a magnetic force field out before him. A thrill of recognition raced over her skin, and the day seemed suddenly hotter and brighter.

She shot Miranda a pleading look. "Stay a while?"

"Not on your life."

Ash braked his bike in an impressive half-moon skid of gravel and dirt and tugged off his helmet. He jammed his fingers through his short, dark hair. The sun winked off the dented chrome of the motorcycle and glinted in his gray eyes. Stubble shadowed his jaw and framed the white flash of his grin. He looked far too sexy for his own good—or for hers. Her eyes must be big as saucers. She turned away and busied herself with her supplies.

Beside her, Miranda waved and called, "Good morning!"

He answered her back, and as always, his deep, masculine voice sent a wash of sensual interest through Abby.

From the corner of her eye, she watched Ash amble over to visit Mae, his latest girlfriend, who woke up enough to coo and wiggle her toes for him. Miranda unhelpfully told him she happened to be on her way out, and he scooped up the baby seat and diaper bag and put them in the back seat of her SUV. Miranda lived near Abby's apartment; they'd been neighbors and buddies for the past few years, but Abby might be inclined to reconsider the buddy part. She really didn't want to be alone with Ash. Not now, just when she'd reached some kind of emotional equilibrium.

Miranda couldn't peel out of the driveway fast enough, curse her.

"Morning, Abby." Ash's shadow fell over her. "What're you up to? Putting on an addition?"

She tugged off her gloves. "Just because the store's not open doesn't mean there aren't things to do."

Even his dark scowl looked sexy. He wore his customary t-shirt, black today, and jeans. His cool eyes assessed her. "I was hoping you were resting."

"Resting? I'm not the one with the broken hip. I've got a full day planned."

"I can see that." His answer came on the breeze. He'd walked over to check out the ramp. Scratching the back of his head, he inspected her handiwork. "What's this?"

"What's it look like? A wheelchair ramp." And he'd better not find anything wrong with it.

Being a man, of course, he had to try it out. His big, sneakered feet thumped up and down the plywood, sending up shaky plumes of dust. The plywood dipped and squeaked. Abby held her breath. If it fell now, she swore she'd have it for firewood later.

"Nice work," he pronounced. Abby let out the breath she'd been holding. "Although, you might want to—"

"Oh, no." She stopped him with a raised hand and hefted her toolbox with the other. "It's done. If you have any bright ideas, save them for another time. I worked on that ramp all morning."

"It's only nine o'clock."

"I got up early. Habit, from the store."

"Ah." He studied her face, probably reading the evidence of another sleepless night in the circles under her eyes. "Well. You look like you could use a break. I'm taking you out for breakfast."

She gave a dry, humorless chuckle. "Sure, we can eat at that cute little deli in town. You know, Lucy's?"

"There's got to be someplace else. How about Leo's?"

"The competition? Perish the thought. What would my aunt say?"

"Think of it as industrial espionage." He strolled toward her, rubbing his hands together. "We'll check out their omelets and bagels, see if they're as good as yours. Steal their secret recipes. Put cockroaches in their salt shakers."

"Oh, you make it sound so appetizing." She squelched her smile a little too late.

"We can take my Ferrari." He jerked a thumb over at the old motorcycle.

She lowered her chin and gave first it, then him, a disbelieving stare. "Nice wheels."

"It was under a tarp in Peter's garage. My old bike." Pride of ownership lit his face. "You and I went for some pretty fun rides on Red Betty, as I recall." His eyebrow raised a perceptive degree as heat rushed into Abby's cheeks.

Many of those rides had ended at secret places, in shaded groves, where she and Ash kissed and caressed until they were breathless and bothered. Her throat gone dry, Abby fluttered her lashes at him. "I can't quite remember. Are you sure that was you?"

Ash gave an evil chuckle. "Maybe I'll have to refresh your memory."

Completely unnecessary, though she wouldn't admit that to him. She bit the edge of her lip. Even now, her skin burned for the sweep of his hands, and her lips tingled as if anticipating the slight tilt of his head that would bring his mouth against hers. Before her face ignited in flame, Abby sputtered, "I can't, really. I have errands to run. I want to pick up some top soil at Martin's and bed Lucy's garden."

"We could do it together."

"On Red Betty?"

"Your car. I drive, I buy you breakfast and a tank of gas. Deal?"

A foot of air separated them, and his body heat swept around her, unrelenting as sunshine. His wind-tousled hair plastered to his brow in short, damp commas. The fierce focus of his gaze made his determination evident.

Well, she was hungry . . . and she could use the help.

"You're not going to take no for an answer, are you?" she said.

"When did I ever? Besides, Abby, I'm only here for a few more days. Let's make the most of it."

A few days? Why did something that should have been good news lie on her heart like a cold stone?

She could tell by the set of his jaw he was grinding his teeth. Bad habit of his. She put her hands on her hips and sighed. "I guess if I say no, you'll wear out your molars."

"Huh?"

She reached up to cup his sandpapery jaw with her hand and gave him a little shake. "You're clenching. Relax. I'll go."

He rubbed his chin, a puzzled expression on his face. As she turned to walk to the garage, Abby laughed.

★　★　★　★　★

He followed her into Lucy's kitchen, doing a very good job of not jumping up and down in triumph. He tracked the tick-tock of her feminine walk as she went up her self-installed ramp. Later, he'd have to convince her to let him pound a few more nails into the top and the base, otherwise it wouldn't last long. But, he had to admit, she'd done a good job with what she had. Independent as always. That was his Abby.

"I see your hand is better," she said.

He'd replaced her overzealous wrap job with a half-dozen band-aids. "Yeah, I'll live. Where is the little monster, anyhow?"

"Tied up out back. You're safe for the moment. Can I get you some coffee?"

"No, thanks, I can wait."

"Are you sure? I might be a minute, washing up."

"Come as you are. You look great." He sounded hungry—for her. He knew it, and so did she, by the way she turned her face away when the color glowed in her cheeks. He walked through the spacious country kitchen and stopped by the window overlooking the back yard. She went into the hallway bathroom, but left the door open. He watched her while she drew out her ponytail and pulled a brush through her long, flowing hair. Like a skein of dark gold silk, it draped her shoulder as she tipped her head and fell almost halfway down her back. The brush shushed rhythmically; he could almost feel the softness of her hair sliding through his fingers.

"Have you spoken to Lucy yet today?" he asked, corralling his runaway thoughts.

"I gave her a call this morning. Hospital days start early, and I knew she'd be up with the sun out of habit. She sounds like her old self already. I'm going to see her later this afternoon."

"Maybe I can come with you."

She tossed the brush in the drawer and didn't answer. Her

mental battle over whether to let him in or keep him out showed in her expressive eyes. Go slow, he reminded himself. You don't have much time, another voice nagged.

Ash glanced around the sunny kitchen. "I haven't been here since I was a kid. I know I keep saying this, but nothing changes. Same teacups and roses on the wallpaper, same old copper kettle on the stove."

She joined him by the sink. "The only thing that's different is that the house is starting to fall apart."

"Yeah, I noticed it could use a coat of paint."

"More than that." She picked up a sponge and wiped the already spotless counter. "The roof shingles are coming up in spots, there are loose boards in the deck. The yard's been mowed, but Lucy's gardens are going to seed. She used to take such pride in them."

"Maybe it's time for her to sell the place."

She started as if he'd sworn aloud. "Where would she go?"

"A condo? There's new elderly housing going up in Westfield, I passed it coming in."

"Elderly housing?" She made it sound so absurd.

"She is . . . elderly. I know it's hard to face."

Abby scrunched up the sponge and pitched it into the sink. "I've been thinking of moving back in. Permanently, to help her out." Her soft lips compressed in a frown. "Maybe get a second job. I don't know."

"Second job? The deli's not doing well?"

"I looked over the books yesterday. It's a pretty grim scene." Her brown eyes filled with worry. "Please don't tell anyone."

"Of course not." He was just glad she was telling him. He had a feeling she'd been keeping all this to herself for too long. "If you need money, I can—"

Her brows snapped down. "Oh, no. No, I wasn't asking—" She threaded her fingers through her hair, a nervous gesture he recognized just as she'd recognized his tooth-grinding. "I'm sorry, I'm sure you didn't come here to hear about my problems."

"You can always talk to me, Abby." He reached for her hand on the counter and curled his fingers around hers. "We used to talk all the time. Remember?"

She eyed their joined hands, then slid hers out from under his. "Some things have changed, Ash."

Her quiet voice pierced him. So serious. So sad. She was right; she had changed, from a laughing, happy girl to a woman with too many responsibilities and not enough time for herself.

Before he left, he promised he would see her smile again.

# CHAPTER EIGHT

Any doubts Abby harbored about taking up Ash's invitation melted away with the first bite of her spinach and cream cheese omelet.

"Oh," she moaned, "this is heaven."

Seated across from her, Ash stared with his hands white-knuckled around his coffee mug and his gaze riveted on her mouth. "Glad you like it," he muttered after a moment, setting down his mug so he could wipe the heel of his hand across his brow.

Abby perused the busy café. It was a small place, bright and sunny, with glass-topped tables and smiling waitresses who seemed to know just about everyone they served. "I've never been here. How'd you find it?"

"I ate here before I got to my brother's. I knew it would be your kind of place."

"My kind of place? What do you mean?"

He waved his fork. "Cozy, cute, with a more creative menu. That's one thing I'll miss about L.A. You could get any kind of food you wanted, any time of day or night. There was a little dive down the road from my apartment that made Thai noodles so hot they could set your hair on fire. Great stuff."

"Cranberry's not ready for exotic food. Although, of course, this is Buckland. Slightly more civilized."

He nodded and dug into his own stack of pancakes and eggs. "How come you never opened that catering business you used to talk about?"

"Never enough time or money. And it's not as if Cranberry has a huge demand for caterers. It's still more of a picnic-in-the-park kind of place."

"You would have had to set up shop in the city."

He said it in a leading way, and she shrugged. "I still might, someday."

"Abby, you'll never leave Cranberry. You're a small-town girl. It's in your blood."

"You never know. The way things are going . . ." She tried to make light of it, but the events of the past few days darkened her tone. She didn't want to finish the thought. If the deli went under, and her aunt moved to a condo . . .

She felt Ash touch her wrist, and looked up.

"I'm sorry," he murmured.

His gray eyes were kind, caring. She dropped her gaze—not that it would do any good. He understood as well as she how she felt about Cranberry, and why she had such an attachment to the town. What he'd said at her aunt's was true; they used to share every thought, every dream. It was too easy to slip into old habits. She found a smile to ease the mood and went back to her breakfast. "With all that good Thai food at your doorstep, what made you leave L.A.?"

"I killed someone."

Abby gagged. Reaching for her water glass, she sputtered, "Excuse me?"

"Are you okay?"

She gulped down the water and nodded, pressing her napkin to her mouth. "For a second there, I thought you said . . . you killed someone."

One arm draped on the table, he took the time to shovel in another forkful before he answered. "You heard right."

"Was it a . . . a criminal?"

Without looking up, he nodded. Abby breathed again. The sounds of the restaurant rushed back at her. She flexed her hands on the edge of the table, just now realizing she'd shoved herself back in her chair.

Good lord. She studied him in a whole new light. The stony jaw, the taut muscles of his arms flexing while he picked over the remaining eggs on his plate. His body was hard and honed, made for meting out punishment and taking the same. He might have been the tough guy in Cranberry, but thrown into the crucible of a dangerous city, he must have been completely unprepared. For the first time, she began to wonder what he'd been through, how it had shaped his heart and mind as well as his body.

When he finally lifted his head, his expression was shadowed, unreadable. If she was an open book, then Ash was an unfathomable well. He'd learned to mask his feelings, she realized. She recognized nothing in his mica-flecked eyes. A cold stillness settled over her. Suddenly Abby felt as if she didn't know him at all.

"It was a kid," he said, just when she thought it couldn't get any worse.

"A child?"

"Sixteen. He had a sawed-off shotgun. We were raiding a house we'd been watching for weeks." He set down his fork and drew his hand over his face. "He got a shot off at me, then wounded my partner. He was wild, in a rage. I didn't want to . . ." His voice was flat. He sat up and shoved his plate away.

"Oh, Ash. It's not your fault. You had to do it."

His mouth flattened, and she sensed he'd questioned his actions a thousand times. He spread his fingers over the top of his coffee cup. "I wanted you to know, in case Peter said something. I wanted you to hear it from me first."

"I'm glad you told me," she murmured uncertainly. She bit

her lower lip. "Did you get in trouble?"

"The usual kind. In most big cities, the public views cops as the bad guys, so when something like that happens, there's an inquiry. A very thorough one. When the dust settled, though, I was cleared."

He said it with quiet emphasis, as if it was important she believe him. Of course, she believed him. "It must have been horrible for you."

"Worse for the kid I shot," he said dryly, and she saw the cold façade he must have built to protect himself. But even the bluntness of his words testified to the fact that it still affected him, that he hadn't forgiven himself.

"You're not going back, are you?" she asked.

"To Los Angeles? No."

"To being a cop."

He set down his cup and shook his head. "No."

"I'm sorry, Ash. I know how important it was to you."

He seemed to be folding in on himself, his mouth grim, dark lashes shielding his eyes. "One man can't make a difference. Not in a place like L.A."

Catching her lower lip between her teeth, she silently disagreed. "What do your father and brother think?"

"My father hasn't said much. I think the whole concept is so foreign to him that he doesn't know how to react. Peter, on the other hand, worries I'm some kind of vigilante who wants to gun down your vandals."

"I can't believe your brother would think that about you."

"We've never had the best relationship. In fact, the only time we've really gotten along is when I wasn't living in Cranberry. Then we seemed to appreciate each other." He said it wryly, but there was an undertone of frustration in his words. "My father wants me to stay and join the force here."

A spark of hope leaped through her. "Have you . . . considered it?"

He shook his head, dark brows lowering. "Peter's going to be the next chief of police. I can't work under him. He doesn't trust me."

"Then he doesn't know you."

At her adamant defense, he looked up, faint surprise evident in his expression. An unspoken question hovered between them. Did Abby trust him, then? The strength of her statement made it sound as if she did. Nerves quivering as if she'd leapt into battle unarmed, Abby didn't know what else to say.

Fortunately, he didn't push the issue. They finished their meals and conversation got back on more casual footing. By the time the waitress came to take their plates away, Abby was comfortably full and the most relaxed she'd been in days.

"That was wonderful," she said, leaning back in her chair with her fingers laced over her tummy. She gave Ash a smile, and he slanted one back at her. No wonder every waitress in the place had stopped by to see if they needed more coffee. Even the most casual glance from the man burned with subtle sexuality. Or maybe it was just that she was sleepy and warm and satisfied, a sensation she'd once enjoyed in his arms, in his bed. It would be easier to stop thinking that way if she didn't have a gut feeling he was thinking along the same lines. Their minds in harmony . . . their bodies moving together . . .

Abby shook her head to clear her thoughts, and Ash pulled out a black leather wallet and waved the waitress over. She gave him the bill, which he paid at the table. Abby stood and got her purse, and they strolled out into the late morning sun.

"Thank you for breakfast," she said, reaching for her keys only to remember Ash had them. She turned at the car door. He was right behind her. "Are you driving?"

"Yes." He stepped forward and slid his arms around her.

She had one second to catch her breath before his mouth made contact. Her muscles contracted. Her sharp inhale brought his sun-warmed scent rushing into her lungs. His firm hand traced the length of her spine, pressed at the small of her back, coaxing her closer. His other hand cradled her head, fingers tunneling into her hair. The hot metal of the car couldn't compare to the fire radiating from his solid body as he pressed her against the door. Her legs nearly buckled with shock, then, as he slanted his mouth over hers and deepened the kiss, with startling need.

One question was answered right away. Her memory hadn't lied. He was everything she remembered, and more.

Sweet desperation filled her. Her purse thumped to the pavement. She reached for him to draw him down. His taut shoulders felt like granite beneath her fingertips. The fabric of his shirt bunched in her grip. Through her closed eyelids, the sun blazed, all her senses suddenly alive. His firm, knowing lips moved over hers, caressing, exploring, too gentle, too patient. By the time he lifted his head, she was trembling.

She didn't want him to stop. Abby bit down a groan and dared to open her eyes. He gripped her waist, thumbs drawing small circles beneath her ribs. Breathing hard, his mouth bent in a frown, he touched his forehead to hers. Oh, God, he had to feel how she was shaking. She couldn't hide it.

Frozen, embarrassed, aroused, she stared down at his scuffed sneakers. Then, traveling up his jeans, her gaze locked on something else. A hot flush raced over her skin from crown to toes. Apparently she wasn't the only one aroused by their kiss. Desire hit her tenfold, a wave that made her knees go weak. Despite the sun beating down on the top of her head, she shivered.

It seemed to be his cue to come to his senses. "You're welcome," he murmured.

He straightened away and took the keys out of his pocket. One corner of his delicious mouth sloped up, and she couldn't decide if she wanted to slap him or kiss him again. He looked terribly satisfied, while she was a messy puddle of nerves and need.

Not fair. Not fair at all.


Abby touched the broad green leaves of a potted shrub and asked, "How about these hydrangeas? Do you think Lucy would like these?"

She said it over her shoulder. Ash smiled to himself. Since the restaurant, she'd been skittish. She seemed to float over the ground, just out of his grasp, but high color tinted her cheeks and she looked more awake and aware than he'd seen since Lucy's accident. He hadn't tried to kiss her again, although the shady rose bower in the side lot of the Cranberry Garden Center looked mighty tempting. For the moment, he was content to watch her. Especially now, when she was bent over with her perfect, curvy—

"Hey, Ash!"

A voice he hadn't heard in ages boomed from the direction of the store. He recognized his old friend, Jim Martin, and grinned. "Jimmy, you old dog."

"Ash, you old bastard." They shook hands and clapped each other on the shoulder. "What the hell have you been up to?"

Abby came over, and Jim put his hand over his mouth. "Oops, hi, Abby, didn't know there was a lady present."

She waved a hand. "Oh, don't mind me. I'm going to wander over to the evergreens."

Ash nodded. "Okay. I'll catch up."

She gave a nervous grin and practically bolted away.

"Didn't know you were back," Jim said, drawing Ash's attention away from the lovely retreating view.

"Only for a while. Looks like you're doing a good business here." Jim's family had owned the garden center for sixty years.

"Yeah, I could complain but who'd listen?" His square white teeth gleamed through his short brown beard. In high school, Jim had been a whiplash-thin basketball star. Judging by his ample belly and domesticated appearance, he must have settled down with that girlfriend of his—what was her name?

"You still with Andrea?" Ash ventured.

"Hell yeah. Married five years. Got a little boy and another baby on the way."

"Congratulations." Ash smiled, but on the inside his mood darkened a little. While he was off chasing bad guys, everyone else had had the good sense to cozy up and start families. And be happy.

"How about you and Abby?" his friend asked.

Ash shook his head. "Just helping her out while her aunt's in the hospital."

"I heard about that. She okay?" After Ash filled him in, Jim hooked his thumbs in the waistband of his dirty-kneed jeans and grew serious. "I was afraid she might have been hurt during a break-in. We've had some trouble lately with vandals and shoplifters. It's unusual for Cranberry."

"What kind of trouble? When?"

Jim swept a hand toward the parking lot. "We put a chain across the driveway at night, but it's not like we can lock away every tree or plant. Two days last week, I came in to find a few big ceramic planters smashed out back. Some shrubs were missing. I found them later, upended in the back woods." He lifted a shoulder. "Who would do that? They didn't even take the stuff, they just destroyed it."

"Lucy's deli was hit, too."

He nodded. "And Johnson's drug store, and Little Angels Preschool. Jodi Faulkner lost most of the tricycles and toys she kept in the yard for the kids to play on."

"That's a shame." Ash rubbed a hand across his jaw. Clenching again, he realized. "You talk to my brother about it?"

"Sure. He came out both times. Didn't seem too upset about it." Although Jim was, judging by his tone. "He said it was a bunch of kids and they knew who they were and would put an end to it."

"He told me the same thing. I had dinner with him last night, and he assured me the parents had been informed and there wouldn't be any more incidents."

Jim snorted. "Parents? I lost about a thousand dollars worth of merchandise. Are they going to reimburse me? Or Jodi, or Clay Johnson?"

"I don't know."

"You're a cop, too, aren't you? Can't you step in?"

"Wish I could, but I'm not official in Cranberry. The most I can do is keep after Peter."

"Well, you do that. Otherwise I'm tempted to sit out back one night with my deer rifle and unload some rock salt into their hides."

"I doubt you'll have any more trouble." Ash glanced over Jim's shoulder at Abby's distant form. She was meandering through a row of berry bushes. "Did you clean up the damage? I wouldn't mind taking a look at it."

"We picked up the ceramic planters, but the bushes are still in the woods, and I haven't gotten around to washing the spray paint off the side of the barn. It's not where customers can see. Come on."

Ash followed him around the back of the nursery's main building. A dirt path led to the old barn they used for storage. Bold red and blue spray paint scrawled obscenities across the peeling gray wall.

"You know, in Los Angeles, some of the graffiti is actually

pretty artistic," Ash quipped, rocking back on his heels. "This is crap."

"Tell me about it. I can see how they concluded it was kids."

"Yeah, younger teenagers, I'd say. Look, they can't even spell Cranberry right. One 'r.' "

"And who spells sucks with an x?" Jim shook his head. "Back in the day, old Mrs. Narley would've suspended us for such shoddy work."

"If we catch them, I'll make sure they spray paint this over a hundred times, correctly." He swapped grins with Jim, then shook his head. "How about the shrubs?"

"They're in the woods here, but I don't know how much you'll be able to tell from that. It's rained since then."

Ash went back there anyway, and looked over the broken pots and ruined plants. "What kind of plants are these?" he asked, crouching down to rub the dying leaves between his fingertips. He sniffed the residue.

"Kenaf. We raise it for livestock," Jim said. "Why?"

"Looks a little like pot."

Jim laughed. "Oh, hell, you think the kids thought I was growing a stash here?"

"Who knows? They're obviously not the sharpest knives in the drawer."

"Then they shouldn't be hard to catch."

"You wouldn't think so," Ash said, but his thoughts were elsewhere. Peter hadn't told him about these other incidents. This was pretty serious stuff, for Cranberry. A surge of protective instinct rose in him. His brother should be taking better care of the town and its residents. He liked Jim, and he remembered Jodi Faulkner from school. She was a nice girl. No one deserved to have their property destroyed. "Jim, if anything like this happens again, call my brother, but get hold of me, too." He waited while Jim drew a pad from his shirt pocket then gave him his cell phone number. "I'm going to ask around, see what I can find out on my own."

Jim slipped the pad back into his pocket and clicked his pen. "Thanks, Ash. Hey, how long are you hanging around? I know Andrea would love to have you up to the house for dinner."

"Maybe another time. I've got a few matters to settle before I leave." Namely Abby. He hoped she wasn't looking for him. Or maybe he did hope she was looking for him. He shook Jim's hand again. "Keep me posted."

"I will. And you do the same."

Abby couldn't deny that Ash had been good company this afternoon. He'd come in handy lifting the heavy shrubs she'd bought to replace the dead ones in Lucy's front yard, hauling fifty-pound bags of topsoil and peat moss as if they weighed no more than loaves of bread. They'd brought their purchases back to Lucy's house and dropped them off, had a quick lunch, and were now on the way to visit her aunt. No more kisses in between. She wasn't sure if she was happy about that or not.

Now, staring out at the passing scenery as they cruised down the parkway that lead to the hospital, she held his cell phone and tapped it against her palm for a moment.

Beside her at the wheel, Ash glanced over. "Aren't you going to call Lucy and let her know we're on our way?"

She leaned back in the seat. "I . . . I guess I should."

"What's the matter?"

She sighed. "I promised Lucy I would call my parents yesterday."

"And you didn't."

"I chickened out. I was so tired and frazzled. And I know she's going to ask me about it. I feel like I've let her down."

"Can't you call them tonight?"

"Of course I can, it's just that—"

"You don't want to."

She cast him a sidelong glance. "Ash, it's annoying when you keep finishing my thoughts."

One side of his mouth twitched in a half-smile. "It's only because I know you so well. Tell Lucy the truth. She'll understand. Then call them when we get home."

"I could do that," she conceded. "Although they're probably in a completely different time zone. I might be waking them up in the middle of the night."

"It won't matter. They're your parents."

"What if I can't reach them? Maybe I should send a letter instead."

"Abby."

"A telegram?"

"No dice."

She scowled and slid a little lower in the seat. He was right, though she hated to admit she wanted his advice on the matter; hated to admit the magic of his kiss was working through her system, making her want to reach for him, lean on him. If only she'd been smart enough to say "no" this morning . . .

Ash found a space in the hospital visitor's lot and parked the car. As soon as he switched off the engine, the air conditioning stopped and the heat of the late afternoon swamped the car. He came around and opened the door for her.

"Come on," he said. "It won't be so bad. Maybe she won't even ask."

But, of course, "What did your parents say?" was almost the first thing out of Lucy's mouth. She smiled up at Abby from the crisp sheets of her hospital bed with nothing but trust shining in her eyes. Abby felt Ash's hand on the small of her back. Moral support, no doubt.

"Actually, I didn't get a chance to call them," she admitted, clutching the metal railing on the side of Lucy's bed. "I fell asleep almost as soon as I got home."

"Oh, dear. You couldn't reach them today?"

Her shoulders slumped a little. "I was busy running errands, Auntie."

"She'll call them tonight," Ash interjected.

"Oh, good." Lucy beamed at him. "Make sure she does, Ash."

Abby bristled at the notion that he had to monitor her. She was twenty-six years old and perfectly capable of fulfilling her obligations. She glared at him, but he smiled mildly back, undeterred by the irritation she hoped was snapping in her eyes.

They spent an hour with Lucy. Her aunt wanted to know how the store was doing, and when Abby informed her she hadn't opened today, she seemed pleased. "I'm glad you're taking the time off, dear. Take tomorrow off, too. I insist."

Abby nodded. "I'm only working in the morning, then I'm devoting the afternoon to the house. There's a lot I need to do before you get home. The yard needs clean up and the roof is still leaking."

"Oh, Abby, I won't have you up on the roof. Hire someone."

She parked her hands on her hips. "I'm sure I can—"

"Do it yourself." Lucy waved a bored hand through the air. "I know, dear. You want to do everything yourself, but it's my house and I've been putting off repairs too long. Ash, I remember when you were a teenager, you used to do some landscaping and construction. Do you know anyone who'd be available to work for the day?"

"I'm sure I can think of someone," he said, grinning like the co-conspirator he was.

Abby shook her head. These two were like a couple of plotting kids, and every time Lucy passed that approving glance toward Ash, Abby crumpled inside. Her aunt was clearly picturing them as a couple and finding ways to make it so. For Lucy's sake, Abby went along with Lucy's plan, tolerating Ash's hand when it lingered on her arm, accepting the chair he solicitously got for her. But when the visit was over and she and Ash were back on the road, she turned to him.

"Please don't get Lucy's hopes up."

"What do you mean? It's really no trouble for me to nail a few shingles on her roof and mow the lawn."

"Not that. It's . . . the touching, the attention, the . . . the being nice to me. It's giving her the wrong idea."

"So I should stop being nice to you?"

"No. Yes." Exasperated, she held up her hands, palms out. "No. Just stop making her think we're together."

"Aren't we?" If his voice hadn't deepened, she might have thought he was teasing, but there was just enough tension in the set of his mouth to give her pause. Her thoughts raced back to their kiss. She closed her eyes.

"Of course not."

"I feel like we've never really been apart, Abby."

"Remember those six years there? We didn't see each other, didn't talk to each other?"

"Doesn't matter. When I see you. Touch you . . ." He glanced at her. Damn his sunglasses. Or bless them. She wasn't sure she could handle whatever emotion would be flaring behind them.

She caught her lower lip between her teeth, tasting him all over again. "You sneaked in one kiss." Shaking her finger at him, she tried to cover her jitters with humor. "Next time, I'll be quicker."

Yet even now she wasn't fast enough to escape him. He seized her hand and drew it to his mouth. Abby's breath caught as he pressed his mouth to the sensitive center of her palm. A spark raced through her, igniting desire so pure and shocking, she gasped—and yanked her hand away.

She knotted her fingers in her lap. "That's exactly what I

mean. Stop it."

"I don't think you want me to stop, Abby. And I sure as hell don't want to."

"And what will happen if we don't stop? You'll go off to . . . wherever you're going, and I'll . . ." *Be left behind again.* She stopped short of admitting that he'd hurt her. It didn't need to be said. Lifting her chin, Abby turned to stare out the window at the blurry scenery rushing by. She'd be damned if she'd give him the satisfaction of seeing her trembling lower lip.

"Miami," he said after a moment.

"Excuse me?"

"Miami. That's where I'm going. My partner and I are starting a security firm."

"Florida." Her mouth went dry.

"Yes, Florida. You've heard of it? Thirteenth state, oranges, beaches, etcetera?"

His sarcasm prodded her into a scowl. "Good. Far away."

"I guess there's no point in asking if you'd visit me someday."

"None at all."

Abby refused to look at him. Irritating man. Florida. Figured. He couldn't even look for a job closer to Cranberry. As if there were no jobs in Connecticut.

"Nothing's set in stone yet, Abby," he said quietly, as if that should be some kind of reassurance.

What kind of game was he playing? Why had he opened up over breakfast, told her about shooting that boy, held her, kissed her? Covertly, she cast him a sidelong glance. He looked thoughtful, remote. She wanted to understand why. She wanted to get inside his heart again. That hurt most of all.

# CHAPTER NINE

Later that night, Abby tried to convince Pawpaw to make the call, but he wasn't having any of it. So finally, around ten o'clock, after doing dishes, putting away laundry and tidying her aunt's already tidy house, Abby sat down in Lucy's softly lit living room with the poodle and the phone in her lap and dialed the number.

She went through a series of long-distance operators. Each one sounded tinnier and farther away than the last. Eventually she was put through to a relief center in the heart of Patagonia.

She had to speak loudly. "Mom?"

After a static-filled delay, her mother's voice, which she hadn't heard in a year and a half, filled the line. "Abigail?" Soft, surprised laughter just audible over the background hiss. "Is it your birthday again already?"

Abby twisted her fingers in Pawpaw's fur. "No, Mom. That was a few months ago."

"Was it? I'm sorry." She didn't sound sorry. Abby could picture her, a young-looking fifty-five year old with her long, gray-streaked chestnut hair pulled back by a simple elastic, skin burnished by years in harsh conditions, hazel eyes undimmed. Probably lived in a tent, or a hut, or maybe a battered camper if she was lucky. Abby shifted in the recliner's deep cushions.

"Mom, I'm calling about Aunt Lucy."

"Oh, dear. Has something happened?"

Abby gave her the details. Her mother remained silent so

long that Abby thought she'd lost the connection. Finally, her faraway voice said, "She'll recover, then?"

"Yes, that's what the doctor says. She's coming home in two days."

Another pause. "Do you need anything from your father or me, then, dear?"

"Need anything?" Pressing her fingers to her brow, Abby shook her head. "No. I . . . I thought you would want to know. That's all."

"Good, then, Abigail. Keep us informed. I'm sorry if I sound out of sorts. It's the middle of the day here, you know."

"I didn't—"

"We're flat out delivering grain and powdered milk. The truck's about to leave. You were lucky to catch me. It's beautiful country here, despite the hardship. I'll send you photographs."

Sure you will, Mom, Abby thought but didn't say.

"Well, good-bye, then," her mother said. "Love to Lucy."

"Sure."

"Sorry, dear, I didn't catch that?"

Abby spoke up. "I said, I'll give her your love."

"That's fine. Good–bye."

Abby hung up the phone with a dismal click. Pawpaw glanced up at her. His round black eyes seemed filled with concern. Probably only concerned that she'd stopped scratching his back. Abby made her fingers move in the dog's fur and set the phone back on the end table.

A hollow emptiness spread in her chest. She sat alone in Lucy's cozy living room. The windows were open and a breeze danced with the white sheers. The grandfather's clock gave a single chime for quarter-past the hour, and from the pond beyond the field, the chirruping of little frogs and crickets carried.

Were there crickets in Patagonia?

She wondered if even now her mother was going to her father to tell him of the funny phone call she'd gotten from their daughter. Silly goose thought Lucy's broken hip was good enough reason to interrupt their adventure in the beautiful country.

Imagine that.

Abby nibbled her thumbnail and stared into the twilit space, wishing she weren't so resentful of her parents' dedication. It was sad when she thought about it, that everyone else, like her parents and Ash, was out in the world having adventures and trying to do great things while she was here, safe and bored. And alone.

At least her parents had each other. Maybe they hadn't been faithful to her, but they'd certainly formed a lasting marriage. Because of them, somehow, in some odd way, she'd developed a belief that love was possible, that love could endure in a harsh world. Even that legacy had twisted in on her.

With a groan of frustration, she searched the ache in her heart. It wasn't all her parents' fault. That pain had been dulled by the grind of years. No, this was something fresher, sharper-edged. Suddenly, she knew what it was: she missed Ash.

She stood, sliding poor Pawpaw to the floor. "Oh, this is impossible," she said to the offended poodle. "Let's go for a drive. Or better yet, a walk. I need some air."

Pawpaw's ears went up as if the very idea of a walk at his age was absurd.

"I'll carry you if I have to," Abby muttered. She pulled on her sneakers then grabbed the dog's leash from the top of the TV. She paused long enough to take a flashlight from the front hall closet before she stepped out.

The evening wrapped around her like a velvet cape, soft and warm and fragrant. By road, the deli was thirty minutes away, but she could walk there in twenty if she went through the field, past the pond. Damp grass swished beneath her feet as she found the thin path that kids used to cut behind houses after school. Abby took a deep breath and let it out, letting her tension seep away into the shadows.

Seeing the light from the buildings on Main Street, she felt her mood lighten. She was almost to the opposite edge of the field when Pawpaw stopped dead. The little poodle began a thin, rumbling growl.

"Come on, you." She gave the leash a gentle tug. "We're almost there."

The dog's eyes trained on the building a couple of doors down from the deli, an old house used as an antiques store. Abby squinted into the darkness. No sound but the crickets in the woods. The breeze passed a hand over the tall grass, and the skin on the back of her neck prickled.

Almost as if someone was watching her.

Maybe Ash's tales of big-city crime had affected her more than she'd thought. Suddenly, all the shadows took on suspicious shapes. The soft night sounds hushed ominously. Curse the man, he made her nervous even when he wasn't there. Although she kind of wished he was there now. She'd feel safer with his big, solid body at her side.

Oh, this was insane. She squared her shoulders. She'd never been afraid of the dark before, and she refused to become dependent on anyone, especially Ash Wheeler, just because an elderly poodle growled at nothing. She frowned down at the dog. "Now you've got me paranoid."

Pawpaw sat. Whatever had bothered him seemed to be gone. Just to be safe, Abby picked him up, cradling his light weight under her arm. Her flashlight beam played across the back parking lot. "Nothing. I told you so." But a shiver zipped up her spine as she stepped onto the pavement. A movement—she gasped.

When the heavy hand clamped onto her shoulder, Abby shrieked and swung out for her life.

Peter tipped back in the plastic chair next to the deli's sandwich counter and groaned as he adjusted the ice bag over his eye.

"I am so, so sorry," Abby said for about the fortieth time, clutching a shivering Pawpaw to her chest. "I didn't know it was you."

Leaning against the deli case with his arms crossed, Ash assessed her pale complexion. He had fielded her frantic call not twenty minutes ago. He'd been playing one of Petie's video games, and winning, too, when his cell phone had gone off and Abby's panicked voice came on the line. Apparently, thinking he was a thief, she'd laid Peter right out on the pavement. Ash had raced Red Betty to the deli in record time. By the time he got there, though, Peter was up and swaying on his feet. There wasn't much more to do than help him inside and get some ice.

"Hell of a shot, Abby," Ash said. Now that it was obvious his brother wasn't badly injured, he couldn't help tease her a little. "Didn't know you could swing a flashlight like that."

She speared him with a glare. "It's not funny."

"Hey, better a flashlight than the attack poodle."

"Watch it or I'll sic him on you."

He raised a brow. She was gorgeous when she was angry, with her hair wild around her face and her cocoa eyes shining. She was probably regretting calling him. With that stubborn pride and streak of independence, she must have been pretty scared to reach out to him, of all people; but she had, and it warmed him down to his sockless feet to know it was his number she'd dialed first.

Peter let the front legs of his chair hit the ground. "Quit it, you two." He dropped the hand holding the ice bag into his lap. "How's it look?"

Bad, Ash thought, inwardly wincing. He knew how that felt. A big egg had begun to rise over the ridge of Peter's brow. It would be dark purple tomorrow, and sore as hell.

Abby leaned forward and gingerly lifted the hair off his brother's forehead. "It's, uh . . . Well, at least I missed your eye." She bit her lower lip. "Better put the ice back on. I'm so sorry."

Pete waved her to silence. "I shouldn't have sneaked up on you like that. I didn't see you clearly in the shadows."

She looked pale. Ash was sure she'd never been physically violent with anyone before. He knew from past experience how that charge of adrenaline could leave a person feeling shaky and hollow. From the percolating pot behind him, he poured a cup of coffee, added plenty of sugar, and pressed it into her hand. She took a sip and made a face.

He poured one for his brother and one for himself, too. "What were you doing so late at the store, Abby?"

"I'm expecting deliveries tomorrow. I need to make room for them." She threaded her fingers through her hair. "Miranda is coming in the morning to help, but I wanted to get a head start."

"Why didn't you drive?"

"It's a nice night, I thought I'd walk."

"At ten-thirty? It's not safe."

"This isn't the big city, Ash. Of course it's safe. And stop interrogating me." Her chin and her tone lifted.

"Cranberry or no, there've been enough weird things happening around town that you should be more careful."

She made a soft *tsk* of disgust and set down her cup. He noticed her hands were unsteady. "Did something scare you, make you nervous?"

"Yes!" She turned blazing eyes on him. "Your brother sneaking up on me!"

Peter raised a hand. "Ash, leave her alone. She didn't do anything wrong. It is her store, after all."

He looked at his brother. "Why were you sneaking around?"

"Don't start," Peter groaned. He shook his head, then winced and lifted tentative fingers to the bump. Muttering a curse under his breath, he got to his feet. "If you have to know, I was finishing up some paperwork at the station. I was on my way home when I saw a light behind the deli. It must have been Abby's flashlight. I went to investigate. I thought I might catch those vandals you're so on about."

Peter's complexion had gone two shades whiter when he stood. Ash gripped his elbow to steady him. "Let me drive you home."

"Or to the hospital," Abby chimed in. "I hope you don't have a concussion."

"I'm okay." He slanted Abby a weak grin. "All in the line of duty." Then he looked at Ash. "What did you tell Merry?"

"Only that Abby needed help with something. I figured you could explain it to her later."

"Thanks." He peered at Abby. "You're sure you're all right? I must have given you quite a shock."

"Don't worry about me." Her lips tightened at the corners. "Maybe we'll have a laugh about this tomorrow, me sneaking up on you, you sneaking up on me."

"Like the Keystone Kops," Ash said to Peter. "What if you had come across the vandals? They seem to travel in a group, and they might be carrying baseball bats or crowbars. You might have gotten your head smashed in by worse than a flashlight."

"They're just kids."

"You should have called for backup."

His brother spread his hands. "Called on what?" He wasn't in uniform, and Ash could see his Volvo was parked outside, not his cruiser. "I was well in control of the situation."

Yeah, until Abby clocked him. Of course, it was useless to point this out. Cranberry bred thickheaded fools who refused to acknowledge that the world was a dangerous place.

He turned to his favorite fool, Abby. "I'll drive you home, then."

"In what? Pawpaw isn't going to ride on the back of your motorcycle."

"Okay, we'll walk." And talk. He wasn't through chewing her out for wandering the wilds late at night.

She picked up Pawpaw's leash. "I don't need a bodyguard."

Before Ash could retort, Peter stepped in. "Abby, maybe it is a good idea. It's well past eleven now, and we figure those kids have been prowling close to midnight. Let Ash go with you."

Her lips pressed in a line, but finally she nodded. Ash said goodbye to his brother. The sleigh bells jingled over Peter's exit.

As soon as they were alone, Ash turned to her. "Ready to go?"

"No, I am not," she said. "I have things to do. If you want to escort me, you'll just have to wait. Or you can leave." She gave him an unpleasant smile. "If anyone tries to assault me, I still have my trusty flashlight."

Ash didn't see the humor in it. He sprawled out in the plastic chair Peter had vacated. "I'll wait."

With her back turned to him, she shook her head. "Maybe I want to be alone."

"Maybe I don't."

She sighed loudly for his benefit, but puttered about in silence for a few minutes.

Ash replayed the scene in his head, with a cop's clear eye for detail and gaps. "What did you see, before you KO'd my brother?"

"Nothing. I told you." She moved around the counter and began to put away the coffee and cups. "Pawpaw and I were

116

walking through the field and as soon as I stepped onto the pavement, Peter grabbed me from behind."

"But you said, 'Me sneaking up on you.' Abby, who were you sneaking up on?"

"No one. I didn't see anything."

Instinct told him otherwise, and he'd long ago learned to trust his gut. "Think back on when you were in the field. You didn't see any movement, hear anything odd?"

She gave him such a look that he imagined if the flashlight were within her grasp, it would be creasing his skull right about now. He didn't take it personally. It was just nervous residue making her jumpy. Legs stretched out, hands linked across his stomach, he held her indignant gaze and waited for her to fill the silence.

Finally, she looked away. "Well . . . I didn't hear anything. But Pawpaw started to growl just as we were about to leave the field."

He flicked a glance at the poodle, who was curled up asleep on his doggie bed. If only animals could talk. "Did he bark, or start pulling in any direction?"

"He was looking toward McCready's, a couple houses down. The antiques place." She picked up a dish, then set it back down, her face drawn in thought. "I figured he'd sensed Peter first. He didn't bark, so he must have recognized him. Still, for a while there . . ."

Ash waited.

She wiped down the counter then paused. "I don't know. It's weird. I felt like someone was watching me."

"Not Peter."

She shrugged. "I have no way of knowing."

"If he was coming from the station, it would have been the opposite direction from McCready's." He got to his feet. "Let's take a walk."

She flipped her dishrag over her shoulder. "You go, I want to finish up here."

"I'm not leaving you alone."

"Ash."

He crossed his arms over his chest and waited. Finally, she rolled her eyes and said, "All right, all right."

They went out the front door. Ash made sure she locked it, another precaution she declared extreme. Pawpaw yawned at the end of his leash and pattered behind them on the sidewalk. The clicking of his toenails echoed between buildings.

The quiet of the streets spooked him. He'd become used to the rush and bustle of the city, even come to thrive on it. All the stores were closed now, of course. Cranberry rolled up its sidewalks at six. His gaze swept over the darkened windows. McCready's was one of four or five antiques stores on Main Street, and there were others toward the fringes of town. It was a little ridiculous how many there were, but as the population aged and people retired, they packed up their attics and rented floor space to sell off their treasures. Antiquing was one of the few cottage industries Cranberry could claim. Maybe his father was right; Cranberry was a fading town, becoming an antique itself.

"Here's McCready's," Abby said, stopping in front of a weatherworn two-story house.

"Is that crack in the window new?"

"No, it's been that way since winter."

Ash stepped up on the creaking front porch. He cupped his hands around his eyes and pressed his face to the window. The first floor was filled with old furniture, spinning wheels, white dishes gleaming dully in the glow of the street lamp. "I suppose whoever owns this place doesn't have an alarm system either?"

Abby's pale reflection appeared in the window. "I wouldn't think so. Zach McCready lives right upstairs."

Ash backed up and looked to the second floor windows. All dark. They walked around to the shared parking lot behind the house. Everything seemed okay, but he stood there for a moment, his mind quiet, his senses alert, waiting for the breeze to carry him a sound or a movement.

Pawpaw stepped in front of Abby to the end of his leash and also stared out into the field. His nose twitched. He raised one paw and his ears went up. Ash held his breath. But then the dog went back to sniffing the ground, and Ash relaxed.

"Okay, I'm satisfied there's no one around now. But that doesn't mean there wasn't someone here earlier. You and Peter might have scared them off."

Rubbing her arms, Abby shrugged. "Maybe." The moon whitewashed her thoughtful face.

"What's the matter?"

"Now that I'm out here, I remember. It was quite a distinct feeling of being watched."

He cupped the back of her arm with his hand. "If anything seems odd to you, any time, call me right away. You've got my cell number. Memorize it."

A fleeting grin swept away her pinched frown. "Ash, you worry too much."

He rubbed his thumb over her skin. "I'm glad you called me tonight."

"You were the first person I thought of. I was afraid I'd killed him."

"Peter's been blessed with an especially thick skull."

"It must run in the family," she commented dryly, but she smiled at him with a warmth he'd hold close on the cold nights sure to come.

By the time they got to the other side of the field, Ash's sneakers and the hems of his jeans were soaked with dew. Red Betty bumped alongside over uneven ground as he walked slowly, watching Abby's animated face in the moonlight. He didn't want to rush back. He would be content to spend all night out here, listening to her talk about nothing in particular.

She gazed up at him, her eyes shining. "Don't you think so, too?"

He blinked. "About what?"

"Oh, Ash, you haven't been listening to a word I've said."

"Uh, you were saying you want the town to buy up vacant property and turn it into a land trust?"

"Yes!" Her enthusiasm lit up the night. "Isn't that a good idea?"

"Sure, if you can get the backing." He considered what he'd learned earlier. "My father was telling me that Cranberry has been losing families, that people are moving to areas with more jobs. Maybe some of that land would be needed for new business."

"Too much of it has been bought up already. The town council is ruining the countryside."

"Hmm. Maybe you should run for office."

"With that old-boy system, I'd never get in. Still, I should try." She gazed ahead with a determined lift to her chin as they strolled across Lucy's lawn. He could practically visualize the mental momentum gathering behind the idea. "When's the next election?"

He laughed softly. "I'm not sure Cranberry is ready for you. You've got those activist genes in you."

She flipped him a worried look. "Am I sounding like my parents?"

"That's not necessarily a bad thing." They'd reached the back porch. He stopped, toed down the kickstand and let the bike lean. "Speaking of which, did you make your phone call?"

She nodded with a weary sigh. "You were right, it was better to just get it over with."

"What did they say?"

"I only talked to my mother. I got the distinct feeling she didn't understand why I was bothering her with this."

"They're not coming home, then."

"Of course not."

The resignation in her voice hit him like a cold rain. He'd never met Abby's parents, since they'd never returned to visit in all the years he'd known her, but out of loyalty, he'd developed a keen resentment toward them. He took her hand and led her to Lucy's old swing. "Come on," he said, settling beside her, looping one arm behind her shoulders. "Tell me all about it."

As if a cork had popped loose, Abby let it spill. The brief conversation, the quick good bye. She stopped short of saying what he sensed lurked beneath the surface: the feeling of rejection she suffered whenever she dealt with her folks.

He slid his hand down her arm and drew her against his side. She laid her head on his shoulder. The old swing whistled with their lazy, rocking rhythm. Pawpaw snoozed in a patch of grass a few feet away.

Ash turned enough so he could inhale her scent, sweet as clover, and feel her hair beneath his cheek. "They don't know what they're missing, Abby."

She patted his thigh as if he were the one needing comfort. Her shoulders rose and fell beneath his arm as she took a big breath. "They're doing good things in the world. I just never fit into their plans. Really, it's okay. I'm fine with it now."

Well, he wasn't. He tightened his grip. She felt good against him, made to fit against his body. Her skin was soft beneath his stroking fingers. The night closed around them like a curtain while the crickets sang a serenade.

Her head lifted a little and she gazed out into the field. "I suppose I wouldn't mind having their sense of dedication. I want to fight for what's important. Cranberry can't turn into Brockville or Camden. They used to be nice little towns, and now they're nothing but fast food joints and megamart stores." Her eyebrows dipped. "Lucy got an offer on her hayfield last year. A construction company wanted to put up houses. I'm so glad she turned them down. Although it might be nice to have the money now."

"I wish you'd let me help you out financially. Cops don't make a half-bad living in the city, and I had nothing to spend my paycheck on except booze and drugs and prostitutes."

She elbowed him in the side and gave him a scolding laugh. "Oh, please. You were probably the straightest arrow on the force. You can take the boy out of Cranberry, but you can't take Cranberry out of the boy."

"No, and I tried to have it surgically removed, too."

Her laughter came for real then, pure as silver bells, and she draped back against his side. For a precious moment, he had his old Abby back, worry-free and happy. He smiled down into her eyes. She shifted a little in the crook of his arm and grew serious again.

"It must have been so hard for you out there. I can't even imagine. Nothing could have prepared you."

Twining strands of her hair around his fingers by her shoulder, he gave a philosophical shrug. "Trial by fire." The silence stretched. He wouldn't burden her with his dark memories.

Realizing Abby was looking up at him with concern, he cracked a smile and said, "It wasn't all bad. I made some good friends, too."

"*Girl* friends?" she teased, but there was an undertone of curiosity in her voice.

He tsked and let his fingers run along the side of her throat. "I lived like a monk."

Her skeptical laughter bubbled up. "Oh, now that I can't believe."

"In bed by eight, up with the sun, good country boy that I am." He grinned.

She turned back to the field and stretched her legs with the rhythm of the swing. A fading smile played around her lips. "California women are beautiful."

He hooked his knuckles under her jaw. "No one," he murmured with gruff sincerity, "compared to you."

She drew away, one eyebrow delicately arched. "Ah, so there were others."

"No one serious. No one I married. Like you've been living in a convent?"

"After Brian, I didn't want to date. This town is so small. People gossip. I felt like all eyes were on me wherever I went. Besides," she said, brushing her hair back over her shoulder, "I like being single."

"Forever? You used to want a home of your own, a family."

"Cranberry's my home. And I'll always have Lucy."

"That's no life for you, Abby. It's like you're just giving up on your dreams."

"And what do you know about my dreams?"

"You used to have them. We both did."

She drew away. Her tone became cool, the walls coming up between them. "Reality set in. Thank God. You don't have to worry about me, Ash. I don't want anyone to worry about me."

She began to rise, but he caught her wrist. He got to his feet and clasped her upper arms.

"I have this fear," he said, "that I'll come back again someday and find you here just as you are now, alone and sad and carrying the weight of the world on your shoulders. You were a free, happy girl once."

"I grew up."

"So did I." He tightened his fingers on her tense muscles and drew her to him. His body burned with her closeness, his senses keen on her every reaction, the subtle softening of her mouth, the unconscious yielding to his pressure. "I know what I want now. There's no question."

Her chin lifted in a last act of defiance. "Miami? Life on the beach?"

"You."

"You had your chance," she murmured hotly.

"I'm taking another."

Ash lowered his head and closed the inches between them.

Her soft lips parted beneath the first gentle brush of his mouth. He cradled her face between his palms. Through half-closed eyes, he watched her lashes flutter down in sweet surrender.

One simple kiss swept away the years, dissolved his inhibitions. She wanted him, too. Through the anger, her need drove her closer. He felt it in the sway of her body, in the clutch of her fingers on the bare skin of his arms.

He suckled her lower lip, stroked his tongue across the seam of her mouth. When she tipped her head, lifted herself to him, he almost groaned with relief and joy. Her soft breasts pressed against his chest, heartbeat to heartbeat. He knotted his fingers in the tumbled silk of her hair. Sweet girl. God, how he'd missed her.

His hands roamed her back, the curve of her hips, brought her against his hardening body. Abby made a soft sound deep in her throat, and need jolted through him. Urgent need. He was ready, so ready. The house, the bed, were mere steps away—then abruptly, the grip on his biceps began to push rather than pull. Abby stepped back, her face turned away.

Cool night air slipped between them. Dazed, Ash stared down at her. Abby's beautiful eyes shone with something too close to pain. "No, Ash," she whispered.

For a moment, he couldn't process her words. "No? No what?" Not to this incredible pleasure, so uniquely theirs.

Abby wrapped her fingers around the iron chain of the swing as if it was all that could hold her up. In a tight voice, she said, "I'm not ready for this. I can't handle it. There's so much going on—" She rubbed her hand over her heart, as if trying to ease an ache. "—and I know it would be so easy to . . . let it happen. But I can't. Not again."

The naked honesty of her words hit him like a hammer blow. The six-year-old ghost of what he'd done to her haunted her still, and he'd been too blind a fool to see it.

He slid his hands over her slender shoulders. Anger bumped up against desire inside his chest. Gotta make it right somehow. "You have to let someone in someday, Abby."

"No I don't," she shot back. She scuffed out a little laugh as if she realized how her abrupt her answer had been and turned a watery smile on him. Her dark eyes were huge and glossy. "In fact, living alone is so peaceful, I'm surprised we all aren't living in caves like hermits."

He wrapped his hand around the iron chain, just above hers. "Hmm. Sounds boring."

A cool smile lifted her lips. "Then again, maybe you're right. Maybe someday I'll find someone. I'll let you know. Maybe this time I'll even invite you to the wedding."

"Ouch." He flinched, but shook his head. Abby had always used words and jokes to cover her hurt, but he knew better. All the sarcasm in the world couldn't mask the deep emotion in her eyes. He covered her hand with his on the chain. "I lied, you know."

She didn't pull her hand away. "About what?"

"About not wanting to see you when I came back. You're all I thought about from the minute I decided to come home."

"Well." Regaining her composure, she said, "You knew where I worked. What kept you?"

"I told myself it wouldn't matter. That I could see you and walk away again. Not want you. Not need you." He rubbed her wrist with his thumb, felt the flutter of her pulse. "Guess I was lying to myself."

Her small fist tightened under his. Moonlight speared through the strands of hair parted around the upturned oval of her face. Bending, he pressed a parting kiss to her soft lips. "Good night, Abby," he whispered.

He stalked to Red Betty, miserably reflecting he'd never seen anyone so beautiful or desirable as Abby looked just then, golden hair haloed by the back porch light, stubborn pride draped like a banner around her squared shoulders. The engine snarled as he gunned it and braked sharply at her side.

"Until tomorrow," he promised. He roared off into the night, alone.

# CHAPTER TEN

Abby drove over to the deli to meet Miranda the next morning, well ahead of the time she'd told her friend to arrive. After staring at the ceiling for another night, she'd found herself wide awake at four o'clock, and by five, figured she might as well shower and head out. The idea of going back to work was shockingly enticing. Too much time alone had clouded her thoughts. Too much time with Ash had fogged her brain. She'd slept with the taste of him on her lips, the subtle scent of him lingering in her hair. Her body had hummed with need until she'd finally found a fitful sleep some time after midnight. She needed something to keep her mind off the man, or else she'd go crazy.

She unlocked the deli's back door and let herself in. Pawpaw skittered ahead of her and went straight for his bed. Abby tucked her purse behind the counter, then let her senses drink in the wonderful atmosphere of the store. The earthy tang of coffee hung in the still air. A swath of golden sunlight spilled across the floor. The cooler ticked and wheezed. Outside, cars whisked by and a few early risers strolled the sidewalks. The serenity of love and belonging enveloped her.

She'd spent most of her childhood playing on the plank fir floor or roller-skating out on the front walk. The folks in town had become her surrogate family as they poured in and out, always giving her a smile or a kind word. Fewer people stopped in now. Most of them preferred the drive-through at the chain donut store at the border of Cranberry and Buckland. Maybe they didn't need Lucy's Deli as much, but she still did. There had to be a way to save it.

After setting a pot of coffee to percolate, Abby picked up a broom and dustpan and began to sweep the floor. She'd seen last night that Ash had cleaned up the mess from Pawpaw's assault. Everything looked tidy and put away. More impressively, there on the windows, winking in the sunlight, were the shiny new locks he must have installed. In the corner sat their old stool, good as new. Or as good as a hundred-year-old relic could look.

Abby propped the broom against the wall and picked up the stool. She turned it over to inspect the new nails holding the leg in place. Ash had done a great job. And not just with that. The more she looked around, the more little touches she spied: the crack in the front window had been patched; the shelves had been wiped down; the fluorescent overhead light that had flickered for weeks now glowed steadily. She'd never gotten around to replacing it, but Ash must have found the time.

She hugged the old blue stool to her chest as if she could press back the wave of emotion rising in her. Allowing herself to believe these little touches meant he cared about her was a dangerous temptation.

A knock at the back door startled her out of her thoughts. The bread van was parked outside with the first delivery of the day. She let in the driver and took a plastic bin of goodies from him. The muffins and pastries looked so fresh that Abby decided she'd take some to Peter as a peace offering.

A little past six, Miranda's smiling face appeared in the front window. Abby let her friend inside.

Mae reached for her as soon as Miranda put the carrier on the floor. Abby unbuckled her and scooped her up. "Oh, you must have given her a bath this morning." She pressed her nose to the baby's fuzzy hair and inhaled. "I love that clean baby smell."

Miranda laughed. "It sure beats the way she smelled before the bath. Whew, it's amazing how something so bad can come out of something so sweet."

"Babies aren't everything they're cracked up to be in those Gerber commercials, are they?"

"Oh, she's all right." Miranda planted a kiss on her daughter's round cheek. "I think I'll keep her for a while."

Abby settled in a chair and propped Mae on her lap. "She's starting to sit up really well. Look at that! Soon she'll be walking, and then you'll be in big trouble."

Miranda said nothing, and Abby glanced up at her. A thoughtful smile lingered on her friend's face. "Abby, I just can't see you going the rest of your life without children of your own."

Usually she had a quick comeback, some wry joke about how a baby would slow down the blistering pace of her corporate career, or ruin her dreams of climbing the Matterhorn. Today, though, she couldn't find the words.

"I don't know," she said finally, patting Mae's fingers together, "I'm afraid it's just not meant to be."

"Nonsense." Miranda shuffled through her enormous diaper bag and found a set of plastic teething rings. "What would make you say that? You're young, you're beautiful, and you're independent."

"Keep going," Abby said with a wry grin. "My ego could use the stroking."

"Why? Did something happen between you and Ash?"

Abby gave her a quizzical look. "I'm telling you, Miranda, you should either start a dating service or a psychic hotline."

"Ah, that explains your sad expression when I came in."

"I wasn't sad." Was she? She fussed with the pink bow clipped to a lock of Mae's golden hair and bit her lower lip. "I'm a little overwhelmed with everything going on. Lucy will be home tomorrow. Tonight is my last night in my apartment, and I don't know when or if I'll go back. Somehow, I have to find a way to run the store on my own. We can't afford to hire anyone else."

"And what about Ash?"

"He won't be here much longer to help out. Although—" She nodded toward the new window locks. "—I see he was busy while I was away."

"He was determined to get everything done that same day. He wants to make you happy."

A blush stole across her cheeks. She lowered her gaze to Mae's tiny white shoes. What exactly had Ash and Miranda discussed while she wasn't around? Good grief, nothing too personal, she hoped. Ash was an expert interrogator, and Miranda only too happy to talk. A recipe for disaster.

Miranda leaned forward and put a comforting hand on her knee. "Well, if not him, then surely there's someone out there for you."

Abby shook her head and found a smile for her friend. "I'm pretty content with life the way it is. Or, should I say, the way it was, before Lucy got hurt." And before Ash reappeared and scrambled her hormones. "We should probably get to work. Thanks for coming today. I know it's not easy for you to do anything with Mae in tow."

"We're only too happy to help out, aren't we baby?" She took Mae from Abby when she handed her up. The baby reached for her mom, and for a moment, the two of them smiling at each other made such a beautiful picture that Abby felt something squeeze inside her chest. A longing. An emptiness.

A need that she was beginning to fear even her work couldn't fill.

★　★　★　★　★

Ash heaved the last bundle of shingles into the back of his brother's Volvo, then swiped his hand across his forehead. Sweat beaded on his brow, and it was only mid-morning. In his mind, he pictured Lucy's roof and tried to estimate how many shingles it would need. Maybe he should buy an extra bundle, just in case. He paused for a minute, rubbing the back of his neck, hoping he hadn't forgotten anything. Once he left Cranberry Hardware and dropped off his supplies, he'd have to bring the Volvo back to Peter. He didn't want to be stuck motorcycling heavy bundles of shingles back and forth in this heat.

"Uh-oh, looks like you're thinking. That can't be good," a voice called.

He glanced up and saw Jim from the nursery approaching. He grinned. "Hey, Jim. What's going on?"

"Just getting some lumber to make potting benches. I'm glad I ran into you, though. I was going to give you a call." Jim eyed the bundles in the car. "What are you up to? Building a house?"

"Fixing Lucy's house. The place is pretty run down."

He held up a covered white foam cup. "I just saw Abby at the deli. Dropped in for a cup of coffee before I head in to work."

Ash nodded. "I'm trying to get this all done before she gets home."

"Mighty nice of you."

He shrugged modestly. "So what were you going to call me about? Was there more vandalism at the nursery?"

Frowning now, Jim jerked a thumb over his shoulder, toward East Elm Street. "It's been quiet at my place, but I was talking to Mr. Cooper at the pharmacy. It appears someone tried to crack open their back door with a crowbar last night. The door is steel, but it was bent. Fortunately, they have a good alarm system. As soon as it went off, the thieves must have bolted."

"What time, can they estimate?"

"Don't know, I didn't ask. Your brother might know."

Peter hadn't said anything, as usual. "Sounds like our vandals are getting more daring."

Jim skritched his fingers in his short beard. "They were doing more than painting graffiti this time. Didn't your brother mention it?"

"No. But I haven't seen much of him this morning. I dropped him off at the station, then borrowed the car. Maybe he didn't know about it. He didn't work last night."

"Makes sense. Well, I'll be in touch if anything else comes up."

Ash thanked him, and Jim walked to his car. Ash slammed the Volvo's hatch shut. Of course, his brother knew about the attempted break-in. He just hadn't said anything. Ash leaned his knuckles on the hot glass and considered. Should he go to Cooper's or the station first? He curled his hands into fists and pushed off. Realistically, he should do neither. This wasn't his beat; this wasn't his town. It wasn't his business. He should go to Lucy's and get on with his work.

But somehow, the Volvo ended up in front of the Cranberry Police Department.

After double-parking the car, Ash strode inside. The air conditioning stung his sweat-dampened skin. He gave a cursory nod to the officer on front desk duty and headed down the narrow, yellow hallway toward Peter's office. Despite what he'd told Jim, Peter had had plenty of opportunity to tell Ash about the attempted break-in. He knew Ash was interested in the case. More than interested. Involved, because of Abby.

He swung open Peter's door and nearly knocked Abby off her feet.

She jumped back, lips parted in surprise. His gaze riveted on her mouth. Suddenly, the air conditioning couldn't chug hard enough. His body flooded with heat. Last night . . . that kiss.

Even as she regained her composure and stood a safe distance from the door, he couldn't tear his gaze from her face. Her golden hair was pulled back in a ponytail, her head covered by a red-checked kerchief. Her sky blue, sleeveless top hugged the firm, rounded breasts he'd come this close to touching. It tied at her waist, emphasizing the sweet curve of her hips outlined by faded, cut-off jean shorts. His avid gaze traced her coltish legs to ankles so slender his fingers could cuff them. Abby had never appreciated her sexy legs. At least not the way he did.

"Well, good morning to you, too."

Her bemused voice splashed over him. He met her wide brown eyes with a crooked grin. Oh, hell, he must look like an idiot. He still had one foot in front of the other, frozen mid-stride, and his hand on the doorknob. And his mouth hung open. Close mouth, release doorknob, straighten with remnants of dignity . . . "Morning, Abby. Didn't expect to see you here."

She turned toward Peter, who lounged in his beat-up chair with his polished black shoes on the desk. He smiled at Ash through a mouthful of the muffin he held in his hand. And what a self-satisfied smile it was, like the cat with the cream. Ash wished he could roll back the tape. The way the air crackled with pure sexual awareness, any fool could tell something potent simmered between him and Abby. He'd never wanted to be so obvious in front of his brother. What he and Abby had, or were trying to have, or were trying to avoid, was private.

Peter broke the awkward silence. "Coming to beg for your job back, bro?"

"Yes," he said, his tone dry with sarcasm. "I can't take another day without filing."

When Peter cocked a brow, the big, raspberry-colored bruise above it lifted, too. Peter waved toward a wicker basket. "Have a muffin. Abby brought them over as a consolation prize."

He glanced at her, but she wasn't talking. A chill settled on the back of his neck. Still mad at him. Man, he shouldn't have run out on her last night, but if he'd stayed, they would've been waking up in each other's arms this morning, and she might really have reason to hate him.

Peter's gaze tipped between them. "Abby, these muffins are so good, I'd be willing to take another beating for more."

She smiled at Ash's brother. "They can't make up for that bruise on your head, but I hope they'll take your mind off the pain."

"Doesn't hardly hurt at all. Don't worry about it."

Ash stepped in and closed the door behind him. "It turns out Abby may have been right last night about hearing someone in the woods. I ran into Jim Martin at the hardware store. He told me there was an attempted break-in last night over at Cooper's."

Peter swiped crumbs off his desk and dusted his hands. "Totally unrelated. There's no evidence linking the incidents."

"Can you be sure? It was the same time of night, possibly the same instrument they used to smash Jim's ceramic pots—"

"Pure coincidence."

Peter's tone alone told him there was more to the story. He was about to respond when Abby said, "Did they get in? Was anything stolen?"

Peter said, "We think the alarm system scared them away. Two of our officers arrived at the scene within minutes of the alarm going off, and they found nothing except some scratches on the back door." He tipped his head. "No harm done."

Worry etched a fine line between Abby's brows. "What time did that happen?"

Picking at crumbs, Peter replied, "Oh, about two a.m."

She cast a glance at Ash. "Then it might have been the same person, or people, I thought I heard."

"No," Peter said, "it couldn't have."

"Why not?" Ash crossed his arms. "They could have been casing joints all night before they decided to try the pharmacy."

Peter's lips curled into a subtle sneer. " 'Casing joints.' Ash, this isn't a gangster movie."

If Abby hadn't been in the room, he would have really had it out with his brother. As it was, though, he didn't want to drop any farther on her respectability scale. After last night, he'd slithered far enough down already, and that wasn't where he wanted to be.

Knowing he wouldn't get anything else out of Peter, he turned to her. "Are you going back to the store?"

She nodded. Goose bumps pebbled her skin from the A/C, or maybe from the tension in the room. She seemed nervous, and he mentally kicked himself for pushing her too far last night. He reached to lay his fingers on the back of her arm. "I'll walk you over."

She murmured a goodbye to Peter, who winked and patted his belly. "Thanks for the muffins. Merry'll be mad when I'm too full for lunch, but it was worth it."

Abby could feel the tension pouring off of Ash in waves. Hard knots of muscle flexed in his arms as he shoved open the door and they stepped onto the sidewalk. His gray eyes were cold as stone. Her own emotions were in just as much tumult. She hadn't been prepared for his explosive entrance, or for the way her body had rushed with heat upon seeing him. Embarrassed, certain her face had lit up like a beacon, she'd tried to hide her reaction behind a frown. Fortunately it seemed as if most of his attention had focused on his brother and whatever battle was being waged between them.

Glad to be out in the clean, summer air, she took a healthy, head-clearing breath. She almost had to jog to keep pace with his long, determined strides.

"What was that all about?" she asked.

He glanced down at her. A muscle ticked in his jaw. "Peter's sitting on the case."

"But you heard what he said. It's not the same people. Or person."

He made a sound of disgust and shook his head. "That's hard to believe. You know this town. How often is there a break-in?"

"Oh, I don't know. Maybe one or two every couple of years?"

"Exactly. There has to be a connection." He stopped a block from the deli and took her hand. "Come with me to Cooper's. Let's check it out."

Ignoring the appealing strength of his fingers wrapped around her own, she hesitated. "I left Miranda at the store. I'm not sure she can handle everything alone."

"Let's find out."

Before she had a chance to formulate a reply, he tugged her to the deli. As Abby suspected, several more customers had trickled in. George Darcy chatted with the Madeleine sisters, two elderly spinsters who always stopped by on their way to their senior exercise classes. They fluttered their fingers in greeting and openly goggled at Ash. Miranda cheerfully assured her she could manage both customers and clean-up on her own, for a little while at least. Abby found herself being tugged toward East Elm.

By the time they were half way to the pharmacy, Abby had regained her wits, if not her common sense. She cast a sidelong glance at Ash's lean, dark form striding beside her. "You really do get your way all the time," she groused at him. "That's not healthy. You'll get spoiled."

"I can only hope."

The sloping grin he gave her stirred her simmering desire. She tried to ignore it, feeling only slightly safer now that they were moving. "I admit, I'm curious about this break-in, too. There's usually not much action in Cranberry."

"Too much, lately. And Peter doesn't seem to be doing anything about it."

"Maybe what this town needs is a tougher police force."

"That's what I think, but it'll never happen while Peter's in charge."

"What about your father?"

"He's semi-retired already. He puts on the uniform for special functions, but for all intents and purposes, Peter's the chief."

"What about you?"

She could see her blunt question caught him off-guard. "There's no place for me here. Peter's got the town all wrapped up the way he likes it." He shrugged, as if sensing the conversation was getting too serious. "I could always go back to my sandwich-making job if the owner would give me a second chance."

Abby grinned and lifted her hair so the breeze kissed her nape. "I'm doing my best, but this pesky man keeps distracting me."

"Put up with me just a little longer," he murmured. His intimate tone curled around her heart. A little longer. That was all they had together. The weight of it lay on Abby's mind, the pressure like a hand on her shoulder, pushing toward an uncertain destination.

They reached the corner of the white brick pharmacy. Ash began to go around back.

Abby hesitated. "Don't you want to talk to Mr. Cooper?"

"No need to bother him yet. First I want to look at the damage."

"Peter said the door was only scratched." She trailed him through the shady, narrow alley between buildings.

"Yeah, I'll say." He stopped, and Abby followed his line of vision. The door of the pharmacy's rear entrance was bent outward on one side. A six or eight inch space gaped between the door and the jamb. There wasn't a knob on this side, just a rectangular metal plate, but even that had been partly wedged off.

"Oh, wow," she breathed.

Ash ran his gaze over the damage. "Jim described this better than Peter." He stepped back and scanned the area. "I wonder if they took prints."

Not wanting to trample any clues, Abby stayed put. "What do you think happened?"

"Someone tried to break in," he said dryly, and she puckered her lips.

"I can see that. I mean, how, and why?"

He picked over the loose gravel at the doorstep. "Crowbar, probably. And the why is easy. Drugs."

Abby shuddered. First vandals, now drug dealers. What was her little town coming to?

He glanced up at her. His gray eyes squinted against the bright sun. "I believe I would like to talk to the owner." He stood and dusted his hands on his thighs. "I'll walk you over to the deli, then come back."

Lucy's was only a few minutes away, and she could see his interest had been piqued. "It's all right, I can find my way home."

"You're sure?"

He looked so sexy when he was serious, his eyes sharp, intensity radiating from him. So formidably male that she had the strongest urge to run her hands across his chest and up to his shoulders and pull him down to loosen that stony jaw with a kiss. Had to be sunstroke making her think that way. "Sure," she said with watery conviction. "But let me know what you find out."

"I will." For a moment, his intensity vanished with a smile. "Thanks."

He looked like a little boy about to play a favorite game. "You love this cloak-and-dagger stuff, don't you?"

"I would have made detective in a couple years." His modest tone didn't mask the regret underpinning his words.

"You would've been great." Both of them had dreams that had gone wrong. Both of them hovered now at forks in the roads of their lives. But Ash would go one way, and she the other before the week was out, unless . . .

He must have seen the emotions fleeing across her face, because he reached for her hand and twined his fingers around hers. "Abby," he started. His voice was gruff and low. "About last night—"

Her breath caught. "It's fine. It's okay. We got carried away."

He tucked a loose strand of her hair behind her ear. "No, I left before we got carried away."

The sweep of his finger against her temple seemed to spread like warm honey over her skin. She made the mistake of looking into his eyes. The world dissolved. Desire thrummed through her, fresh and strong as if they'd never parted.

"I only mention it because you looked angry in Peter's office. If I did anything wrong, I apologize."

"No. Nothing wrong." Words hopscotched through her overheated brain. If anything, he'd done things too right.

"Good, then." His lifted her hand and brushed his lips across her knuckles. "I'll see you at Lucy's later. I stopped by the hardware store and picked up what I need for the roof."

She blinked owlishly. "The roof?"

"Remember, you asked me to fix it?" His voice dropped to a wicked, silken murmur and he traced the slope of her hip with his fingertips. "Please, Abby, don't fire me now. I need something to do with my hands."

Electricity zinged along her nerves. She hopped back, laughing. "You're incorrigible."

"I've been called worse." His even, white teeth flashed in a devilish grin, and her heart spun like a top. He knew exactly the effect he had on her. "I'll see you later," he said.

"All right," she said a bit breathlessly. "Later then."

Abby turned and began to walk back to the deli, her knees like jelly, the pavement beneath her feet about as solid as marshmallow.

Crazy, that's what she was. Absolutely certifiable.

# CHAPTER ELEVEN

If he was going to talk Abby into going with him to Miami, he had to have a plan.

Of course Lucy would be on his side, and that was key. He wouldn't rip Abby away from her aunt in her moment of need, but once Lucy recovered, say in a few months, and he had an apartment established and his job underway, Abby could come and live with him. Try it out. Get away from Cranberry.

Pounding a nail into the thick eaves, Ash frowned around the extra nails he bit between his teeth. A metallic bitterness flooded his mouth. It tasted a lot like defeat. Already. If she hadn't followed her husband, why should she follow him?

Because, his mind whispered, there was still something incredibly hot, raw and unsettled between them. And it wouldn't be resolved in the few days he had left.

He shifted around on the sun-baked roof, sat hard and dragged his forearm across his brow. He'd stripped off his shirt an hour ago. He'd be lobster-red tomorrow. He pressed a finger into the skin of his shoulder and the indentation flooded back deep crimson.

The afternoon sun bouncing off the black roof was brutal, as bad as any beach day in California. Worse, because there was no sea breeze. Gathering clouds had barely muted the relentless glare. Good thing he was almost done—with the roof repairs, at least. Next there was the lawn, which could use a baling as much as a mowing. The place had really gone to pot.

Abby couldn't keep up with it all. She needed a break. Maybe he could try that line of attack. No, that would backfire, because he'd be suggesting she leave Lucy with the responsibilities. Anyhow, the one thing that made Abby dig in her heels was telling her she couldn't do something.

Reverse psychology? Bait her with the idea that she couldn't cut it in Miami? Nope. Ash took the nails from his mouth and made a fist around them. He pulled up his knees and crossed his arms over them and stared out at the forested expanse of this God-forsaken corner of Connecticut. That was too close to the truth. He'd have to be smarter than that.

Honesty? He pictured himself saying, "Abby, I know you don't want to get married, and neither do I, but let's go shack up and do the dirty and buy ourselves a little amnesia about the family baggage and bad memories back home."

Who knows? Maybe that would have a perverse appeal for her. It sure did for him.

"Somebody call the cops! There's a naked man on my roof!"

Ash took a quick look over his shoulder. Down below, one hand shading her eyes, Abby grinned up at him as if he'd conjured her from his daydreams. She must have taken the short cut through the field. Pawpaw snuffled at the end of the leash she held.

He called down, "I was just thinking about you."

"Uh-oh, that can't be good."

But she looked pleased—and adorable in her shorts and tied shirt. She'd lost the red bandanna, and her hair flowed free around her shoulders.

He waved. "Hey, come on up and join me."

"Forget it, California Boy. That's a little too high for my blood."

"You're missing a beautiful view. You can see all ten square miles of Cranberry."

"I've seen it. Besides, there's a storm brewing. You better get down from there before God figures out where you are and hits you with a well-deserved lightning bolt."

Forget the sweat and sunburn. The grin on his face widened, as it always did when Abby was around. He got to his feet, one work boot planted on either side of the peak. "Okay, I'm coming. Catch me."

Two stories down, Abby hefted the handles of a plastic bag she held in her left hand. "I have a better idea. Meet me on the widow's walk in front of my old room. I brought lunch."

"Throw in a cold drink and it's a deal."

The back door creaked, then slammed when she let herself inside. Ash picked up his box of nails, stuck his hammer in his belt loop and eased himself down. His work boots thumped on the steep roof. He snatched up his t-shirt on the way and mopped the sweat from his face and chest, but it was too damned hot to put it back on.

A well-placed hop, and he landed on the widow's walk, a little porch just the right size for the two old folding chairs that were on it now. He tossed his shirt over his shoulder and tried the gold handle on the narrow french doors leading to Abby's old room. Unlocked, of course. He shook his head and closed the door behind him. Did it never occur to Abby or Lucy that anyone could just walk in? Including a tired, sweaty hired hand in search of a sink.

The rush of cool air soothed his skin. The scent of lavender and mothballs hovered. He peered into the semi-darkness of the quiet room. A pale pink floral bedspread covered the double bed set against the opposite wall. A dried flower arrangement collected cobwebs on a tall white dresser. Wow, talk about a time-warp.

Abby had invited him up here only a couple of times while they were dating, and even then all they'd done was sit on the

143

edge of her ruffly bedspread and talk. She'd been a shy, good girl, and he'd been the guy with the bad reputation, but he'd never violated her trust, or her, until a few weeks before he'd left. She'd touched something inside him he'd never known he possessed. Some quality of worthiness. Something he'd lost.

He raked his nails over his scalp and turned for the half-bath in the corner. He flipped on the overhead bathroom light, filled the sink with cold water and dunked his head. The chill braced him.

He heard a feminine gasp.

Backhanding water out of his eyes, he glanced up. From the shadowed room, Abby stared like the proverbial deer in the headlights. He savored her priceless expression as he straightened. Water streamed over his face and down his bare chest. He grabbed a hand towel from the rack and swiped the rough terrycloth over his skin.

"Sorry," he said, even though he wasn't. He didn't make the least effort to hide his amusement.

Recovering, she shifted the tray she carried to her hip. "Well, I see I'll have to fix the lock on that door. The wildlife's wandering in."

"You're lucky you haven't had more visitors. Honest to God, Abby, anyone could break in." He folded the towel and dropped it on the edge of the sink.

To his surprise and delight, she gave him a slow once over and said, "That might not be such a bad thing."

Well. The day was looking up. He strolled into the room. "Wouldn't be the first time I snuck in through your window."

She gave a soft, husky chuckle, less sure of herself. "We were lucky we didn't get caught."

"Doing what? Talking?"

"Being alone together."

"As if Lucy would care. She always liked me."

She caught her lower lip between her teeth. "I'm not sure how much she would have liked finding you on my bed."

"Probably not," he agreed, moving past her. "Does it still squeak on the left side?"

The tray came around across her stomach, as if to put a barrier between them. "I didn't even remember that it squeaked."

Liar. "Or was it the right side?" He scratched his chin, studying the bed and the thick, quilted pink comforter. He reached down and rubbed his hand over the fabric. A rush of pure lust thundered through him so strong it sapped the strength from his joints. So easy to picture Abby . . . her long, toned legs wrapped around his waist, her full breasts swaying to the rhythm of their love-making; her hot, responsive body yielding . . .

They'd had only a few nights together, yet the echoes of their passion still rocked him to the core.

He sucked in a breath and took a quick step back.

"It does bring back some memories, doesn't it?" She appeared by his elbow, and her innocent smile made it pretty damned clear she wasn't remembering the same things he was.

"Yeah." His voice sounded strangled. Served him right that his teasing backfired on him. "Oh, yeah."

"I love this house. I guess it won't be so bad moving back in, if it comes to that."

He stared down into her face. "Haven't you ever wanted to live anywhere else? Get a house of your own, a fresh start?"

Her eyebrows tucked together as if the idea were preposterous. "This house has been in my family for over a hundred years. My great-great-great grandfather built it when he came over from Ireland. Then each generation added something. A room, a porch, a renovation." She crossed to the dresser to pick up the tray she'd set down. "When it's mine, I'm sure I'll make a few changes, but I could never abandon it."

Abandon. The commitment behind the word brought the

flavor of defeat into the back of Ash's throat again.

Abby grinned. "Ready for lunch?"

He shoved his fantasies from his mind. "Sure. Need some help?"

"Grab that folding table?"

He took a metal tray table from where she'd leaned it against the wall and followed her out onto the widow's walk. He squeezed the table between the two chairs and took a seat. Humming a tune under her breath, Abby arranged sandwiches and dewy bottles of iced tea.

"How's the roof coming along?" she asked.

"Fine. I was just wrapping up and thinking about starting on the yard."

"I appreciate all the work you're doing." She placed blue paper napkins off to one side, and a green plastic soda bottle filled with bright yellow black-eyed Susans in the middle. She was going through some effort here, he noticed. "This will mean so much to Lucy. And it does to me, too."

When she bent across the tray, her butterscotch hair unfurled over her shoulder and his fantasies burst through his flimsy mental door. Her face glowed with porcelain purity that only living in fresh country air could bring. She looked like an angel, an irresistible vision. He reached out and lifted the fall of hair from her cheek.

Abby jumped a little at his touch. She tucked the golden strands behind her ear and smiled shyly.

"You're beautiful," he murmured.

She gave a self-conscious laugh and shook her head. "You're only saying that because I brought food."

The tightness around her mouth belied the levity of her tone. She wasn't comfortable with flattery; never had been. And right now he knew she wasn't wholly comfortable with him, either, but the fact that she'd brought this offering was a promising gesture. Probably wouldn't pay to question her motives too deeply.

"Well, this is nice," he said, lacing his fingers behind his head and lounging back so she'd relax. "What's on the menu?"

"Pastrami on rye, for you. Hot mustard, of course."

"Of course."

"Chips, soda. And . . ." Like a magician producing a rabbit out of a hat, she pulled out a separate brown paper bag. "Chocolate chip cookies I baked at the store this morning."

He groaned when the delicious smell wafted under his nose. "Did I say you were beautiful? I meant you're gorgeous, fantastic, incredible."

Back in high school, Abby had gotten him hooked on her chocolate chips. Then, she'd done it because she wanted something. What was it? Oh, yeah.

"I remember the first time you baked cookies for me. You were trying to get me to quit smoking," he said

"Oh?" Eyes widening, she tugged at the tie on her sky-blue shirt. "I'd forgotten about that."

"It worked, too. You kept me so full of cookies that summer, there wasn't even room for smoke."

"It doesn't seem to have done any permanent damage." Her gaze lingered over his bare torso. Appreciatively, he hoped.

He raised his arms and arched his spine, stretching luxuriously, watching her eyes grow even wider. "You and I always found a way to burn off the calories."

"It pays to keep active," she murmured raggedly. He caught the telling glow in her cheeks before she turned away. Not so unaffected after all. Thank God. He'd hate to be the only one stewing in sexual agony.

Bemused, Ash studied her. She could have avoided him today, stayed at the store. Yet here she was, bearing gifts, no less. Something was up. He knew what he wanted, but what goal did

Abby have in mind? Not seducing him. She had only to ask. Something else then. He'd coax it from her; then maybe they'd both get what they wanted.

"Let's eat before the rain starts," she said and handed him a paper plate loaded with chips and a thick sandwich. "It seems like it's been raining every afternoon lately."

Opening to push plan A? "In Miami," he mentioned, "it's beautiful and sunny almost all the time."

"And hot," she said, uncapping her drink.

"No snow to shovel."

She sat, stretching her endless legs out before her and crossing them at the ankles. "I like the snow. I don't mind shoveling. Besides, I would think all that sunshine would get monotonous."

He cleared his throat, and cleared his mind of how he'd like to run his hands and his mouth over her shapely calves. "Some days, there's crazy thunderstorms, with jagged lightning and buckets of rain. Then it blows out as quick as it came and leaves everything misty, like a rainforest."

She slid him a mildly suspicious glance and hesitated before recapping her iced tea and picking up her sandwich. "We get thunderstorms here, too. And look at the land. Nothing but those scraggly palms in Florida." She swept a hand to encompass the acres and acres of oak and maple trees interspersed with towering evergreens. "And listen to that!"

"Crows?"

Her long lashes rested against her freckled cheeks while she took in what the breeze carried to her. "The rumble of the big tractor working the field down the road. Frogs and crickets in the swamp behind Kutchner's. Sometimes I hear cows mooing from Willowby's farm, or a hawk screeching overhead. Everything's so alive here. Isn't it wonderful?"

"How about the sound of the surf." Determined to generate equal enthusiasm, he leaned on the arm of the chair and bent toward her. "Florida beaches are incomparable. You've never seen anything like them, Abby. Endless stretches of white sand, speedboats racing through the breakers. The water is blue as a robin's egg."

"And full of sharks. Give me Miller's Pond any day."

She smiled brightly, and he gave in to his frown. Plan A was not going as planned.

Well, he'd known it wouldn't be easy. He slumped back in his chair and bit into the pastrami. "Great sandwich," he said without much enthusiasm, and tried to concentrate on the flavor rather than on the despair in his gut.

Abby's hope crumbled like the cookies she'd brought in the bag. Ash couldn't have made his excitement for Miami more evident. Boats and thunderstorms and sand. Is that what he wanted? Her strained smile faded as she ate her sandwich. Why couldn't he see how perfect Cranberry was? She felt as if she were stuck in a rerun of *Green Acres,* only she wanted to live in the country, and he was insisting on the penthouse view.

Silence engulfed them for several long moments. She risked a sideways glance. What a scowl on that face. His eyes had gone remote again, cool and gray as marble. Unreachable, unreadable. Why that should cause the seductive tightening in her belly went against all logic. Except, of course, that she'd always been drawn to his dark nature. She loved his humor and his kindness, but it was the strong, dark side of him that roused this long-dormant need the way no one else ever had. It was a problem whose solution defied logic and required pure, sensual instinct. Yet it seemed her instincts had gone way off-kilter.

This impromptu picnic was supposed to start Ash seeing things her way, and instead, she sat frustrated while he looked ready to bite through brick.

He happened to glance up just then. Their gazes snagged,

and at the same time, each said, "Are you all right?"

Agonized silence collapsed around them again. Nibbling her lip, Abby spoke first. "You'd think after six years apart, we'd have so much to talk about."

He put aside what was left of his sandwich. "We do. It's just knowing where to start."

As if they could start over. Abby tried a tentative smile, a real one this time. He reached across the gap and closed his hand around her wrist. Her pulse leapt. The urge to pull away was strong. The urge to let the heat of his palm seep into her skin was stronger.

His eyes narrowed, and his thumb swept along the sensitive underside of her arm. "Miller's Pond," he said. "Is it still there?"

"Sure. I mean, I guess so. I haven't been there in years."

"Don't go swimming anymore?"

Hard to think when the simple friction of his thumb was doing wild things to her insides. "Not . . . not since . . . no." Great, now she wasn't making any sense at all. She shook her head. "Why?"

"Let's go for a swim."

She laughed. "In Miller's Pond?" Serious gray eyes tipped back at her. Her laughter died. "Oh. I don't have a bathing suit or anything."

A slow, dangerous smile curved his lips. "Good."

"Besides, remember old Mr. Miller who used to chase us off with his shotgun? He's just gotten older and meaner since you left."

"I can take him. Come on." He stood, grasped her hand and pulled her to her feet.

"Ash, we can't—"

Must have been the heat getting to her, too, because the world wobbled beneath her feet when he stepped close enough that she could see the mica flecks in his eyes and said, "Grab the cookies, and let's go. Let's at least ride down there, check it out. I need immersion in cold water. I mean, look at me." He gestured to his cooked shoulders.

Her hungry vision filled instead with his hard, flat abs and solid, sexy body. What a temptation, to trace every contour with her burning fingers. She curled her hands into fists by her side. None of that, naughty fingers. "A cold shower and some aloe would be better."

"But not as much fun."

"I'm not even sure I remember how to get there," she said in a last-ditch grasp at sanity.

"Red Betty knows the way."

That old death trap? "Oh, no."

But her backward step was halted by his hand curved around her hip. She froze. The hand slid lower. Determined fingers cupped her left cheek. And squeezed, with delicious pressure. Before she could slap his face, which would have been the lady-like thing to do, or draw a ragged breath, which would have been the least she could do, that merciless hand drifted to the small of her back and drew her against him. The heat from his skin melted through her thin shirt and lacy bra. The latter suddenly felt too small, constricting her breasts, making them ache. Making them want.

A challenge gleamed in his eyes as he bent his head.

"You can sit on the shore and watch," he murmured into her ear, "but Abby, I think you really want to get wet."

# CHAPTER TWELVE

As Red Betty growled down the rural road, Ash replayed the moment when Abby had gone boneless in his arms. When he'd breathed into the shell of her ear and she'd given a shaky, shivery moan that made him instantly redwood-hard. He'd resisted kissing her, settled instead for the lightest brush of his lips along the side of her throat and the slow crawl of his hand toward her breasts. Toward, but not touching. Not yet.

She'd swayed into him and her pebbled nipples pressed against his bare chest. If they gave medals for self-control, he'd be sporting one right now for not dancing her backward into the house and testing that squeaky mattress.

The bike bounced over a pothole, and Abby's arms convulsed around his waist. "Okay back there?" he called. The wind carried his words away, but he felt Abby nod. The helmet she wore clunked into his sunburned right shoulder, setting off sparks of agony. He gritted his teeth. It would all be worth it, if he played his cards right. He gave her hands, locked in a death grip around his middle, a reassuring pat.

Finally, they turned a shady corner and the deep blue bowl of the pond became visible through the heavy forest.

"Told you I'd remember," he said.

The trail they used to take down to the water wasn't quite overgrown. Twin tire tracks flattened the weeds and led through the forest. They weren't the only ones still sneaking behind Miller's back. Ash smiled. Good to see teenagers were still teenagers, even in this stiff-necked town.

He eased the bike over the bumpy road, remembering . . . a turn here, a jog there. Suddenly, the woods cleared out to a small strip of brown beach. Across the pond sat Miller's house, a weathered, gray, slat-sided monstrosity surrounded by scraggly weeds and patches of brown lawn. A few yards down, a white outboard, paint peeling, rode low in the water. Docks stretched like accusing fingers on either side, the one on Miller's side longer and better maintained than the one down the beach. A platform for sunning floated in the center, a good swim out. Give it another acre and Miller's Pond could be called a lake. It was a nice piece of property, but Miller had never been one to share.

Ash stopped the bike and cut the engine. "Suppose kids still sneak down here to skinny dip like we used to?"

He turned enough to watch Abby pull off the helmet. She shook out her damp hair. "We never skinny dipped."

"No? You sure?"

"Well, I know I had *my* clothes on, at least."

He grinned. "Gotta loosen up, Abby."

She made a face at him, then peered across the water. "It's still beautiful here."

"Doesn't even look like Miller's house is occupied." He swung his leg over and slid off, taking the helmet from her and hanging it on the handlebars. "Are you serious? You've never been skinny dipping?"

"No way. Not even been swimming since I thought I felt something grab my ankle in here once."

"Sure that wasn't me?"

She tsked. "Couldn't have been. I was with Brian."

"Then it was psychic intervention on my part. I was haunting you."

"You can't be jealous of my ex. You never even met him."

He wrapped one arm around her waist and tugged her close, hip to hip. "Jealous . . . jealous isn't the right word." Envious. Hateful, spiteful, bitter and mean, all the territorial, Neanderthal things he shouldn't be feeling but was, in buckets. He waited for her to reproach him. He deserved it. Instead, she draped her arm around his waist and sighed.

"Now I wish I did have a bathing suit."

He bent his head and nuzzled her ear. "I'm sure we can have just as much fun without one."

Abby's emotions flowed through her like waves on sand, eroding her resistance. With a touch, a seductive word, he lured her like an undertow her heart would never escape. As if she hadn't known he would. As if she hadn't known she would want him to.

He took her hand and she let him lead her down to the shore. The mossy ground cushioned their footsteps. Electric blue dragonflies burred around them, scared up by their passing. Her heart beat double-time in her chest. "Where are we going?"

"Down to the dock. We can sit on the end—or you can, at least. I'm going in."

She eyed him up and down. "Wearing your clothes?"

His sly grin let her imagination do the calculations. Then he squeezed her fingers and said, "We'll see. Maybe my shorts. We brought towels, and I'll air-dry on the way back. Do you mind?"

Her throat dried up, constricted. "Uh . . . no."

They stepped up onto the unsteady, dried-out boards of the small dock. She gripped his hand for balance. "This doesn't seem safe."

"It's fine. What'll happen, you'll fall into three or four feet of water? I'll save you."

"I'm a better swimmer than you are," she tartly replied.

"You were. Before I moved out west. Swam all the time there, in the ocean, against the waves. Got pretty good." He turned, took both her hands in his and reeled her in, looping her arms around his waist. He leaned down so his lips brushed her cheek. "Take off my shirt for me. I'm too burned."

Abby closed her eyes and turned her face into his shoulder. He smelled so good; clean sweat, hard work, hard man. She drew the edge of his t-shirt through her fingers, the skin of his lower back hot against her knuckles.

"Lift up your arms," she whispered. He knew perfectly well what he was doing. What he was doing to her. Since their eyes had met in her bedroom, she'd been melting like a candle caught in a white-hot flame. Why hide it? Why not make him melt, too?

He lifted his arms, but she took her time. She could feel the near-tangible pressure of his stare on the crown of her head. Before she tugged off his tee, she slid her hands under the sweat-dampened fabric and ran them over his taut skin. Bunched muscles. Knotted sinew. Deep breaths ruffled her bangs as Ash gulped air and let it out. She trailed her fingers over his ribs down to the waist of his shorts. The faded denim was damp and cool. His skin twitched everywhere she touched, as if little sparks stung him from her fingertips.

Knowing she affected him so made her own breath come short. She wanted to lie down, curl herself around him, here on the dock, in a puddle of sunlight. She drew her lower lip between her teeth, sucked on it to swallow down a groan.

"Abby." His husky voice broke through her haze. His hands lowered, slid over her hair. His forearms rested on her shoulders. "We can always go home and take it off there."

"Sorry," she murmured, then offered a small grin. She was every bit as insincere in her apology as he'd been in his. He smiled into her eyes, but it was a wicked smile, knowing, inviting. "Arms up," she said, and this time pulled the gray t-shirt off in one fluid movement.

His pained grunt made her put a hand on his bare chest. "Are you okay? You're as red as a cranberry. Get it? A cranberry?"

"Har har, yes I get it." He shuddered. She felt it through her palm. "Next time, sun block."

"Definitely."

"This time," he said, catching the waistband of her shorts with two fingers and walking backward, tugging her toward the end of the dock, "cold water. Ice cold, as I recall."

She leaned against his pressure. "I . . . I really don't want to go in."

Laughing, he let her go and bent to yank off his boots. Sleek muscles curved his shoulders as he peeled off his socks and tossed them on top of his boots. "Sit on the edge and stick your feet in, at least."

"What about Old Man Miller?"

"He can stick his feet in, too, if he wants."

A cautious glance across the water still showed no movement from the creepy house. She toed off her sneakers and set them beside his big, clunky boots. "Hope he doesn't still have that mean dog."

"We'll find out soon enough."

She'd just taken off her socks when she heard the splash, and looked up to see Ash swimming toward the platform in the middle of the pond. Could he be any noisier? Kicking like a dolphin, he went under for a few seconds, then burst upward. Water sprayed like diamonds from his short, dark hair when he shook his head. He turned and waved. His white smile flashed. Abby suffered the most absurd urge to strip off her clothes and dive in after him. Probably the water would evaporate in a great puff of steam from the combined heat of their two bodies.

With a self-suffering mutter, she plunked down on the edge

of the dock and dropped her legs to the knees in the clear water. The pond was spring-fed, and cold. Her pale feet kicked languidly back and forth while she rested her chin on her fists and stared at them.

Absurd, absurd . . . this behavior of hers. She was setting herself up for a fall, and she couldn't even blame Ash. She knew what she was getting in to and what she was up against. It wasn't too late to pull back, to stop things before they went so far that she'd have regrets. What had they shared so far? A few kisses? A few hot, wonderful kisses that had brought the color and light back into her world?

How wonderful would it be to make love with Ash? The potential depressed her. Of course, it would be unforgettable. Their few nights together had been forever imprinted on her mind. More might break her. Ruin her for all other men, as the saying went. She raised her chin enough to watch him, on his back now, leisurely stroking a u-turn around the float. She frowned and scooped up water, rubbing it over her the undersides of her wrists.

With Brian, sex had been pleasant. Polite. They'd never seemed to bridge the tentative newness of their relationship. Their noses had bumped when they kissed. When she made the littlest noise during sex, he'd stop to ask if she was uncomfortable. He always made the bed afterward. You could bounce a quarter off it. No wallowing in sweaty, tangled sheets for him. Or for her. She'd gone along, not wanting to offend. Always feeling guilty because she'd married him when she didn't love him.

Abby dropped her gaze to her toes wiggling beneath the surface. That had been the source of the awkwardness with Brian—she'd thought. Or was it that she'd felt like she was cheating somehow, on Ash, who had left her without a backward glance or qualm?

Absurd.

Hard hands grabbed her ankles and she startled, blinking from her thoughts.

"Daydreaming?" Ash's wet smile gleamed up at her. His strong, tanned fingers flexed, manacled her ankles and began a slow slide up her calves.

She leaned back on the heels of her hands. "Don't sneak up on me like that."

"You looked sad." He touched a dripping, cool finger to a furrow between her eyebrows. "Still not too late to hop in."

She sniffed, hoping to appear indifferent, and wiped the rolling bead of water from her nose. "It's awfully chilly."

"Not nearly chilly enough." The gravelly tone of his voice made his meaning crystal clear. His wandering hands reached her knees and slid beneath them, easing them apart while he moved between her legs.

Brows knitted, unsettled in her own mind, Abby reached down and wiped the water from his forehead, brushed her palm over his thick, short hair. She traced the straight length of his nose, and each eyebrow. Just a face. Just a man. Just Ash, who made her pulse ring through her veins. For his part, he didn't move, but let her explore, gazing up with trusting, lusting granite eyes.

Was this love? Rolling through her in almost painful rushes of heat and light, making her belly tighten, making her curve her feet around his bare waist where he stood in the clear water and draw him in?

Heck, if she thought about it, she'd do nothing but think about it. She wanted to act, to feel. To be free. She shut off her brain and cupped his face and leaned down to kiss him.

Ash pressed up to meet her halfway and oh, it was good, so good. A shiver tripped the length of her spine. Abby rode the sensation, opened her mouth a little, touched her tongue to his lower lip. His half-day's growth of beard abraded like sandpaper against her upper lip where she rubbed back and forth. He tasted of sweet water and iced tea and desire. His dripping arms lifted and circled her hips. Moisture seeped through her shirt.

Off balance by their awkward positioning—him in the pond, her on the dock—Abby put her hands on his slick shoulders and looked down at his face.

"I liked that," he said, his voice low. "Don't stop now."

She laughed softly. "Have to, or I'll fall." In love or in the pond? Who knew?

One eyebrow arched, he exerted pressure and she began to slide off the wood toward him. Her laugh grew nervous. She clung to the old boards. "Ash, cut it out!"

"But the water's fine," he crooned.

She unhooked her feet from his waist and gave a playful push against his chest with her toes. "I thought you preferred the ocean."

"I'm learning to appreciate pond life." But he relented. He came forward again, hands sliding along her legs, and rubbed his raspy cheek against her thigh. His breath coursed over her skin, flame in contrast to the ice-cold water dripping from his hair. With a muted gasp, Abby gripped the rotting boards and leaned back. His open mouth trailed a sucking kiss from her knee and up, up, up. His fingers worked under the hem of her shorts, drawing firm circles, moving toward where she wanted them most.

"Oh! My gosh—" She scooted back, yanking her legs up in a spray of water.

He gazed at her where she sat panting on the dock. A grin curved half his mouth. "All right, I'll come up there, then."

"Ehh . . ." She breathed out, "how about a couple more laps?"

He laughed, the sound pure male satisfaction, as he heaved himself up and somehow turned himself so he sat beside her on the edge. "You started it."

She bit her lip. "Yeah . . ."

He put a hand on her knee. "Please, feel free to start it again any time."

The things his smile did to her . . . Abby felt as if she were glowing from the inside out with some kind of rare, feminine radiance. She put her hand over his. "You did used to get me into all sorts of trouble. It's coming back to me now."

"Me?" he said in mock innocence. "You had plenty of ideas of your own. You always were a rebel."

"No way. What would I rebel against? Lucy?"

"Against circumstances. Life. Against your parents, or lack thereof."

That cut a little too close. Abby lifted her hand and ran it through her tousled mess of hair. She stared out over the calm waters. "I told you, I'm all right with that."

"You'll never be all right with it, any more than I'll be all right with my family."

"It's not the same."

"Sure it is. We were both outcast kids. My father never wanted more than one child because he couldn't stand my mom's side of the family. They thought she'd married down. Never let him forget it. It was always a sore spot between them, got worse over the years. He suspected my mother got pregnant to spite him. Probably she did. She was a rebel, too." He leaned back on his elbows. "When I ended up looking like her, it only made things worse. Then I wouldn't follow his plans for my life . . ."

She reached out to run her fingers over his hair. "I can't believe he still feels that way, especially now with your mom gone. He was really brokenhearted when she died."

"Too little, too late." He shrugged brusquely, clearly uncomfortable that he'd said so much.

"You never gave him a chance once she passed on. Maybe if

160

you'd stayed, things would have been different."

He squinted at the sun, forehead furrowed against the glare. "Don't know. Can't say I'm sorry things worked out the way they did." She drew back, rubbing her arms, and he looked at her. "Except for you. I am sorry for what happened between us."

Ash cupped the underside of her calf, his palm smoothing over her skin. Beneath him, the water lapped against the sides of the dock, clouds passed overhead, and he realized the last thing he wanted to do was make Abby upset. "I was a jerk."

No reply. He cast a sideways glance at her pensive expression. "This is when you're supposed to say, 'No, Ash, you did what you thought was right.' "

Staring out over the water, she rubbed the bridge of her freckled nose. "I'm thinking it over."

He gave a low chuckle and lay back on the boards, stretching his arms over his head. "You're a tough nut, Abigail."

"When you left, I was too young to know how to feel. Hurt. Relieved. Mad. But I've learned a lot since then."

"And *now* you're mad?"

"Maybe." She eased to her side, propped on one elbow facing him. "Why didn't you ever give this place a chance? You were always itching to get away."

"You know why. I never fit in. I'm like a bird in a cage here."

"I think you fit in just fine. You look pretty comfortable right now, for instance."

Closing his eyes, he drew in a long, slow inhale of fresh air and sunshine and Abby on the breeze. The peachy shampoo she used, and a touch of fresh-baked cookies, lingered in her hair. He twined his fingers in the soft strands draping her shoulder. "Yeah. Can't complain, I admit."

She touched his cheek with her fingers, stroked his temple.

He loved her touch. He wanted to purr like a big cat. He sensed her leaning closer. "Couldn't you give it another chance?" she whispered.

Frowning, he turned his head to stare at her. "Live here?"

Guileless chocolate eyes assessed him. "Sure. Why not?"

"I'm already committed to this deal with my partner."

"If it weren't for that, would you?"

He felt like a fish wriggling on the line, being drawn with infinite patience from his cozy den of bachelorhood and Life the Way He Liked It. "No" formed on his lips, but rumbled out in a disgruntled sigh instead when Abby trailed her fingertips from his elbow to his shoulder and back again.

He set his back teeth together. Abby had never used her wiles to get her way before. Had she? Thinking back, maybe she had. There'd been the quitting-smoking thing, and the staying-in-school thing, and the try-to-get-along-with-your-family thing. She'd always been the little moral angel on his shoulder. Oh hell. Any man who thought he ran the show around a pretty woman was only fooling himself. And she wasn't an untried girl anymore; she knew what she was about.

Her hand drifted to his bare stomach, and he caught hold of her wrist, pressing her palm against his belly. "Careful, Abby," he murmured.

Her gaze dropped. "Sorry, I forgot, your sunburn—"

"It's not the sunburn." His gaze traced the curve of her lips. "Just out of curiosity, sweetheart, what's in it for you if I stay?"

Now it was her turn to wriggle. Her fingers flexed beneath his palm, but no force in the world could convince him to release her.

She nibbled her lower lip, making it plump and damp. "This is your home, that's all. I . . . Maybe because of what happened to me, I think you should want to make peace with your family. Don't turn your back on them again."

Her voice had gone soft. Turn his back on her, she meant. He understood. Rolling to his side, he scooped her elbow out from under her and had her on her back before she could blink. Holding her wrists in a gentle but unyielding grip, he crossed them over her chest and gazed down into her surprised eyes. A halo of wild blond waves framed her sweet face.

"You know," he said, "if I stay, you won't ever get rid of me. I'll be checking up on you all the time. Every man you date, I'll be watching. You might not like having me around."

Her brows knitted. Her hips moved beneath his in the mildest protest. Her sky blue shirt strained against the rise and fall of her breasts. "I told you," she said, "I don't date anymore."

He gave a raspy laugh as his body reacted to the silk of her thigh against his and the smoky awareness mellowing her gaze. "That's too bad. I was going to ask you to the town's Fourth of July picnic."

Oh, if looks could kill. Her fingers clenched and her lush lips puckered. "Ash Wheeler, you are a jerk."

"At last we agree."

"Let me go."

"If I do, will you slap me?"

"Most likely."

He let her go, slid his hands around her ribs, and rubbed his cheek against her breast. God, she had a great body. Warm and wonderful, with all the right curves to fit his hands. Seeing as no slap had landed—yet—he unbuttoned the first button of her shirt. Pressed his mouth to the exposed skin. She stroked his hair, tentative at first, then bolder, hands mapping the back of his neck, his shoulders.

He slipped the second button. No resistance. The third. Delved inside to cup one lovely—

Abby made a breathy sound and rolled toward him.

He moved his body over hers. Need pulsed through him,

163

crushed the breath from him, narrowed his world to the taste, feel, smell of her. Holding himself up on one elbow, he studied her softening gaze, her parted lips. Through her lacy bra—angel pink, he noted appreciatively—he teased her with his fingertips. Drew light circles. Watched her pupils widen. Murmured, "I don't think this day could get much better, do you?"

"Maybe . . . a little . . ." she whispered. She lifted her head to meet his kiss.

And a thunk resounded off the dock.

A fist-sized rock thudded by his bare foot and splashed into the pond. Ash jerked up his head at the same time Abby yelped as if she'd been pinched and yanked away.

"Peter." Muttering a curse, Ash swung to a cross-legged squat. A few yards away, Peter stood at an angle, facing away enough that he wasn't gawking, but not enough to hide his smirk. When Peter turned, Ash gave his brother the scowl of death.

Peter closed the gap and set one polished shoe set on the gray planks. "Miller called and said there were two kids necking out on his dock. I was going to send Preston, but then I got the description." He nodded toward the old house. "Seems Miller replaced his coon hound with a high-powered telescope."

Cowering behind him, Abby uttered a strangled groan. Ash didn't have to look to imagine her fumbling with her shirt buttons. He dragged his hand over his jaw. "Well, thanks so much for doing the honors yourself."

Peter thumbed up the black brim of hat and laughed. "Nothing changes, bro. Still jumping into hot water feet first."

With his wrists dangling over his bent knees, Ash covertly gave his brother the finger, which only made Peter laugh harder.

Peter leaned, bracing a hand on his thigh. "Dinner's at seven tonight. Merry's making something we both like, for a change, fried chicken. Pop'll be there. You coming?"

"Yes," he growled.

"Hey, Abby," Peter called, "you're invited, too."

She huddled against Ash's back, probably wanting to dive into the pond never to be heard from again.

"Hey, I might have some news on your aunt's sign. I'll tell you more at dinner." Peter's teasing grin was merciless. "You okay back there, Ab?"

Her red cheek popped up above Ash's shoulder. "Peter, for God's sake, yes, I'm fine."

"Great. See you tonight?"

"Fine! Just, just—"

"Go away," Ash finished for her.

With a wink and a nod, Peter gave them a mock salute. He turned back to his cruiser, which was barely visible through the trees. "Be sure you two clear out right away. Had to talk Miller out of using his pellet gun. Not sure I was wholly successful."

They sat until the car door shut and the cruiser pulled away.

Scrubbing the heel of his palm over his brow, Ash began to laugh. "Timing is everything . . ."

Abby elbowed him. Boy, did she look ticked. Dried his laughter right up.

"I've never been so embarrassed . . ." she muttered through clenched teeth.

He swung around to face her. She'd fastened her buttons all wrong, the collar on one side too high. Ignoring her swatting hands, he undid them then buttoned them up again properly. "It's okay. It was only Peter."

"Still," she snapped, "he . . . he knows."

"Honey, you're a divorced woman of legal age, and I'm a thick-skinned old bachelor. We weren't doing anything wrong."

Her eyes shut tight. She pressed her palm flat against her forehead and took a heavy breath. "Right. I guess."

"So is it a date?" He held up a finger. "Oh, forgot, no dating.

Well, it's just Merry and Peter's. Accompany me to their house? We won't use the dirty 'D' word."

One corner of her mouth pressed down. "Between the two of you Wheelers, I don't know which is worse."

"You have to even think about it? I'm insulted."

Across the lake, a harsh clap shattered the afternoon. Water spackled skyward. Abby clutched his wrist. "Mr. Miller! He's got a gun!"

Shading his eyes, Ash lifted a shoulder. "We're out of range. But maybe it's our cue to leave." He pulled his t-shirt back on, keeping an eye on the irate old man pacing the opposite shore. Good thing it was a big pond. Miller seemed plenty ticked off, too. Abby fumbled with her sneakers, and then they were jogging to the motorcycle.

Ash handed Abby the helmet, helped her fasten the chinstrap when her shaking hands wouldn't cooperate. A spatter of rain smacked his bare arms and the back of his neck. "Easy, Abby, it'll take him a few minutes to find his way around."

"I suppose." Peering over his shoulder, she relaxed a hair. Her teeth caught her lower lip.

Ash rapped his knuckles on the helmet. "Bet you haven't had this much excitement in a dog's age."

She eyed him ruefully. "Not since you left, that's for sure."

He studied her face framed by the battered fiberglass helmet, captured a mental picture of her freckled cheeks, mussed bangs over her brows and the disarray of her clothes. He remembered how they got that way and his body tightened. With his thumbs, he smoothed the hair off her forehead. "Hey, after dark we could come back, try that skinny dipping. Broaden your education."

Abby cocked her head and swayed toward him. She put her palms flat against his chest. "I'll have more time next week, and it's supposed to be hotter," she said in a low, breathy tone that made his joints turn to jelly. "Then I might be tempted. But oh—" Brows lifting, she gave him a little shove. "—that's right. You'll be gone by then."

And it obviously bugged her. Ash started to answer, but then another barrage of pellets kicked up the water, followed by an acidic cussing. Miller, making good time.

Abby hopped onto the motorcycle's seat, scooted back to make room for him, and gestured impatiently. "Can we go now? Please?"

He swung on in front of her and gunned the engine as soon as her hands locked around his waist. The rear tire spat up clods of weeds and dirt as the bike leapt forward. At the edge of his vision, Miller burst out of the brush. Thin gray hair on end, his face a pinched mask of fury, he shook his old rifle at them as they whizzed by. Abby laughed, plastered against Ash's back, her arms clamped around his ribs.

Bending into the storm, Ash grinned like a devil. Abby wanted him to stay. She wanted him. That was half the battle won.

# CHAPTER THIRTEEN

Standing in the bedroom of her small apartment, Abby decided she should go with jeans. Jeans and a simple top. This yellow dress . . . too obvious. She posed sideways to the full-length mirror, hands in the pockets of the sleeveless, daffodil-colored dress she'd pulled out of mothballs. It had a low, square neckline, a tailored waist, and fell to her knees with a little flare that made her look very feminine. And very June Cleaver. Sheesh, all she needed was a string of pearls and a short, tight perm.

She had nothing to wear on a . . . No, no, not a date. Just dinner at Peter's. Abby scratched a mosquito bite at the base of her throat and turned to scowl at the heaps of clothing on her bed. Jeans, sweats and cut-off shorts. That's what her wardrobe had been reduced to after a few years of not . . . dating. Except for this stinky yellow thing, which, the more she looked at it, the more it looked like something out of a fifties sitcom. She rolled her worry stone around in her pocket and pondered. A knock at the front door made her jump. Oh, no. Hadn't Ash said six-thirty? She glanced at the red numbers on her alarm clock and groaned. Six twenty-two.

Spinning on her bare heel, she ran to the door, skidded to a stop, groaned again and balled her fists by her ears. Over eager. Over anxious. And playing dress-up for a night out. Ash was a cop; he'd sniff out her nervousness in a heartbeat. She sucked on her lower lip and patted her hair. Well, she couldn't let him stand out there in the rain.

She jerked open the door and blurted, "I'm not wearing this."

Ash's gaze devoured her on the way down and enjoyed a second helping on the way back up. "Then who is? Introduce me. She's beautiful."

Abby flicked her fingers in the air. "God, Ash." She stepped back letting him in. "Where do you come up with those lines? Do they work in Los Angeles?"

"Why? Not working here?" He had on a nice pair of black slacks, good shoes, and a light jacket over a slate gray shirt, open at the collar. The fabric looked fine and expensive, and flattered his eyes. He'd shaved, and brushed his hair, and he smelled like absolute heaven. Apparently, somewhere in California, he'd contracted a sense of style.

Which only made her feel even more like the next Betty Crocker candidate. Abby took a step back. Her heart thumped like a puppy running up the stairs. "You'll have to give me a minute to change."

"Why? What's wrong with what you've got on?"

"This?" She yanked out the skirt on either side and let it drop. "I can't wear this to . . . to Peter's."

He followed on her heels right to the doorway of her bedroom. "I like it. It's cute."

"Cute," she muttered. She could feel his heat all up and down her back. At the threshold, she stopped, spun, put a blocking hand on his chest. "Five minutes."

But he gazed over the top of her head, into her bedroom. "Looks like you've already tried on a few things."

"I was cleaning my closet."

Pressed against her, he smiled. Knowing.

"Don't look so smug, Mr. Detective."

"Smug? Me?" He backed off, letting her breathe. The fitted top on this dress hadn't seemed nearly so snug a few minutes ago. She gave his arm a little push. "Go make yourself homely. I'll be out . . . soon."

He took another scan of her bedroom, like a preemptory perusal, made a "hmmm" of approval before he slid past her and right in.

Not for the first time since his return, Abby's jaw dropped. She crossed her arms and propped herself against the doorframe. "You know, you're early."

"Not by much."

"I knew I should have driven myself."

"That wouldn't have been very gentlemanly of me. Besides . . ." He grinned over his shoulder. "I wanted to see where you live."

She heaved an exaggerated sigh.

Ignoring her, Ash stopped beside her bed to peruse the piles. His fingers stroked down the leg of a pair of old jeans, across the waistband of a paisley skirt, drifted over a black velvet halter top, settled, fingers spread, just about where her right breast would be, if she were wearing it. He had big hands, square and strong and competent-looking, and there was something unbelievably erotic about watching them explore the textures and shapes of her clothing. She could feel her breasts tingle and tighten in response, as they had earlier, on the dock . . .

"Don't see anything I like better," he drawled, assessing her with shadowed eyes.

Abby realized her own hand traveled the neckline of her dress, fingertips skimming inside. Her fevered skin needed air. Ash's presence spread through her small bedroom; his masculinity, his intensity dominated the soft pink lighting and flowery wallpaper.

She moved toward him on bare feet as if drawn by a string. His avid gaze tracked her. Riveted, as she had been. Hip to thigh with him, she slid her hand from his waist to his shoulder, under his jacket, over the exquisitely soft shirt and the tense muscle beneath. Noted a little line forming between his drawn brows. She licked her lips and, with a Mona Lisa smile, whispered, "Then move over, so I can put this stuff away."

"What?" Ash stared for a second, then rasped out a chuckle deep in his throat. He edged aside and shook his head. "My God, Abby, you have come into your own."

"My own what?" She batted her eyelashes. She picked up the black halter and shook it out, as if she could shake the lust off it.

"You know," he grumbled. "You're a real woman now. Not a, uh . . ."

"Innocent virgin?" she finished when he hesitated.

"Mmm-hm."

"Well, you saw to that."

He paused by her tall dresser. "Regrets?"

She turned, the jeans folded over her arm. "No. I'd heard . . . for a girl, to lose her virginity can be painful. It wasn't. You made it wonderful. I don't know if I ever told you that."

Perhaps the somber tone of her voice puzzled him. Rather than answer, he touched the silver edge of a frame holding a photo of her parents, moved on to one of Lucy. "No pictures of your ex," he observed.

"Not here." She put the jeans in a low drawer, closed it with her knee. "I have a wedding album. Somewhere. Do you want to see it?"

"No," he said, a little too quickly.

Turning back to her clothes, Abby balled a turquoise t-shirt in her hands. Her palms were damp. Her heart rocked in her chest, but not with desire now. With edginess. Maybe some part of her did want to hurt Ash back.

"Was he good to you?" he asked quietly.

Puzzled herself now, Abby stared at him. "Why this sudden interest in my husband?"

He flinched at the last word, a brief flexing of his jaw. "Being with you this week . . . I've been thinking."

"Regrets?" she echoed, with a small, tight quirk of her lips.

"Maybe." He came beside her, glanced at her stacked garments, then at her. "Are you going to change?"

Abby wondered at the double entendre in his tone. Her body hummed at his tempting proximity, and a tearing happiness ringed her heart simply because he stood beside her.

With a quick shake of her head, she stepped away and stood before the mirror. The muted light glowed on the sunny yellow fabric. She held out the skirt again and sighed.

"I guess I don't have the energy to find something better. You're sure this doesn't scream 'old maid'?"

"You're lovely." Ash stood behind her, close, his chest brushing her shoulders. His right hand circled her waist, slid around to rest below her breasts, where he could surely feel the wild beating of her heart.

She plucked at the wide belt cinching her waist. "It's hard to know what to wear to the house of a woman whose husband you KO'd with a flashlight."

"Better let me go in first, in case she's waiting to ambush you."

Ash's slanted grin reflected back at her, above her left shoulder. His dark frame, his broad shoulders, silhouetted her pale coloring and slender body. Like a page from the past, shocking in its clarity. Abby's breath caught. All that talk of could have been, might have been . . .

She let herself drift back against the strong wall of his chest. Their eyes met in the mirror.

Uncertainty flickered in his expression. His fingers spread across her belly. "Abby . . ."

He said her name as if he'd wanted to ask her something. Something serious. She put her hand over his. "What is it?"

He hesitated, holding her tighter. Then his lashes lowered to mask his eyes. He trailed his fingers across the bare skin of her throat and shoulder. "Nothing. It's nothing." His hands dropped away. "It's time to go."

The woman was going to give him a heart attack.

After the third distracted attempt, he fumbled his jacket onto the hook in Peter's front hallway. He couldn't drag his gaze away from her. Radiant. He'd never attached that word to any woman, but it fit Abby tonight. Driving over, he'd worried he'd have an accident, he'd had such a hard time keeping his attention on the road. His eyes just naturally wanted to turn, drink in her quicksilver smiles, the way she tipped her head when she laughed, the curve of her fingers as she brushed her hair from her temple.

Man, he was in deep. Sunk like a stone into something he hadn't counted on, and it scared him and lured him at the same time. At her apartment, his plan had been to pass his grand idea by her. Test it out, see how she felt about moving down with him. He'd chickened out.

In the past six years, he'd run into burning buildings, faced gunfire, hunted down vicious criminals, but he'd choked on his own nerves when Abby seemed about to read his mind. Women could do that. He knew from past experience that Abby was especially adept. Only a matter of time before she figured out where he was going with all his heavy-handed hinting about Miami. And if she said no . . . Ash's throat went suddenly tight and dry.

He watched her smile her way into Peter's living room. Charming and gracious in her pretty dress, she greeted Merry and bent to say hello to the kids, who made for him like a wave of friendly pups.

"Uncle Ash!" Little Pete clutched at his hand. "Did you ride the motorsickle in the rain?"

"No, buddy, I took the car."

Petie made a disappointed "aww," and Ash affectionately mussed his nephew's neatly combed blond hair. "I had a lady with me tonight. It wouldn't have been right."

The boy glanced behind him. "I know her. She works at the candy store."

Figures he'd remember the deli for its treats. "Yeah, that's right." Then Missy grabbed hold of his other hand, well, two fingers of it anyhow, and Clay, the toddler, anchored himself to his pants leg. Abby glanced over just then and laughed. He gave a lopsided grin and shrugged. If letting kids hang on him made her eyes shine like that, he'd give each one a nickel to follow him around all day.

Merry, next to Abby, shook her head. "I don't know what they see in him, but the children do love their uncle."

Petie got defensive. "He's gonna teach me how to drive the motorsickle."

Merry raised a finger. "Over my dead—"

"When you're old enough," Ash cut in to appease the boy. "If your mom says it's okay," he added, to appease Merry. Didn't want to cross her. Beneath the carefully styled hair and crisply ironed blouse beat the heart of a Marine sergeant's daughter, and it showed. Like now.

She clapped her hands. "Come along, children, help me set the table."

Missy, a petite brunette like her mom, skipped toward the kitchen. Barefoot and bow-legged, a diapered Clay followed, but Petie tugged on Ash's hand. "What if she never says it's okay?" he asked mournfully.

"We'll sneak—"

"Sneak?" Abby had come over, and now tipped her head at him.

174

"Eh . . ." Ash sighed, looking down into the boy's anxious brown eyes. "We'll speak to your father. Maybe he'll be on our side."

"Oh, fat chance," Petie said. "He's hen-pecked."

Abby gasped. "Petie, where'd you learn language like that?"

Ash tried to dodge his nephew's conspiratorial grin, but the heat rose up his throat anyhow. "Uh, go help your mom, okay?"

The boy trotted off. Ash rubbed the back of his neck. "Kids these days."

"Yes, and the bad influences in their lives."

Her tone was stern, but a smile flirted at the corners of her mouth. Ash touched the back of her wrist. "Well, he's got eight years before he turns sixteen, but I'd be shocked and amazed if he wasn't on a dirt bike way before then."

"Giving Merry gray hairs."

"Peter, too."

She looked at him thoughtfully. "You know, I think you'd make a good dad."

"Yeah?" He stood a little straighter. She smiled again, one of those perceptive, feminine smiles that made his heart squeeze while his bachelor brain went "uh-oh." But the message from his brain faded like a cry in a storm as he trailed her into the kitchen. She thought he'd be a good dad. Well, that was something.

The kids had set the table and Merry, with Abby's help, laid out dishes of fried chicken, corn, potatoes and fresh, hot rolls on the big oak table. After he'd dropped her off, Abby had baked a rhubarb-strawberry pie for dessert. With sugar sparkling on a lattice crust, it looked like the first-prize winner at a country fair.

Merry handed a stack of green paper napkins to Missy. "Pete should be home soon. He got waylaid by an accident out on Blue Spruce."

"Anyone hurt?" Ash asked.

"He didn't think so."

Ash kept the kids entertained and out of the women's way. A few minutes later, the front door squeaked and Peter walked in, still in uniform, shaking the last of the day's rain from his hat. "Greetings, all."

Ash nodded. "How was that accident?"

"Cow versus car. The cow won, but not by much." He shrugged out of his windbreaker. "Somehow this one heifer keeps getting through the fence. Third time this month she's wandered into traffic."

Trying not to laugh, Ash rubbed his chin. "Maybe put her under house arrest—or farm arrest."

His brother caught Petie under the arms and swung him up for a hug. "She's a crafty criminal, that one. Ain't she, Petie?"

"Gonna shoot her." The boy made a gun of his fingers. "Bang, bang."

"Now, none of that. Just a poor, dumb animal with a bad case of wanderlust." Peter set his son down so he could scoop up Missy and smack a kiss to her cheek, then he leaned over to peck Merry's cheek as well. Merry turned and kissed him on the lips instead.

"Good to have you home," she said. "I was afraid you'd miss dinner if the accident was serious."

"No worries." He patted his belly and surveyed the laden table. "Damn, it smells great in here."

"Peter," Merry chided.

"Darn," he corrected himself. Too late. Little Pete said, "Can I have one of those damn rolls?"

Ash turned to Abby. "See, it's not just me."

Peter Senior, ruddy-faced from the rain, came in a few minutes later, made the rounds amongst the grandkids, and they all sat down and dug in. Once it became clear no one was going to mention the bump on Peter's head or the incident at the dock, Abby visibly relaxed. Conversation flowed as easily as the white china platters around the table. Merry inquired after Lucy, and she and Abby caught up on local gossip.

Ash's dad asked about the latest goings-on at the police station. Peter filled him in. There was more happening in Cranberry than Ash had guessed, but pretty typical small-town stuff. A few domestic quarrels, neighborly disputes, kids causing trouble. Lately, a pack of underage teens had got hold of a fake ID and managed to buy themselves some liquor.

"They might have gotten away with it," Peter said, scraping up the last of his mashed potatoes, "if they hadn't started a ruckus with some other boys."

"A ruckus?" Ash pointed his fork at him. "Lucky it didn't boil over into a fracas."

"Or escalate into a brouhaha," Peter, Sr. grumbled with a perfectly straight face. "Hain't been a brouhaha in this town for fifty years."

Peter buttered a roll for Missy. "You're forgetting the town council meetings. They're forever brouhahaing."

"Speaking of which," Abby chimed in, leaning forward to look at Peter, "you said you had news about Lucy's sign?"

"Yeah, it's fine. I twisted some arms, threw my weight around a little."

"In other words," Ash said, "you forgave a few parking tickets and promised some votes."

Peter rubbed at the bruise on his forehead. "Yup, that's about the size of it."

"Well, thank you for that." She gave him a relieved smile and straightened the paper napkin on her lap.

Ash shook his head. "Small town policing."

"You know you miss it, being a cop," his brother said.

Ash stabbed at the last of his green beans with his fork and thought about it. "Sure I do. Sometimes."

Peter set his elbows on either side of his empty plate. "Have you considered what we talked about?"

Ash passed the pitcher of lemonade to Abby, who seemed to be listening in rather intently. Man, he hated Peter putting him on the spot like this. All eyes were on him. He shook his head. "I don't know. I've already got this business deal rolling."

He knew he sounded unresolved, more so than he'd intended. Now why was that? The two Peters exchanged significant glances, but Merry popped to her feet, her face set in a frown, and started to clear dishes. Clay began to whine. From the sink, Merry said, "Pete, could you take care of the baby? He needs a diaper."

With resigned amusement, Peter met Ash's eyes over the rim of his glass. He heaved to his feet, wiggled his youngest out of the plastic high chair and headed for the bedroom, murmuring nonsense to the baby as he walked.

A bit of envy crept into Ash's soul. Peter had good kids, a good wife. A good life.

He glanced at Abby, who regarded him with those beautiful, hopeful doe-eyes. Is this what she wanted? Of course it was. A settled, domestic existence in her little hometown. Rosy-cheeked babies filling her ancestral farmhouse with love and laughter. And him . . . ? Where'd he fit into the equation?

Ash tried to picture himself sprinting down Blue Spruce after the swishing tail of a black and white heifer. He pressed his fingertips to his forehead and silently groaned.

The rain had stopped and the night had gone foggy and cool. Tendrils of mist rose from the pavement like pale fairies. A mostly-full moon hung low, wearing a skirt of wispy clouds. Abby rolled down the window of Ash's rental car and inhaled deeply of the sleepy, pine-scented breeze. It seemed a night fit for dreams and . . . possibilities.

They'd stayed for dessert, the group migrating to sit around the TV to watch the end of the Yankees game. She and Merry had sipped coffee, while the men drank beer and the kids dug into pie and juice. She savored the simple pleasures of good friends and family, and Ash sitting next to her with his arm draped over her shoulders. She couldn't ask for anything more. Except that the dream that he would be there always, and that someday, those would be their own children playing on the carpet, might come true.

The evening was ending all too soon.

She stretched her arm out the window and let the playful wind curl about her fingers. "Well, that wasn't such a bad time after all," she said, curbing her wayward thoughts. "Especially since Merry didn't exact revenge for Peter's bump."

"I'm glad you enjoyed yourself. I did, too." Ash drove with one hand on the steering wheel. The other rested on his stomach. "I bet I gained ten pounds tonight. Between the fried chicken, the potatoes, your pie—"

"Two helpings," she reminded him, flush with satisfaction that he'd gobbled down her home cooking with such enthusiasm.

"Not to mention the two dozen chocolate chip cookies you left with me this afternoon."

"You'll lose your girlish figure," she remarked.

He patted his lean torso. "Pretty soon, I'll be too fat to chase after bad guys."

"Would you be doing that anyhow, in the security business?"

"Probably not. We'd call the cops now, instead of being the cops."

"Thank goodness," she said, then caught herself. "I mean . . ."

He flicked her a glance and waited. A flutter of nerves winged through her. Would he want to talk about this? Hesitantly, she said, "I can't get what you told me out of my mind. Shooting that boy. Shooting anyone. Guns and violence. Living with that danger every day."

"Yeah." He put both hands on the steering wheel. "There was always something happening in the city, that's for sure. It was interesting work. Challenging."

"Not just chasing cows."

"You read my mind." He nodded. "But I miss the excitement, and the friendships."

"Like your partner?"

"Oh, heck, yeah. He's a great guy. You'll have to meet him someday. Excellent street cop. Best man to have at your side." Even in the dim light, she could see his expression sobering. "We'd been partners for four years when he got shot."

"I'm so sorry. Was he badly hurt?"

"At first, we didn't think he'd walk again. Worried he'd even lose his leg. But Ryan's a fighter and he proved the docs wrong. He uses a cane, but he thinks it makes him look debonair." He chuckled. "God knows the women still love him." Then his brow creased. "Hmm, maybe I won't introduce you after all."

"Ryan, eh?" She went along with it, touching her hair. "Is he good looking?"

"No, he's hideous," he said, sounding alarmed.

Abby laughed. "Don't worry. One handsome policeman in my life is enough."

He smiled back, teasing. "I'll let Peter know."

"Just don't tell Merry. She already seemed grumpy. I couldn't figure out why tonight."

He sank back into his seat. "She's upset with me for not visiting more often. Little Pete is the only one of their kids I've actually seen before recently." An appropriately guilty tone underscored his words. "There was just never a good time to get away."

"Their children are adorable." Fighting her own pang of longing, Abby could relate to Merry's position. If the kids got attached to Ash, and then he disappeared again for another six years . . . She dropped her gaze to her hands, linked together in her lap. "It was nice to have everyone together tonight. You don't know how lucky you are, to have a family that . . . wants you."

He pulled the car in front of her apartment and parked. The engine shut off, leaving them in misty silence for a moment. Then Ash cupped her face in the palm of one hand and leaned toward her. "I want you, Abby. I want you so much I can hardly breathe."

Abby curled her fingers around his, bent her head to press her cheek against his knuckles, and closed her eyes before letting him go again. Longing and desire rose in her, all her hopes crowding around her heart.

With a heavy sigh, she sat back and stared at the moths that flitted around her front door light. One after another dove against the glass, getting only so close to the heat and light they craved; if they got what they wanted, of course, they'd burn. But it was worth the risk. And Ash was waiting for her to answer.

"Come inside," she whispered. Then more firmly, looking at him, drinking him in. "Come inside. Please."

# CHAPTER FOURTEEN

She barely remembered the short walk to her door. She dropped the key once, suddenly beset by nerves, and Ash took over and guided them in, his hand on her shoulder, turning her to him even as the door closed out the world.

There was nothing tentative or questioning in his kisses now. Firm, hungry lips parted hers, swallowed her little gasps. Heat and need welled inside her like a hidden spring, flooding her limbs, washing away her hesitation. In her dark apartment, they bumped hips, staggered, unbalanced by their urgency. They groped for buttons and buckles. When she stepped on his foot, a shaky laugh escaped her. "You're sure we remember how to do this?"

"It hasn't been that long." He moved back, swiped his hand over his dark hair. "We must be doing something wrong, though, we're both still fully dressed. Let's slow it down and see if we can figure it out. Come on."

When he looked at her with that wicked grin, she'd follow him anywhere. He took her hand and led her through a patchwork of moonbeams to her bedroom.

He drew her to him in the silvered shadows. Abby pressed the length of her body against his and hummed beneath his touch as he slid fingers through her hair, eased the zipper down the back of her dress, caressed the bare skin of her throat and shoulders.

She found those buttons that had frustrated her before and

began to free him from his shirt.

"Slow, slow," he murmured, catching her hands. She glanced up. He smiled, his voice like silk, hypnotic. "No rush. Tonight we have time, all the time in the world."

"Until morning?" she whispered, hopeful.

"At least." He twined her hands up behind his neck and kissed her, long and soft, reminding her again why this was so special, why they were so special together.

He undressed her first. Though she wished he'd hurry, Abby stood quiet while he slipped her dress from her shoulders. The cool air whispered across her heated skin. When he unclasped her bra, she couldn't contain an earthy sigh. The gleam in his silver eyes was all masculine knowing and desire. His big, coarse palms cradled her breasts, and she tangled her fingers in his belt loops to keep from drawing his head down to her aching nipples. "You're a terrible man," she muttered, leaning into his touch.

"I know." He rubbed his thumbs over their tips, dragging a groan from her. "But you love me anyway."

Love? Abby started, but any quick reply died on her parted lips as he nuzzled and suckled first one breast then the other. Her knees couldn't hold her. She melted onto the bed. One hand around the back of his head, his hair rough silk against her palm, she drew him down with her.

There were no further protests when she finally managed those buttons and peeled off his shirt, then his pants. They worked their way to the center of her bed until they were skin to hot skin, her hands in his clasped over her head, kissing and rubbing and driving each other wild.

"About that waiting," he gasped, lowering his solid body onto hers.

She smiled into his eyes and rolled her hips. "I'd say we waited long enough. Who's counting, anyhow?"

The hard length of him burned against her thigh. Now *that* she hadn't forgotten. The sweet, aching pleasure. Undeniable, incomparable. She wanted . . .

He slid his hands over her breasts, tender now from his attention, down her belly, and parted her thighs with a brush of his fingers. "You're sure, Abby?"

Suddenly he was serious again. She looked at his face, really looked. He was all sharp planes and angles, dark hair brushing his forehead, a muscle working in his cheek. He had changed. He wouldn't have asked six years ago. Would have simply seduced and taken. Instead, tonight, he offered a gift, which she could refuse. Or share.

She pressed a hand to his rough jaw and smiled. Warmth ringed her heart like a halo. "Aren't you?"

He laughed low in the back of his throat. "Stupid question," he murmured, and eased her legs wider with his knees. "I'm sure. Sure I need you," he rasped, bending his head to her throat. "How I need you . . ."

His fingers sought her first, tested her. Abby arched her back and pressed her nails into the firm muscles of his shoulders while he stroked and teased and slicked her own wetness over her sensitive flesh. His mouth found her breast again, his tongue swirling over her sweetly sore nipple. She groaned through gritted teeth. So good, so close to heaven. His hot scent filled her senses. She sucked at the skin below his ear, dug her fingers into his hair, curved a leg around his lean hip. "Ash, Ash . . ." She didn't care that she begged.

He kissed her as he entered her. He swallowed her cries as he moved in her. Sweat slicked their bodies. Harsh breathing and low moans floated through the shadows. Abby closed her eyes and concentrated on the prickle of his chest hair rubbing against her breasts. On the grip of his fingers on her waist. She slid her calf over his strong thigh and molded herself to him. Tightened her inner muscles to hold him, smiled at his throaty groan, turned to catch his kiss. Every whispered word told her he cherished her. Every caress made her feel beautiful, feminine. Loved.

They found the stars together and floated back down to earth tangled in the safety of each other's arms.

Remember, she whispered to herself long moments later, as he soothed the tremors from her tired muscles with long sweeps of his hands. He tugged the soft blanket up over her cooling skin. She snuggled into the curve of his shoulder and closed her eyes against bittersweet tears.

Tonight, at least, he belonged to her.

Ash was mired in a dream when the cell phone rang. One of those damned running dreams where he couldn't move fast enough, his legs leaden. Abby needed him, and he couldn't reach her. He woke with a start, unsure if the repeating chime was part of the nightmare or not. Stifling a groan, he turned his head and eyed the blurry red numbers on the bedside clock. Half past midnight.

A wonderful, warm weight shifted in the crook of his arm. Abby's silky hair slid over his shoulder. Her fingers flexed against the bare skin of his chest, and she smiled although her eyes were closed. He smiled, too. Maybe she was having a dream. A better one than his.

The cell phone persisted. Easing Abby onto the sheets, he tucked her in before feeling around on the dark floor for his pants. He tugged the phone off his belt and padded barefoot and naked into the tiny kitchen before punching the call button.

"Hey, Ash. It's Jim."

Ash yawned. "Hey, Jim. What's up?"

"It's those vandals. They're down here at the nursery. I was working late in the office and I heard noises out back. Can you get down here?"

Of all the nights for those deadbeats to act up . . . Ash scratched his scalp and muttered, "Yeah. You're sure it's them?"

"Who else would be sneaking around at one in the morning?"

"I don't know, raccoons?"

"Don't think so. Come on, it's gotta be them."

"Mm. Okay. I'll head over."

"Great. I got my buckshot loaded."

"Don't do anything you'll regret later," he said, coming fully awake. If for no other reason, he had to get down there to make sure Jim didn't do anything stupid. "I'll see you in a few."

He clicked off, yawned again, contemplated the warm bed he'd be leaving and muttered something nasty under his breath. Probably just varmints. It was a school night. Wouldn't kids be missed?

When he shuffled back to the bedroom for his clothes and caught sight of Abby's tousled hair splayed across the pillow, it took all his will not to call Jim back and tell him to forget it. He scowled as he snatched up his shoes. Extra motivation to wrap this business up quickly and maybe get back before Abby even woke.

She looked so sweet there, sleeping deeply after their lovemaking. He'd pulled the coverlet up to her chin, but her gentle breathing lifted a strand of her hair and her small hands were folded beneath her cheek. Ash paused, his legs as leaden as they'd been in his dream. To think, he'd been asleep and missing this. Just looking at her. His chest ached. God, he was moonstruck.

And worse, now that he was up, he was . . . up. Ready to love her again. He imagined sliding back under the coverlet, nuzzling her throat. With the lightest touch, he'd trace circles around her sensitive nipples until they were taut buds begging for his mouth. He would stroke her shoulders and the curve of her back, then taste her from throat to belly, kissing softly so as not to wake her, savoring the salt of her skin. Then he'd ease down to linger between her thighs. She'd open her eyes on the crest of pleasure, gasping his name . . .

Oh, man . . . He clenched his eyes shut. He'd never felt this intense connection with any other woman. She was everything he wanted, but in the wrong place, and the wrong time. For him, anyhow.

Brusquely turning with his clothes bundled against his chest, he strode back to the kitchen. He tossed his shoes on a chair and pulled in a bracing breath. The cozy room smelled of cinnamon and apples, and the scent of cut grass wafted through the open window. Sweet and wholesome, like Abby. No car exhaust polluted the night. The squeal of sirens and chaotic street life were a world away. He pulled on his clothes, frowning.

How could he ask her to leave this, to live in a foreign world of noise and fear? He'd heard the worry in her voice when she talked about his old job. Security work was safer than being a city cop but still held its dangers. And in the back of his mind, he knew some day he might go back to the streets. He did miss the excitement, the risk. It was in his blood. The more he talked about it with his brother, the more he recognized the pull of his old life. If he was unattached, he could easily make the decision.

But with Abby involved, everything would change. And both of them would lose.

Wrapped in the coverlet, Abby stood in the kitchen doorway, watching Ash leave. He hadn't heard her yet. Somehow she'd managed to swallow down her grief and not make a sound. But she'd heard him as he stumbled around in the kitchen, tugging on his pants, pulling on his shoes. Leaving her.

He stood with his shirt hanging open and glanced around the floor.

"Lose something?" she asked softly.

He just about jumped out of his skin. "Jesus, Abby—" He straightened, rubbing his palm over his chest. Guilt shone in his wide eyes. Somehow, even with rumpled clothes and his short dark hair standing all at angles, Ash still looked like a dark angel. Her insides twisted with humiliation to know he so obviously didn't want her the way she wanted him.

She pulled the coverlet tighter around her shoulders and lifted one eyebrow. "I guess technically it is morning. You're free to go."

"I'm not leaving." He shook his head sharply. "I mean, I am, but I'm coming back."

She'd heard that one before. Caught in the act, how could he deny he was running for it? She could handle anything except a lie. "So, when would that be?"

He hesitated. "Soon."

She rubbed her face and sighed.

"I mean it." When she didn't answer, his mouth tightened. He finished buttoning his shirt and shoved the ends into his pants. "I got a call from Jim. He thinks the vandals are at the garden center, and he wants me to check it out."

"It's all right. You don't have to make up stories."

"I'm telling the truth. I wouldn't just take off." He took an angry swipe at the kitchen table and caught a piece of paper. "Here, see? I was writing you a note."

There was nothing on the paper. He slapped it down. "If you don't believe me, come along for the ride." His voice dropped to an irritated mutter as he looked down to buckle his belt. "Probably nothing but 'possums or 'coons anyhow."

The cold shell that had hardened around Abby's heart the

moment she realized she slept alone began to crack. Maybe he wasn't lying. He sounded sincere. Grouchy, but sincere. Sniffling back a stray tear, she fisted her hands gripping the coverlet beneath her chin. "You really were going to come back?"

"And stay." He closed the gap between them with two strides and kissed her hard on the mouth. "Until morning, and every morning until I—"

*Leave,* her stricken heart finished for him. *Well, here we go again.* It hardly mattered, though. "After tonight, I'll be sleeping at Lucy's. That wouldn't be, uh . . ."

He frowned. "Hm, no." He slid his hands inside the coverlet and settled them on her bare waist. They were cool against her hot skin, sending pleasant shivers through her. "I'm sorry our one night is getting ruined," he murmured. "Maybe we can find a way to make up for it later."

He bent his head and kissed her again, softer this time, a sweet melding of lips and tongues that dissolved the last of her anger. A cloud of heat suffused her. Her bare toes curled against the chilly linoleum.

Oh, my. Shivers chased up and down her spine. Her eyes might be gritty with sleep, but her body certainly was waking up nicely. "Can't the 'possums wait?"

Much to her disappointment, he drew back and tugged on his jacket. "I hope it's 'possums, but if it's not, I'd like to catch the vandals in the act."

"What about your brother? Isn't that his job?"

"I'll call him if it looks like trouble. No point in pulling him out of bed just yet." He traced the tip of one finger down her nose. "We know what a disappointment that can be."

"Mm." Abby caught the edge of her lip in her teeth.

His dark eyebrows slashed down. He caught her chin in one hand. "Are you crying?"

She pulled from his grasp. "No."

"Well, if you're not, you were. Abby, did you really think I'd just take off in the middle of the night?"

Pressing the edge of her mouth down hard, she looked away and shrugged.

"I wouldn't go if I didn't have to," he said.

Just like everyone else in her life. But she opted to take his words the way he meant them, and nodded. "Wait a minute, I'll get dressed." She turned for her bedroom.

"If you're sure," he said. "You can always stay here, keep the sheets warm for me."

He thrust his hands into his pockets and relaxed against the doorframe. He looked scruffy and rugged and entirely male, and she wanted to haul him back into the bedroom and make him forget about the bothersome world outside.

Instead, she whipped a pair of jeans out of the drawer. "I have an electric blanket to do that for us," she said, then stood and let the coverlet slip from her shoulders to the floor.

Dressed only in moonlight, she laughed at his appreciative groan.

"Better hurry," he said in a tortured tone that left no doubt as to the direction of his thoughts. Abby's mood lifted, almost enough to make her forget that this rare happiness would soon be another faded page in her past.

They took Ash's car to the garden center and parked down the road, by the edge of a cornfield. Ash had a flashlight, but the night was clear enough for them to sneak their way to the main building. Abby stumbled in the parking lot, scattering gravel.

"Sorry," she whispered. "My heart is pounding. I can't believe I'm this nervous."

Ash held her hand and squeezed it. "Fun, huh?"

"I hope I didn't blow our cover."

He leaned aside to peer in a window. "I spy with my little eye

190

someone in dirty overalls." He tapped on the window. "Jim!"

The nursery owner waved them in, and they slipped inside through an unlocked side door. When he saw Abby, Jim looked surprised but had the good manners not to ask any questions. "They're out behind the barn." He tipped his head toward the old building, a hulking gray shadow behind the trees. "They left for a while, but came back just before you showed up. I was about to go out there and see what they're up to. I heard popping sounds."

"BB gun?" Ash asked.

"Firecrackers, maybe," Jim said.

"Then it's not animals, I guess," Abby said.

Ash slid her a telling glance. She could imagine he thought the same as she, that it would be a while before they were nestled again in their cozy cocoon.

She caught the edge of Jim's curious gaze before he discreetly turned away. Feeling her cheeks heat, Abby closed up the lapels of her navy blue windbreaker and edged away from the men.

She hadn't considered Jim when she so boldly volunteered to ride along with Ash on this little adventure. Worse, she hadn't thought at all about Ash's family. What must Peter and Merry be thinking right now? Oh, heck, they would have figured it out. Probably shaking their heads with pity: Poor, gullible Abby, falling for Ash just to have her heart broken for the second time.

Had she really believed she could share her body with him and not be changed by the experience? Waking to find him gone had rattled her to her core. The cold shock of it had stirred all kinds of awful memories. And the reality was, whatever words of reassurance he offered tonight, nothing altered the fact that he was still moving ahead with his plans. Plans that didn't include her.

She started when he straightened and turned to her.

"We're going to head around on opposite sides of the barn,"

he said. "We'll stay far enough away so we can make an ID on whoever is out there, but not scare them away. If it looks like trouble, we'll call down to the station and have them send someone over."

"So you're not going after them yourself?"

"No." He rubbed the back of his neck. "I'm not in a position where I can do much, unfortunately, but this way, if they run, at least we'll be able to say which way they went."

"What if they do have guns?"

Even in the anemic light, she could see the corners of his eyes crinkle in a reassuring smile. "We'll keep our distance. No one's going to get hurt."

"I wasn't worried," she lied, forcing her furrowed brow to relax.

"Mm-hm." Obviously not convinced, he turned for the door.

Abby followed. He stopped and held up a hand. "You're staying here."

"No I'm not."

He caught her by the elbows and made her take a step back. "I need you to stay here."

"Why? If no one's going to get hurt—"

"If no one's in the way, then no one will get hurt."

How rude. She pulled back her shoulders. "Why do you assume I'll be in the way? Maybe I can help. Most of the kids in town come through the store. I'll probably recognize their faces."

"If it is kids," he said.

"Who else would it be?"

"I don't know. That's what Jim and I have to go find out."

Jim popped his head around just then. "Is there a problem?"

Abby crossed her arms over her chest and said, "No."

Ash held up a finger and opened his mouth as if to scold her. Maybe it was the stubborn tilt of her head or the look in her eye, but his hand dropped and he let out an exaggerated sigh.

"All right. Just stay close to me, okay?"

Not a problem. As long as she remembered it wouldn't be forever.

# CHAPTER FIFTEEN

He couldn't believe it. Abby had gotten her way again. Why couldn't he ever say no to her? It was the tears. He'd made her cry. What a jerk.

Mentally berating himself, Ash grasped Abby's clammy hand in his and crept silently along the edge of the woods a good ten yards from the barn. He could hear her breathing. She was nervous. He was distracted.

Even if there were guys with guns waiting for them, he couldn't pull his mind away from her anguished expression when she'd thought he was leaving for good. Her sad brown eyes would haunt him through his nightmares. As soon as this was over, he had to do something to make it right. What that miracle might be evaded him at the moment, of course.

Muffled voices pulled him from his thoughts. From here, up on the hill looking down at the barn, he could see figures moving. Shadows danced in a flickering light. A small fire snapped and popped, and laughter rose like sparks on the breeze. "Sounds like kids. Teenagers," he whispered to Abby.

She crowded by his shoulder. "What are they doing, having a campout?"

More focused now, Ash studied the scene. "Let's see if we can get closer."

"Where's Jim?"

"Should be coming around the other side, down the utility road." He crouched low. If they could get as far as the John

Deere parked halfway between the woods and the barn, they'd be close enough to see faces and hear conversation. "Let's make a run for that tractor."

Hunkered beside him, Abby whispered, "Okay."

She was a good trouper. He gave her hand a squeeze to get her attention. "You doing okay?"

"Sure." She tucked an errant strand of hair behind her ear. "This is kind of fun. I feel like Jane Bond."

"Ooh, can I be your sidekick? I've always wanted to be a Bond girl."

Abby bumped shoulders with him. "You need a skimpier outfit."

"It could be arranged."

Ash grinned. What other girl would be having so much fun, torn from bed, out in the middle of the night, shoes soaked with dew, circling in on a bunch of rowdy troublemakers? His chest squeezed again. Either he was having a heart attack, or he was in love. Right now, he didn't want to contemplate either possibility.

Side by side, they scooted across the damp grass, using the shadows for cover, and made it unseen to the tractor. One of the trespassers heaved a ceramic pot over his head and smashed it near the fire. The others hooted with laughter, and the chatter escalated. A black-shirted kid and one with blond hair lined up more terra cotta planters near the fire and dropped lit strings of red firecrackers into them. The fireworks shot off in a series of percussive pops, and two pots shattered. The boys went wild.

"Well, that's not good," Abby whispered. "There go more of Jim's planters."

"Pretty sure that's new graffiti, too." Large red and blue letters spelled out a couple of nasty phrases behind the vandals' backs. "When Jim sees that, he's gonna be pissed. I hope he doesn't shoot them."

Abby grabbed his arm. "He has a gun?"

"A rifle. He said it's loaded with rock salt. Wouldn't do much damage, but still, it'd hurt like hell and probably get Jim in more trouble than it'd be worth." He pulled thoughtfully at his lower lip. "There're more guns in Cranberry than there are in Los Angeles."

"Most farmers still keep them for scaring off animals. You should have been here for Mr. Willowby's crow cannon last summer." She peered around the front of the tractor, then sat back on her heels. "I recognize the blond boy. That's Charlie Dawson. Remember him from the store, the day Pawpaw bit you?"

"Dawson? Why's that name familiar?"

"Town councilman. Maybe Peter mentioned him. He's head honcho of the old-boy system. I can't stand him, but Charlie's never caused any trouble."

"Looks like he's fallen in with a bad crowd." Ash recognized the dark-haired boy who'd stolen candy from the store. He and two others smoked cigarettes and dangled long-necked beer bottles from between their fingers. "Do you know any others?"

"That's Joey Cooke, local football hero." She pointed to the dark-haired boy, then to a redhead. "And Mike Whitmore. He's on the team, too. I don't know the one with the green jacket. I've seen them all at the store at one time or another. Sometimes during the day," she admitted. "Playing hooky. Lucy always let them hang around. Figured they were better off there than roaming."

And they'd repaid her kindness with vandalism, Ash reflected. By her tone, he figured Abby was thinking the same. He said, "They can't be more than thirteen or fourteen."

"They're not bad kids," Abby said with conviction in her voice and worry in her eyes. "Let me go talk to Charlie."

She began to rise, but he put his hand on her shoulder and

pressed her down again. "They've been talked to enough."

"What are you going to do?"

He tugged his cell phone off his belt. "The only thing I can. Call Peter. Now you and Jim and I have witnessed them in action, he'll have to do something."

"But he won't arrest thirteen year olds? Will he?"

He thought back to the screwed-up teens he'd encountered on the streets of L.A., abandoned kids hardened by drugs and crime, and set his teeth together. Some had been saved by tough intervention. "It might be the best thing for them."

Her eyes pleaded with him. "Their reputations will never recover."

"They're doing a good enough job trashing their reputations as it is. And their parents obviously aren't helping. Look, Abby, they need a wake-up call. Maybe it'll scare some sense into them."

He hit the speed dial for Peter's house and tried to think of how to break this to his brother. Peter would not be happy that he was involved. Maybe Jim would explain. He peered into the shadows, where his old friend waited. While the phone rang, a vague movement caught his gaze, near the road.

Firelight glinted dully off a rifle barrel. Ash cursed softly.

Didn't look like Jim was waiting after all.


"Get Peter," was all Abby heard as she caught the phone Ash tossed to her. Open-mouthed, she watched him bolt behind a low line of bushes toward the gravel road. What the heck . . . ? Then Peter's tinny "hello" broke through her shock, and she brought the phone to her ear.

"Peter," she stammered in a harsh whisper, "it's Abby. Ash and I are down at the garden center and the vandals—"

"Abby?" She could picture him sitting up in bed, probably switching on a light, waking Merry. Inside, she cringed.

"Where are you?" He sounded sleepy and gruff. Abby heard Merry's questioning voice in the background.

She took a breath and told him again.

"Oh, hell." He sounded less gruff than annoyed now. Really, badly annoyed. "Get out of there, Abby. Go home. I'll send someone over."

"I can't." She knew she babbled, but her heart raced a mile a minute. "The kids are here, they're breaking stuff, they set a fire, I don't know where Ash is, and Jim has a gun."

There was a heartbeat's hesitation, then he asked for a few quick details. When she finished, he said, "Abby, listen to me." Peter's voice dropped to dead serious calm. "Stay where you are. Help is coming."

She tried to find reassurance in that news. Folding the phone in her trembling hand, she scanned the dark row of balled and burlapped evergreens off by the utility road, the same ones she'd been shopping through the other day. Ash had disappeared into the shadows.

Huddled alone, she felt the chilly dew settle on the back of her neck. She put her hand on the cold steel of the tractor and peered over the gears. The boys watched one of their friends inhale deeply on a cigarette. Oops, not a cigarette, she thought as a resinous odor coasted over the oil-and-cut-grass smell of the tractor. Pot. Geez, she hadn't smelled that since she'd gone to her first rock concert, and even then an older friend had had to explain to her what it was. She slid down and sat with her back against the tire. Peter wasn't going to like that.

She waited only a few moments when staccato pops spiked the night. Hunched over, she put her hands over her ears. More firecrackers. Each explosion plucked at her raw nerves. Then over that barrage, suddenly, a shout, yelps from the kids and a scrabble of shoes on gravel. Heart pounding, Abby leapt up.

Hand on his still-holstered gun, Bill Preston tore around one side of the barn yelling at the top of his lungs for the kids to get down, get down. Like a herd of frightened deer, the boys bolted to their right. Another uniformed cop trapped them there, screaming commands. Wide-eyed, the boys scrambled, all their bravado fled.

To her unending relief, Charlie put his hands on his head and dropped to his knees by the fire. So did Mike. But Joey and his green-jacketed friend spun for a moment, seeking escape.

All at once, floodlights from the barn washed the area in blinding light. Abby threw up her hand to shade her eyes. Joey unleashed a stream of obscenities. He pitched his beer and the last of the firecrackers into the flames, then he and his pal charged for the utility road. Preston made a quick grab, but the kids banged past him and knocked him down. Ash burst from the bushes, hot on their heels.

Adrenaline lent wings to Abby's heels. She took off after him. At the edge of her vision, the other cops dealt with Charlie and Mike. Thank goodness. At least they were safe.

"Ash!" Between the bang-bang-bang of the firecrackers and the pounding of feet, he must not have heard her. He swallowed ground at a flat out run, yelling.

Yelling, "Peter, no!"

Peter ran out from the front of the barn, his pistol up and aimed at the boys. Cold dread made Abby stumble. The fire-crackers—

She'd told him there was a gun.

He thought—

Her heart flew into her throat.

Ash plowed into his brother just as a sharp crack rent the darkness.

For a second, all Ash could do was lie there and wait for the pain to start. Or not. That would be good. The bullet had gone somewhere. But not, he realized at last, into him. Huffing like a locomotive, he stared down into Peter's surprised eyes. "You okay?"

"Yeah," Peter wheezed. "Except you're crushing me."

Ash had pinned him under his body weight, and now dropped off to one side. "You're not shot?" he clarified.

Peter said, "No," and sat up.

Relief as intense as any pain scored through Ash. He lay flat on his back against the cold earth for a moment, stared up at the starry sky and gulped in air. Man, that had been close. So close.

Once his pulse had slowed a notch, he palmed a thin layer of sweat off his forehead and sat up.

Peter rolled to his feet. "Those kids—"

"Long gone." Ash was certain now the shot had swung well wide of the boys. Though it might not have if he'd been one second slower.

"I almost . . ." Peter stammered.

Ash held up a quelling finger. "But you didn't. I know you didn't." He stood, as wobbly as a colt on his overstressed legs. Down the moonlit road, two small figures raced. Ash pointed. "There they go. Probably going to cut through the corn field back to town."

Peter stared. "I . . . I didn't know who it was, coming around the corner. I heard shots."

"Firecrackers," Ash explained.

"I shouldn't have fired, shouldn't . . ." Muttering, Peter tried to put his gun back in the holster slung low on his jeans and missed. And missed. And missed. His hand shook so badly, he finally swore under his breath and had to look down to replace the weapon.

He almost jerked it out again when Abby sprinted onto the scene. Ash gripped Peter's arm to calm him.

"Jeez, Abby," Peter groaned.

She ran up to Ash and spread anxious hands over his chest as if feeling for wounds and blood. "Everyone okay? No one hurt?"

He caught her by the shoulders and shook his head. "How many'd they get?"

"Two." Out of breath, she gave a limp wave toward the back of the barn. "Charlie and Mike. Where's Jim?"

"Right here."

Abby startled and spun. "Oh, Jim, you almost gave me a coronary. I'm halfway there already."

"Sorry, hon." He patted her shoulder. Ash had convinced him to leave his rifle behind and hit the floodlights instead.

Jim swung his gaze toward the main road. "Guess the others got away."

"It's okay," Ash said. "Abby knows one of them, and I'm sure the other won't be hard to identify."

"Joey Cooke and some other kid," she said.

Peter dragged a hand down the side of his face. "Joe Cooke and Steve Pater," he said, his voice hollow.

Abby put her hands on her hips and studied him. "Both councilmen's sons."

Accusation laced her tone. Ash looked from her to his brother. Then two and two added up with a hollow mental clang inside his head, and Ash almost staggered. It couldn't be. Peter?

He looked at his brother, who stared down the empty road, his lips drawn tight and his forehead lined with stress. The picture of guilt. A knot tightened in the pit of Ash's belly. He slid his gaze to the ground and puffed out a heavy breath.

Jim said, "What?" but Preston and Childs, the uniformed officers, appeared with the two captured boys in handcuffs.

Abby gasped. "Is it really necessary to handcuff them?"

"We found dope," Preston said, all business. "And illegal

fireworks. Also, beer and an empty pint of whiskey."

Charlie pulled against his restraints, his eyes pleading toward Peter. "My dad's gonna kill me, Chief."

Peter looked nervous. "I'm not chief yet."

"And won't be," Mike spat, " 'less you let us go."

"I don't think I can do that."

This time, Ash finished for him in his head. Yet even faced with the truth, he couldn't get his mind around it. His morally upstanding brother, protecting the town councilmen's kids to save his job? Sure, he had to be voted in, but still . . . This was Peter they were talking about. Ash's steady, reliable, upstanding big brother. Disappointment sat on Ash's chest like a stone.

Abby put her hand on his elbow. "Isn't there anything you can do?"

He hesitated, filtering her meaning. "For . . . the boys?"

"Yes."

Not her, too. He shook his head in raw disbelief. "Abby, these are the kids who smashed your window and spray painted obscenities on the side of your building. They ransacked Jim's place and vandalized half a dozen other businesses in town. They tried to break into the pharmacy for drugs, for God's sake."

She backed off, her eyes huge. "You don't know that for sure."

"Come on, Abby." Couldn't anyone see what was happening here? Escalating anger heated his words. "It's time they stop getting away with murder. Before they really *do* get away with murder."

"They're only kids," she said in a shrinking voice. "I didn't expect them to be people I know."

"You're just like your aunt, living in a dream world where every bad guy can be turned around with a little love and kindness."

"I should hope so." Her spine went ramrod straight and her hands bunched into fists. Hurt and outrage warred in her eyes.

"I wish it did work that way, but it doesn't. These kids need to understand that what they're doing is serious. Maybe a night in jail will cool them off."

Her jaw clenched. In the sudden, pressing silence, Ash became uncomfortably aware that Peter, Jim, and even Charlie and Mike gawked, awaiting the outcome like spectators at a boxing match. Aw, hell. He reined in his runaway anger with an iron grip.

This wasn't what he wanted, to argue with Abby. Especially not in front of everyone. He took a deep breath and a slow step back. His frustration was his to deal with.

In a tight, controlled voice, he said, "Do what you think is best, Abby. Peter. It's your town. You're the ones who have to live here."

He refused to give them the satisfaction of seeing him storm off to the car. Instead, he waited them out. Jim finally cleared his throat and said, "Well, I'd like to press charges. They destroyed about two hundred dollars' worth of inventory."

Peter nodded. "How about you, Abby? If they confess to the vandalism done to the deli, do you want to press charges, too?"

She wouldn't. She looked at Charlie and Mike as if they were kicked puppies, victims instead of perpetrators. If she said "they're just kids" one more time, Ash thought he'd pull out his hair. When she answered in the negative, it seemed to surprise none of them.

Mike, the tough guy, spat on the ground and let out a line of vitriol about the stupid town and the rotten cops and how much he hated them all. Charlie gave him a none-too-subtle kick. "Shut up, Mike, our dads will get us off. Don't make it worse than it is."

Peter wouldn't meet Ash's gaze until Preston and Childs

loaded the boys into their cruiser and drove away.

"I'll have to make out a report," his brother said at last. His voice was flat. "I'll need you to come down to the station. All of you." He included Abby and Jim with a glance.

Jim agreed readily. Abby said, "Sure." Her shoulders slumped, and she wrapped her arms around herself, clearly drained from the night's experience.

Ash's anger faded. He wanted to hold her close and apologize, although for what he wasn't quite sure. The wounded depths of her cocoa eyes warned him he should be feeling bad about something, though.

Jim went to clean things up, leaving the three of them in tense silence. "Peter," Ash began.

His brother held up his hand. "Later," he said. "I have to drive out to the other boys' houses and collect them."

"Want some company?" Ash asked.

His brother's cool gaze touched him. "I think you've done enough. Besides," he said, "you're a civilian. It wouldn't be right."

"Yeah." His brother's tone pricked at him. The outsider, as always. Still, he wondered what Peter would say to the parents. He wished he could be there. His brother was in a conundrum and, despite his initial anger, Ash felt a twist of sympathy.

"I'll see you in my office in about twenty minutes." Peter walked off to his Volvo, head down and looking for all the world like the last man on the battlefield.

Ash stared after him. "God, what a mess," he muttered.

Abby shot him a caustic glare. "I'll be in the car."

Back stiff, she strode off in his brother's wake. Utterly baffled, Ash stood alone with his palms up.

How'd he become the bad guy in this scenario?

# Chapter Sixteen

Abby poured hot coffee into a Styrofoam cup and stirred in sugar. The bright overhead lights of the police station and the domestic atmosphere seemed oddly unreal to her after all the excitement. She and Ash still had a while before Peter came in, and Jim was being interviewed by Officer Preston. Time enough to cool off and relax and avoid each other as best they could.

What a night. She'd been alternately scared, worried, terrified, then furious, first at Peter, for letting things get this far, and even more so at Ash. How could he have said what he had about Lucy? If it hadn't been for her aunt's kindness, he would have ended up like those boys. In fact, *despite* her aunt's kindness, in many ways he had.

She poked through the clutter of straw wrappers and paper napkins for the cream. Ash came beside her. "Milk's in the fridge." He'd already gotten it and handed it to her. Abby pressed her lips together and took it.

"The silent treatment's getting old, Abby," he said.

She narrowed her eyes at him. "You should be glad I'm silent, because if I said what I wanted to, you'd . . . you'd be sorry."

He shrugged broadly. "I am sorry, for whatever ticked you off. Wouldn't you like to at least tell me what I did that's so horrible?"

She took a sip of coffee and burned her tongue. Again. She always seemed to do that around him: didn't think, moved too fast. Got hurt. She walked to the tan vinyl chair and sat. The two of them were liked caged tigers in the small room, prowling around each other.

"Okay," she said, exasperated, when Ash sat beside her. "It's what you said about my aunt."

"Lucy? What did I say?"

He couldn't be that dense. Or could he? "About how she believes bad kids can be helped with love and kindness."

His gray eyes studied her. "She does believe that, and so do you."

"You made it sound stupid. Naïve."

Leaning back, he frowned. Her gaze tripped on his mouth, and a primal yearning stirred in her belly. He'd kissed her and loved her with those scowling lips just scant hours earlier. Abby swallowed hard and turned away. Good grief, she was an emotional wreck. A ten-car pile-up of head-on feelings.

Disgusted with herself, she sniffed and set down her coffee. "I don't care what you say about me, Ashton Wheeler, but leave Lucy out of it. She always . . . loved you." Oh great, now her voice cracked. She picked up the coffee again and took another sip. She could blame her tears on the burn.

He leaned his elbows on his knees and scrubbed his hands over his face. "You know I didn't mean anything bad by it."

"It sure sounded like you did. Like small town hicks don't even know a criminal when they see one."

"Well . . ." Wide-eyed, he waved a hand in the air. "To be honest, I can't believe you're letting them get away with it. Not just what they did to your place, but the damage they've done elsewhere, too."

She started to speak, but he stopped her. "And please don't say they're just kids."

She clamped her lips shut. Then said, "You were just like them once. Maybe worse."

"I didn't do drugs."

"If it weren't for Lucy, maybe you would have. You were wild, Ash, admit it."

He shoved back in the chair and glowered. Before he could argue, she shook her finger and said in a tautly hushed tone, "And don't tell me you didn't get away with a lot because your father was the chief of police."

That swung his head around. "What are you saying?"

"You don't think the whole town knew the mischief you got into? Everyone talked about it. The chief's son smoking behind the bleachers, playing hooky, setting fires in the hay field."

"That was an accident. I thought no one knew about that."

"Oh, Ash. Now who's naïve? Your father took a lot of heat because of you."

"Hmm."

"Hmm," she echoed. "How about when you let Feeney's pheasants loose? He'd been raising, what? A hundred pheasants to release for hunting season? You busted them out and released them in the state park."

"Hey—"

"You didn't think I knew about that one, did you?" She glowered smugly. "Everyone knew it was you. There was no one else in town with the—guts to do it."

She couldn't help the note of admiration that crept into her voice, even though she forced her mouth to frown. That was probably one of the first events that had made her take a second look at the town's bad boy.

Ash scratched at his jaw. In a thoughtful voice, he said, "You know how hard it is to catch a hundred baby pheasants, stuff them into your two-door Mustang and not get caught?"

She tsked and sipped her cooling coffee. "There's still pheasants on that mountain."

"But no hunting." He quirked a brow.

She eyed him wryly.

"I didn't think anyone figured out it was me," he said. Then, as if he still couldn't believe it, he said reflectively, "I spent days scrubbing bird poop out of my seats. Days."

Abby coughed rather than laughed. She wasn't ready to forgive him yet. "You know they had a name for you after that?"

"What?" His eyes darkened. "Well, you have to tell me now that you mentioned it."

"The bird man of Cranberry."

He groaned, tipped back his head and pressed the heels of his palms to his forehead. His rusty laughter bounced off the walls. "Oh, no, and here I thought I was so cool."

She crossed her legs primly. "Lo, how the mighty have fallen."

"How could you not have told me?"

"I don't know, I guess I thought it was cute."

"Cute? Insult to injury."

"If I hadn't thought you were a nice guy under that macho exterior, I never would have even spoken to you."

He humphed, his face growing serious. "And now you thought I was a nice guy only to find I'm a jerk underneath."

"You're not a jerk. Well, not usually." She sighed and swirled her coffee in the cup. "I just think you have a very black and white way of seeing things. You decided early on that Cranberry was a hostile place, and nothing has ever changed your mind."

He seemed to ponder that. His sweaty hair had dried in spiky disarray, and she wanted to brush it back from his forehead and place a kiss between his furrowed brows. Why'd he have to look so lost and needy? She touched the backs of her fingers to his lean, stubbled cheek. "There's a lot of love in this town, even for rebels."

He drew down her hand and toyed with her fingers. His mouth angled in a frown, and his gaze turned inward. "I never felt it. Except from you."

His revelation tugged at her soul. There was such sadness in his voice, such loneliness. Abruptly, he sat up as if the whole conversation had become way too serious. "And from Lucy," he said, more briskly. "You're right, of course, as usual. I should be grateful she kept me out of trouble."

"Not completely out," Abby replied. He smiled, a flash of white teeth and mischief, and such warmth suffused her that she forgot to breathe.

He laced their fingers together. "I shouldn't have said that about you and Lucy. I'm sorry."

"You should be," she said haughtily, and turned to hide behind her coffee once again. Her heart thundered in her ears and she'd begun to tremble. What was wrong with her? Love. That's what it was. Why not admit it? She loved him so much she felt physically ill at the idea of his leaving. It wouldn't do. She pulled her hand from his and searched for her worry stone.

"What is that in your pocket?" he asked, leaning too close, his heat wrapping around her. "I've seen you fooling around with it before."

"It's . . ." She opened her palm to reveal the smooth white pebble. "It's a worry stone. At least that's what I call it."

She dropped it into his open hand. He rolled it back and forth.

"Just a little thing," she said, embarrassed by her emotional crutch. It looked like an ordinary bit of driveway gravel in the cradle of his big hand. "I like to fiddle with it when I've got something on my mind."

"Huh. You had it a long time?"

Her face froze. She hadn't thought about it, so many years had passed.

His gorgeous gray eyes found hers, the eyes of the man she loved asking her. "Abby?"

"That night, remember?" She blurted it out. "You told me you had a surprise for me. You took me to the shoreline fair."

She looked away as the memories flooded her mind. The color-ful paper lanterns, the music. The salt tang of the ocean mixed with the smells of fried food and beer. And her eager anticipa-tion, quickly crushed. "I thought . . ." She closed her eyes and opened them again. "Well, it wasn't what I'd expected. The surprise was that you'd been accepted into the police academy in Los Angeles."

"It was what I'd always wanted." He rolled the stone around. "Being a cop is—was in my blood. But I knew I could never work with my father, and I wanted something . . . bigger. More important."

"It was a great opportunity."

"Even though my father was against it."

She touched his knee. "But he helped you get in."

"Once he stopped trying to change my mind. I can't understand why he did, after all our arguments, even though I'm grateful."

"Ash, I don't think you know your father very well at all. Whenever he came into the deli after you left, he always spoke about you with a glow in his voice. He's proud of you."

"Huh. Why didn't he ever let me know?"

"He was born and raised here. He's a small town guy through and through. Maybe he didn't understand your restlessness." Even she understood it only partly.

He caught her hand before she could pull away and laid his over it on his thigh. "So the stone. Where'd you pick it up?"

"Well, after you told me your news, I couldn't help but . . . *act* happy for you. Inside, though, I was scared. All I knew about city cops came from TV, where people get shot and killed in every episode."

"Yeah, I almost got 'cancelled' a few times myself," he joked, but it just made her shiver.

"See, that's what I mean. To you, that's exciting. To me, it's terrifying. So while we were sitting on the beach and you were telling me about all your big plans, I found this pebble. It was smooth and white and pure. Like a perfect circle. Like something that couldn't be broken. A kind of lucky charm, to keep you safe when you weren't near me anymore." She shrugged, and a blush stole up her throat. Words failed her. "I know, it's silly."

He held it up between his thumb and forefinger and studied it. "Pretty little thing. Who knows, maybe it did divert a few bullets headed my way."

He held her hand and placed it in the center of her palm. He leaned close. His face was inches from hers, his eyes luminous with feelings she could only hope mirrored her own. "I wish you had come with me," he murmured.

"Oh, I couldn't." She drew her hand from his. That old torn-in-two anxiety rushed back, fresh again as it had been six years ago. "I love this town, and Lucy, and all the old characters who come to the deli." She saw his mouth hardening, his lashes dropping to shield his bitterness, and reached to squeeze his hand. He had to listen. "And I was afraid I could never stop worrying about you. Even if my perception of Los Angeles wasn't exactly right, what you were going into was dangerous. To spend every day wondering if you were going to come home alive, or if our . . ." She stumbled only a moment, took a breath for courage. ". . . our children would grow up without a father." She licked her dry lips. "I wasn't brave enough for you, Ash."

He cocked his head. "But you wouldn't mind if I joined the force in Cranberry. I might get kicked by a cow or run over by a tractor."

He teased, but she could see the wheels turning in his head. He took both her hands in his and rubbed his thumbs over her knuckles, his expression somber. "You should have told me."

"Would it have made you stay?"

"I don't know."

"You wouldn't have been happy. You always would've had one eye on the horizon, wondering what you'd missed."

Turbulent emotions roiled beneath his dark lashes. "Funny, that's what my father always said about my mother. More or less." He let her go and stood, leaving her bereft of his warmth. He went to stare out the window into the parking lot. "I always hated Cranberry for keeping you from me. Now I see that *I* was keeping you from me."

A knock came on the metal door. Jim entered, looking vaguely guilty. "Ash, your brother's back. He wants to see you."

"How'd it go?" he asked.

Jim's gaze dropped to the floor. "Okay, I guess. I do feel kinda bad for the boys. I'm having second thoughts."

Abby couldn't resist shooting Ash a glance, and his pained expression almost made her laugh.

He massaged his temples with his fingertips and groaned. "You thick-headed Cranberrians. I'll never understand you."

She gave him a bittersweet smile, and he came over and kissed her, a brief caress of his lips that sparked a craving so intense she feared the world wouldn't feel solid under her feet until she was in his arms again.

His gentle fingers touched her cheek. In a whisper meant only for her, he said, "Don't count yourself short. You're one of the bravest people I know."

He turned and brushed by an embarrassed Jim, and left Abby to contemplate what revelations the rest of the night might bring.

"We refuse to say anything until our lawyer gets here."

Ash followed the strident voice into Peter's office, not sure what to expect. The bull-necked man wearing a groove into Peter's carpet stopped his pacing when he entered.

Peter, tight-lipped as ever, sat behind his desk. The reading lamp starkly illuminated his drawn face. "Ash." He stood. "This is Richard Cooke. Joey's father."

Ash didn't bother to offer his hand. Waves of anger leapt off the man. Cooke said, "Wheeler here says you witnessed my son in an act of vandalism. I say he's wrong."

"If your son is the dark-haired kid I passed in the detainment cell, then he's the one."

Cooke pivoted aggressively toward Peter. "This isn't the first time you've wrongly accused Joey."

"Rich, calm down." This from a blond-haired man Ash hadn't seen sitting in the corner chair. Ruddy faced, dressed in worn khakis and a rumpled shirt that looked as if it had been pulled on in a hurry, he shook his head. "If anything, Pete's been more than fair with our boys." He drew a black checkbook out of his shirt pocket. "Pete, I'm sorry for the inconvenience our boys caused. I'm more than willing to pay for the damages, and I'm sure Rich will be, too, once he's cooled off a little. Then we can all go home and get some rest."

Peter cleared his throat. "It won't be that easy this time, I'm afraid. They were caught in the act. Charges are going to be pressed."

"With your own brother as a witness. How convenient." Cooke slammed his fist on Peter's desk, startling them all. Ash tensed for trouble, but caught his brother's warning glance. Cooke growled, "The town council will be very interested in your latest incompetence."

The poorly veiled threat hung between them. Peter leaned forward on his knuckles, face to face with the burly man. "I've let your son off the hook too many times. You had plenty of opportunities to get him under control, and you failed."

The blond guy, whose resemblance to Charlie Dawson made Ash think he had to be his father, stood and assumed the hands-out, smiling position of the negotiator. "Pete, boys will be boys," he wheedled. "What's a few ceramic pots? And it's close to the fourth of July. Don't tell me you never let off a few firecrackers when you were their age."

"It was more than firecrackers," Ash cut in. "They were drinking, and smoking dope."

"Yeah?" Cooke turned his anger on him. "Joey says it wasn't his. I think you cops planted it."

If Ash had a dime for every time someone claimed his drugs belonged to someone else, he'd be a very wealthy man. He and his partner used to joke that "drugs got legs." He held Cooke's twitchy glare. "Abby McGuire witnessed them smoking it."

He sneered. "Then why isn't she pressing charges? 'Cause your story's full of holes, that's why." He swung his head toward Peter. "Wheeler here's just trying to blackmail his way into the chief's office."

Dawson gripped Cooke's shoulder from behind. "He knows better than that. You and I are on the town council, and there's not a member on there who would see your son or our star quarterback spend even one night in jail without an uproar." His tone was mellow, but his meaning was razor sharp. "He'll do the right thing. Come on, Rich." He slapped his friend on the back. "Let's go wait for the lawyers."

Without waiting for Peter to dismiss them, they shoved out of the office, sucking all the hot air out with them. Peter dropped heavily into his chair and rubbed his face before turning a weary eye on Ash.

Ash shut the door and sat across from him. "You want to tell me what that was all about?"

Peter picked up a pen. "As you see it."

"I see that you've painted yourself into a corner with those idiots." Ash crossed his ankles and folded his hands over his belly. "Why'd you let it go this far?"

Peter waved his hand expansively. "It's small town policing, like you said." He closed his eyes, pressed the heels of his palms to them and sighed. "How do you deal with this crap in the city?"

"You didn't pull me in here to ask my advice."

"No. To show them I did have another witness. But since you're here . . ."

Ash shrugged. "We deal with it the right way the first time. We might keep it out of the press if it's a bigwig's son or daughter, but it doesn't stop us from processing the paperwork. Let the courts deal with the rest."

Peter tapped his pen against his blotter. He looked about ten years older than he had this morning. "I don't know what to do."

"Yes you do."

"Well." His brother opened his desk drawer and pitched the pen inside before slamming it shut again. "It's out of my hands anyhow. Jim's going to press charges, and probably other folks will, too, once word gets out. The daycare and the pharmacy. How about Abby? Rethinking it?"

"No, but Jim might be." He put his hands behind his head and tipped back the chair. "Don't let him back down, Peter. I was serious when I said these boys need to be taught a lesson."

"That sounds so Draconian. Taught a lesson. What are they going to learn in juvie hall? They're country kids. They'll get eaten alive in there."

"Is that what stopped you?" Ash held his brother's pale gaze, daring him to look away. "Worried about the kids or worried about your job?"

Peter pondered a moment and turned to the open window. A soft breeze curled through the screen. Silence settled. "It's a beautiful night," he reflected after a moment. "Stars are out. Crickets are chirping. I'll bet there's not a car on any road for

215

miles." He looked back at Ash. "But by tomorrow morning, this'll be gossip fodder at every breakfast table in town, and the peace will be over, for me and for those families."

Ash pressed his mouth in a grim line. "I didn't do you any favors identifying those boys, did I?"

Peter grunted. "No. You couldn't stay out of it, could you?"

"Not when Abby was involved. And Jim." He let his gaze wander the wall of framed awards and dusty photographs. "I felt the welfare of the town was on the line. For all I never liked the place, I found I did care after all." He caught his brother's eye. "It doesn't pay to let these things fester."

"Yeah." Peter rubbed the back of his neck. "I remember when you were raising hell, and Dad kept covering for you." He shrugged. "But you turned out all right. I hoped the same for these kids. Given enough time and some parental intervention, they'd come around."

Ash slumped down in the unforgiving plastic chair and studied the worn carpeting. Never had he been reminded so often of what a pain in the neck he'd been, or of the sacrifices people had made for him. Shame nagged at him. Shame and embarrassment, and a growing awareness that he'd made a terrible misjudgment of his family and even the town.

Peter said, "I always was jealous of you, you know."

Ash picked up his head. "Me? Why?"

"You got all the attention. Granted, negative attention. Still. When you left, I thought it was my time to shine, to prove myself to Dad."

"You were always his favorite, though."

"I didn't see it that way. You went off to be a big city cop. He was . . . in awe. I was already married. I couldn't take a risk like that. So I stayed on the force here. Worked my way up the ranks without Dad's intervention. I was careful about that." He canted back in his chair, his face falling into gray shadows. "I wanted to be chief in my own right, my own way. Now . . . I think I blew it." His smile was sad, but resigned.

"Mm, maybe not. It's their first offense. They'll most likely get community service."

"Me, too." He laughed without humor. "I'll be searching the community for a new job."

"What if you offered to speak up for them at their hearing? Outline a plan of intervention. In the cities, they have programs, kind of like a Big Brother deal, to help kids find better role models. I could get you more info on it."

A faint hope lit Peter's eyes. "Maybe."

"Jim would probably take a couple under his wing, and there are other good men in town who would find something for those boys to do."

"You want to be a Big Brother, little brother?" Peter asked, grinning.

"Don't think so. I won't be around that long."

"Ah. Right." His brows tucked together and his grin faded. "You made your decision?"

"The decision was made before I even came into town."

"What about Abby?"

"Yeah . . . What about Abby?" Ash said softly.

He rubbed his eyes, suddenly fatigued. They'd revealed so much to each other tonight, yet he knew they'd only scratched the surface. If they kept digging, who knew where it would lead. "Haven't figured that one out yet."

Officer Childs knocked on the door. "Lawyers are here, Chief." He disappeared again.

Pete stood and hitched up his jeans. "Well. Sometimes it feels like Fate's got you in her pocket and there's no escape."

"Yeah." Ash unfolded to his feet. "Good luck."

"Thanks. And, uh, thanks for what you did tonight."

"What was that?"

Peter's expression darkened. "For blocking the shot. I . . . I can't even think about what might have happened."

"It happens fast, doesn't it?"

"Yeah."

It took something for his brother to bring up the topic. Ash could see it in his eyes: the guilt, the self-doubt and blame. Peter would be replaying that scene in his head many times before he put it to rest. On some level, maybe now Peter understood what had happened to Ash. He could only hope, although he was eternally grateful his brother wouldn't have to carry a load of guilt for the rest of his life the way he did.

On his way out the door, Peter clasped Ash on the shoulder. "I'll see you in the morning, then?"

"Or maybe sooner. She was pretty upset with me. Don't know if she'll take me back."

"Well, then . . ." He lifted one brow and gave a crooked man-to-man grin. "Good luck to you, too.

# CHAPTER SEVENTEEN

Ash needn't have worried about Abby's temper. By the time he got back to the waiting room, her eyelids were drooping and her hair hung in lank waves around her pale face. She slumped off to one side in the plastic chair with her cheek propped up on two knuckles. The night's commotion and the lack of sleep had caught up to her with a vengeance.

Ash bundled her into the car and drove back to her apartment. It was almost four a.m. by the time he got her mostly undressed and tucked under the covers.

"The store," she mumbled.

"Don't worry." He smoothed her hair from her pale face. "You've got hours before you have to open."

He'd already decided to do that for her.

She started to rise on one elbow. "Lucy."

"Not until afternoon, remember?"

Her head dropped to the pillow, and he thought she'd fallen asleep until she whispered, "Ash?"

He bent over her. "What is it, sweetheart?"

Eyes still closed, she reached up to cup his cheek, and her soft lips curved in the hint of a smile.

He covered her hand with his. Did she forgive him, then? A weight lifted from his heart. He placed a kiss in her palm and tucked her arm beneath the covers. "Go to sleep," he whispered.

Careful not to disturb her, he rose from the edge of the bed. He turned the clock around so she couldn't see the glowing red numbers, then backed out of the room, shutting off the light as he went.

He took a quick shower and sneaked back to Peter's for a change of clothes. A little before five, he pulled up to the deli.

The pale sun gleamed on the shingles he'd installed. The newly replaced front window reflected the deserted street with perfect clarity, and the tenacious pansies he'd thought he'd drowned actually looked better for the over watering. Ash hooked his thumbs in his belt and surveyed the building.

Yeah, everything looked pretty good. He'd be leaving the store in decent shape, as he'd hoped.

He got everything ready for the day: coffee percolating, newspapers out. He took a delivery of delicious-smelling baked goods from the driver, who made Ash laugh with his joke of the day. The old regulars drifted in. George Darcy thanked him for the paper and stopped to chat about the weather. The Madeleine sisters tottered by for lemon Danish and fragrant Queen Anne tea. The old gals giggled over how he'd grown, and Ash felt like a squirming ten-year-old under their motherly scrutiny.

Others rolled in as the morning progressed, and every one of them had a bit of news, a compliment about his work on the store or a kindly inquiry after Lucy's health. A few repeated the rumor they'd heard about the vandals being caught, but Ash played dumb. He didn't want to fuel any gossip. Still, it was truly amazing how quickly word had gotten around.

By the time the breakfast rush slowed, around ten, Ash was tired all over again, but a permanent smile had settled on his face. As he washed dishes, he couldn't help but chuckle over bits of gossip folks had told him. Then he caught himself whistling as he wiped down the tables.

Awareness swept over him like a cool breeze. Finally, he understood what Abby saw in this place. Why she loved the people. Everyone knew everyone else's business, but they all cared, in a good way. They even cared about him, though he'd been away so long, and when he had been here, he'd been nothing but an aggravation.

He tossed the sponge into the sink. That sense of close-knit community that had irked him so in his youth now felt like . . . home. He could actually envision himself coming back to visit more often, without the needling dread that had dogged him this time around.

In a fine mood, Ash picked up his cell phone and put in a call to his ex-partner. Ryan would get a kick out of his latest adventures, and Ash wanted to see how their new venture was coming together. After all, everything rode on it. His future, and Abby's, too.

Abby found him in the storeroom, sorting cans. His back was to her, and he was humming absently under his breath. Didn't know she'd come in. She'd sneaked in through the back way so the bells wouldn't jangle. Surprise was her objective.

She'd panicked when she'd woken up and seen the clock. Never in ten years could she remember sleeping so late. But, Lord, had it felt good. She felt rejuvenated. Once she'd spied Ash's note explaining that he was opening the store, Abby relaxed. It didn't hurt that the note was propped against a vase of black-eyed Susans and other wildflowers he must have gone out in near-darkness to pick for her.

The little voice in the back of her head had warned against the rush of love that filled her. Be careful; be prudent. Remember what happened last time.

Abby had taken a sweet inhale of her flowers and promptly given the voice the boot. For one day, one of the last days she'd have with Ash, she was going to allow herself to be happy. He was here, Lucy was coming home, and for this precious stretch of hours, all was right with the world. She'd be a fool not to appreciate the time she had.

She also appreciated how good he looked in jeans right now, and decided she'd like to find out how the bare skin of his nape might feel against her lips. But she wouldn't give him that satisfaction. Not yet.

Instead, she adopted an imperious tone and said, "Just how late were you going to let me sleep?"

He spun around, eyes wide, and Abby laughed.

"Abby." He clutched a can of spring peas over his heart. "You gotta stop sneaking up on me like that."

"Why? It's fun." She walked in and set her purse on the stool. "Besides, you deserve it for not waking me."

"Honey, nothing short of an ice bucket over your head was going to get you out of bed before five." His silver gaze took in her clean white blouse and tan slacks and ended with his approving smile. "You look fresh as a daisy."

"Thank you for mine," she said, tipping her head shyly. "Daisies, that is."

He set the can on the shelf and scuffed his nails over his hair. "You're more than welcome. It's far less than you deserve after I dragged you out on a bust last night."

She grinned, and he came over to drop a kiss on her upturned face. Not in the mood for a quick peck, Abby twined her arms behind his neck and, with a soft sigh, pulled him to her. Desire whispered through her as he accepted her invitation and drew on her lips then tasted her deeply.

The joy they'd sampled last night had lingered in her dreams, whetting her appetite for more. His broad shoulders reminded her of the passion and tenderness he'd shown in bed. His clean cotton and soap scent surrounded her. She was starved for him. She couldn't get enough. By the time they broke apart, they were both swaying on their feet.

Ash held her tight. His strong hands swept her spine and

threaded through her hair, raising delicious goose bumps over her skin.

"Now that's the way to start the day." He nudged the door closed with his foot.

Her brain groggy with desire, Abby eyed him with suspicion. "What are you doing?"

"You know how there's always that dead time between ten and noon?" His voice dropped to a sexy rumble as he trailed tiny sucking kisses along her jaw and moved down her throat. "Breakfast is over. Lunch hasn't started . . ."

The door shut with a click that her moan masked when his wandering hands eased over her breasts. Abby quivered beneath his talented caress. Oh, she'd only meant to get a kiss, but this was so nice. She pressed against him, feeling the enticing evidence of his desire, reveling in it for a moment. But when he started to unbutton the blouse she'd carefully chosen for this important day, she moaned again, this time with regret.

"I only wanted a kiss," she breathed out, not quite able to pull away.

"I've got plenty of those." He proved it by running his hot mouth along the path his fingers took from the base of her throat to the top of her bra. One button and one kiss at a time, he brought every inch of her skin to sparkling life.

Oh, no, no, no; this was getting way out of hand. She tried to pull up his head by tugging on his hair. It was too short. What a shame. Then somehow he'd caught the top of her bra with his teeth and pulled it down. She really should try harder to stop him. "Ash—"

He caught her nipple between his lips, drew it into his mouth, and the world went away in a burst of white-hot light.

How and when they got their clothes off would remain a mystery to Abby hours later when she thought back on the event, but somehow her tidy outfit became a puddle on the floor, Ash's shirt lifted away with a brush of her hands, and then he was shoving papers and clutter aside on the old wood desk in the back and lifting her to sit.

The cold surface heated quickly under her bare bottom. *Everything* heated, from her pounding blood to her swelling breasts, which Ash so skillfully pleasured, to the secret place that yearned only for him.

He scooped up her thighs and moved between them. Off balance, Abby leaned back on her hands, skidding on loose order forms, laughing until he covered her mouth again with a ravaging kiss that left her breathless.

He scrabbled in his pocket for a condom. Thank heaven he'd remembered one. She sheathed him quickly. He growled deep in his chest when she squeezed and stroked his exquisite length. Her undeniable effect on him made her heart soar. He was beyond words, his eyes molten silver, boiling with need.

They came together like two rushing rivers, blindly reaching for what they desired, and found it in a fierce, driving rhythm. He urged her on with hot words and relentless strokes.

Abby surrendered. The sweet tension built, coiled. Pleasure poured through her like warm cream. She flung back her head and cried out. He followed quickly, shuddering in her arms. He claimed her with a deep, possessive kiss before she fell back on her elbows, exhausted.

After a moment or two, the world stopped whirling quite so wildly and the soft rasp of their labored breaths filtered into her consciousness. Abby lifted her heavy eyelids and reached to stroke his short, damp hair. Her own hair clung to her cheeks and fell over her eyes as if she'd been through a blender.

A crazy smile curled her lips. Crazy as what they'd just done. She edged up on her elbows.

"So," she asked dryly. "Did you remember to order the egg salad?"

Resting with his palms on either side of her hips, sweating and out of breath, Ash closed his eyes and started to laugh, low and intimate. She loved that sound. Loved him. Wasn't everything easier when she didn't fight it?

He bent over to kiss the top of her breast, slipped his tongue along her throat. She stroked the nape of his neck and rubbed his taut, muscled shoulder. Her eyes closed to sleepy slits. Her body tingled and ached pleasantly.

What a nice good-morning kiss that had turned out to be.

He started to pull out, but she issued a sincere little mewl of disappointment.

"Enough, woman," he said, cocking a dark eyebrow at her before he withdrew and bent to pick up his jeans. "You'll run the hired help ragged."

"Too bad. I could think of plenty of things for you to do."

His voracious gaze devoured her. Abby could only imagine the picture she made, naked and sated, lying back on her elbows on the wooden desk. She hoped it was a good one. Judging by the way his face darkened as he swiped the sweat from his brow with an impatient hand, it must have been.

"I take it you got my note?" he asked. A bit of desperation touched his voice, as if he needed to exert some control over the situation before he found himself on her again. As if that would be such a bad thing. But they did have a busy day ahead.

"Yes. Thank you." She accepted his hand as he helped her to her feet. "That was very nice."

"Oh," he said, actually blushing a little. "My pleasure."

She patted his delightful bare butt. "I meant opening the store and giving me a break."

He gave a strangled chuckle. "If this is my reward, I'll do it every morning."

Her smile cut short. They wouldn't have the time to try out his offer. But she'd resolved not to dwell on that, right? She accepted the clothes he handed her and balanced on shaky legs to pull on her slacks.

The familiar chime of sleigh bells on the front door made her pick up the pace. "Reality," she sighed. There were probably customers out there.

"I'll get it," Ash, ever the faster dresser, said and pulled her close. He bent his head but stopped a few inches from her mouth. "Is it safe to kiss you, or are you going to have your wicked way with me again?"

Now that sounded like a fine idea. If only they had time. She reached on her tiptoes to press her lips to his. A quiver of heat raced through her, and she drew back reluctantly. "Safe. For the moment."

"Aw, too bad. You're dangerous, woman." He slanted her an off-kilter grin then stumbled a little bowleggedly out the door.

Ash enjoyed a mellow inner glow all morning, like nothing he'd ever known. Peter stopped by to give him a brief update. Not much to report yet. The boys would go to court with their angry fathers and obnoxious lawyers, but Peter had pitched the community service/mentor idea, and there'd been nods all around. At least that was one fire put out.

Miranda showed up early in the afternoon. Ash played with Mae while Abby and Miranda went over the day's to-do list. The baby gurgled and picked her nose, then tried to pick his nose, and he chuckled. Babies were okay. Kind of chubby and cute. And Miranda seemed so happy. He'd like to see Abby happy that way, too. He imagined her rounded out with motherhood, eyes shining with anticipation.

"I don't know, Mae," he whispered to the drooly infant. "What's your take on this situation? Think I can get her away from this one-horse town?"

Mae burped.

"Yeah." Ash put her over his shoulder and rubbed her back. "That's what I'm afraid of."

Abby hitched her purse onto her shoulder. "Ready to go?" she said, and smiled at him.

She'd been smiley all morning. The two of them couldn't seem to stop grinning at each other, and touching each other, and wasn't that a wonderful thing? Between their talk last night and her surprise seduction this morning, she seemed to have come to some decision. He dared to hope it was in his favor.

He handed Mae over to Miranda. The baby started to cry. "I'm not good with kids," he said, palms lifted in exasperation.

Miranda bounced Mae and laughed. "The problem is, you're *too* good with them. Mae likes you. She doesn't want you to go."

Abby stroked Mae's cheek. "There are other fish in the sea, sweetie."

Huh, he didn't like the sound of that. When they got outside, he said, "Other fish?"

"For her," she said mysteriously.

*Women.*

He glanced sideways. Abby, gazing out the open window and letting her hand cup the rushing wind, still wore that enigmatic, Mona Lisa smile.

He wanted her. He needed her. He had to have her.

What was that old saying? A bird and a fish could fall in love, but where would they live?

Well, he had the answer: Miami.

# CHAPTER EIGHTEEN

They brought Lucy home, at last. After he'd hovered a while and made sure they were settled, Ash had gone back to his brother's, and Abby and Lucy were alone together. Late afternoon sun filtered through the gauzy curtains and twinkled on dust motes. The world wound down to its normal rhythm.

"You've been seeing a lot of Ash this week?" Lucy asked from the comfort of her own bed. A steaming cup of tea rested on the lace doily that covered her bed table. Fresh pink roses sprang from an old glass jar.

Abby leaned on the arm of the wooden chair she'd dragged in from the kitchen and decided to pussyfoot around the implication in her aunt's tone. "He's been a big help, I have to admit. He fixed up the store, repaired the roof. Nailed a few shingles onto this house, too."

"I noticed some of the work when we pulled in. Did he build that clever wheelchair ramp?"

Abby couldn't keep the touch of pride from her voice. "Nope, I did that myself."

"Well, aren't you handy?" Her aunt took a sip of tea and sighed. "Oh, that's good. No Earl Grey in the hospital. How I missed it." Her blue eyes took in the rose-patterned wallpaper and worn oak dresser lined with photos, including more than the tea in her statement. "Is he getting on with his family?" Lucy asked.

"Yes, much better." Abby thought about the children crowding around him, and Peter inviting him to stay on. Even his father had shown signs of affection in his gruff, awkward way. "I think in the future he might visit more often." She didn't sound too depressed, did she?

Maybe so. Her aunt's head tilted sympathetically. "He'll always have a special place in my heart. And in yours."

Lucy's perceptive understanding almost undid Abby. She and Ash had had such a wonderful week together. She didn't want their time together to end. Dipping her head, Abby fussed with the satin edge of the blanket.

Lucy touched her arm. "Tell me all the exciting gossip I missed."

Grateful for the change in subject, Abby pulled her chair up close. "Well, it's been a hectic week." She skipped her intimate activities with Ash, of course, but recounted everything else. Lucy laughed over Mr. Miller's attack, and gasped at the events of the previous night.

Abby lifted one shoulder in a helpless shrug. "I didn't want to press charges, Auntie. We both know those boys."

"Of course, you did the right thing." Lucy patted her hand. "As long as their mischief stops, I'll be satisfied."

Would Peter stop it? Her faith in him had been sorely shaken. If only Ash would stay. He displayed the kind of tough leadership that boys would respect. He'd told her about the mentor program he'd proposed to Peter, and Abby couldn't help but think he'd be perfect to lead it.

"They're working out some kind of compromise," she said to her aunt. "Community service." She brightened. "Maybe they can come sweep the sidewalk and take out the trash the way Ash used to."

Lucy's smile faded and she set down her tea. "Abby, I need to discuss something with you.

Bad news; Abby could tell by the sea change in her aunt's

tone. She fought not to let her mind leap ahead to worst-case scenarios.

"I had a long time to think in the hospital." Hesitation weighted Lucy's words. "I've decided to sell the deli."

Abby's heart stopped. "Why? Auntie, what's wrong? You're going to get better, aren't you?"

"I'll mend, don't worry. But Dr. Herbert thinks my high blood pressure is tied to job-related stress. He also says it'll be difficult for me to be on my feet for long periods now. You know how I'd love to prove them wrong, but I'm afraid they're probably not."

"I can handle the store. I've been doing it all week."

"Abby, the deli needs at least two full-time, able bodies to run, and I don't want to put everything on you."

Abby straightened her back against the chair. "I've got Miranda and Candy to help."

"Miranda's busy with the baby now. Since we've known her, she's wanted to be a stay-at-home mother. And Candy . . . Well, she's a sweet girl, but she's in school full time. Soon she'll be leaving for college."

"I can run an ad—"

"There isn't enough income to hire another full-time person." She huffed a little and raised her silver brows. "There's barely enough for the two of us. The last few years, our profits have been steadily decreasing. With the Shop & Save and the convenience stores opening on the north end, fewer people want to make the drive into town and find a parking space on that narrow street." She pressed her lips together. "The era of the mom-and-pop stores is over, even in Cranberry."

"That can't be true." Abby clutched the arms of the chair. "I can make it work. I'll revamp the menu. Run some specials."

A tired smile graced Lucy's face. "If I've been one thing in my life, it's a good businesswoman. And part of being a good businesswoman is knowing when to call it quits. The deli has stood on Main Street for forty years, but we're just not making it any more. I'd be happy to go over the books with you."

Abby flexed her tense fingers and surrendered to the truth. "I've seen them."

Some of Lucy's formidable inner strength became evident in her determined expression and squared shoulders. "We'll sell the building. You'll have your nest egg, and I'll be able to retire. At last! I'm ready to spend my days puttering in the garden instead of buttering hard rolls."

Abby couldn't find the heart to share her enthusiasm. She threaded her fingers through her hair. "What else will I do?"

"There should be enough profit that you can take some time to decide. Maybe go back to school, or travel. There might be something outside Cranberry that would interest you."

"Are you trying to get rid of me?"

Lucy laughed. "No, dear. Just giving you the push out of the nest I probably should have years ago." She must have noticed Abby's crestfallen expression because she laid gentle fingers across the back of Abby's wrist. "Don't be mistaken. I've loved every moment we've had together running the deli. You're every bit a daughter to me, and I couldn't be more proud. But I've always felt it's held you back in your personal life."

"I did get married. Remember?"

Lucy tsked. "Oh, Brian. He was no match for you."

"He was a nice guy!"

"I knew you didn't love him, though."

Shock rippled through her. "Why didn't you say something when I told you we were engaged?"

"I did, but you wouldn't listen." She squeezed Abby's fingers. Affection softened her tone. "You're as strong-willed as your mother. You have to do things your own way."

Abby began to protest, but Lucy gripped her hand with a

steady strength. Abby bowed her head and acceded to her aunt's wisdom.

"I meant that as a compliment, dear. I truly believe you could accomplish anything you want, if you set your mind to it." Lucy's blue eyes twinkled with love and compassion. "You just need to find your heart's desire."

Peter pulled up to the Cranberry Savings Bank and parked his car along the curb. "You're really going to do this, eh?"

Ash nodded. "I love her. And I'm pretty sure she feels the same."

"Pretty sure?"

He echoed his brother's wry smile. "Yeah, I know. It's a long shot, isn't it?"

"She's got a life here."

"Yeah." Ash wiped his damp palms on his jeans. He couldn't stop fidgeting, wanted to get on with it. His rapid pulse beat all the way to his fingertips, but he felt oddly light, too, as if reaching his decision had somehow lifted a load off his shoulders. "We could have a life together . . ." Out of useful words, he gave a self-conscious shrug.

Old married Peter appraised him with a critical eye. "That's a good line. Maybe you can use it on her later."

Ash managed a choked laugh. "I'm sure I'll need a few."

On wobbly legs, he walked with his brother up the three cement steps and into the bank. At eight o'clock, the only folks in the lemony-smelling building were bank tellers.

A prim, older blonde in a frilly white blouse waved them over. "Good morning, Chief."

Peter stepped up to the gleaming counter. "Morning, Marjorie. My brother and I need to see a safe deposit box." He produced a key from his wallet.

"Why, of course." She found her own keys, came around and

walked them to the steel vault in the back of the bank. Her practical navy blue heels ticked on the marble floor. "I was relieved to hear your officers caught up with those vandals."

"Just kids," Peter said.

"Nevertheless," Marjorie fussed, a hand pressed over her heart, "if those boys want to live in Cranberry, they need to respect the town. I've lived here all my life and I haven't seen anything like it since—" She cast a glance toward Ash and sucked her lips between her teeth as if she would swallow her words. Must have recognized him all of a sudden. Ash winked, and she colored furiously.

Back to business, Marjorie unlocked the vault and pulled the great door open. Cool air rushed out, crisp as new dollars. She resurrected her smile. "Here we are, gentlemen. Go right in." She followed Peter to the correct box and they used their keys to open it. "When you're done, I'll be just over there at my station."

Marjorie closed the door enough to give them privacy.

"I've never been in here," Ash said, more to fill the looming silence than anything. He swore his heartbeat echoed off the steel walls.

Calm and cool as ever, Peter sat at the single small table occupying the tiny room and set the box down. "I've come a few times. Our wills are in here, Merry's and mine, and our life insurance policies."

Wills. Life insurance. God. Ash swallowed dryly. The signposts of a settled life. Permanent bonds to another human being. But his human being was Abby. He thought of her face, her laughter, and found he could breathe again. He sat opposite Peter, who shuffled through sheaves of paper. Metal scudded around in the bottom.

"Dad's old coins," he said, handing Ash half a dozen plastic-bound coins. "And his medals from the war."

Ash put down the coins and laid a red ribbon and silver cross across his palm. He wondered what it was for. "He was quite a guy."

"Still is." Peter looked up, then said, "You should give him another chance."

Ash rubbed his upper lip. Damp with nervous sweat. "Yeah. I realize I've been wrong about a lot of things. A lot of people."

"Well, I think we're all having the same thoughts about you, Ash."

"Really?"

The corners of his brother's eyes crinkled. "You're not the little prick you were in younger days."

He'd settle for that. "Glad someone noticed."

Peter's broad shoulders shifted and he dropped his gaze. "I, uh . . . I admit when I heard about the shooting in Los Angeles, I figured you finally went overboard. That your headstrong temper got the best of you. But, uh . . ." Peter paused to massage his jaw, as if he was having trouble loosening it enough to voice his apology. "Now I don't believe that's what happened."

Ash curled his fingers and pressed his father's medal into his palm. His mind raced back. "I've replayed that scene in L.A. a thousand times in my head. We planned it, we executed it perfectly. But no one expected the kid. He wasn't supposed to be there." He opened his hand and the medal clinked to the bottom of the box.

"It wasn't the first time I'd shot at someone, even hit someone, but . . ." He held his brother's suddenly rapt gaze. "They used him to run drugs. He was a throwaway, a street orphan. No one even came to claim the body. And it made me wonder why I was there, who I was helping. When no one even cares about kids, what's the point?"

Peter let out an audible breath. "Makes me glad I live in a small town."

"Yeah, but it's coming. Parents are too busy for their kids. Kids have too much money and privilege. You saw what happened."

His brother nodded once. "I know. I should have handled that all differently. Stopped it at the very beginning."

"Think they'll vote you out?"

He pursed his lips. "No. I've got the town's support. It'll all work out. I just have to be tougher in the future." He quirked a smile at Ash. "More like you."

Ash grinned back, eyes narrowed. "How ironic."

He couldn't resist the ribbing, but inside he glowed with the new respect he heard in his brother's voice.

Peter said, "Here it is. Thought it was in a box, but no."

He opened a tiny manila envelope, and into Ash's palm dropped a diamond ring. Ash held it up between his thumb and forefinger. Light twinkled in the facets and gleamed on the unbroken circle of gold. Perfect as hope, shiny as a new beginning.

"Mom's engagement ring," Peter said, a bemused expression on his weathered face. "She always wanted you to have it. I bet somewhere up in Heaven, she's cheering you on."

Her heart's desire, Abby griped silently. This *was* her heart's desire.

In the mid-morning stillness, bent over the deli's glass counter, she scanned the neatly penned columns in the leather-bound ledger and tried to make the numbers do a dance. Unfortunately, the figures hadn't changed since the last time she'd tallied them.

She worried the edge of her fingernail. Carrying on from here was one thing; the bigger problem would be getting un-mired from the accumulated debt, even though every dollar could be justified. The furnace had needed replacing. The back lot required plowing. Every month brought new bills for electricity, heating or air, to say nothing of their perishable inventory. When they made money one cup of coffee at a time, no wonder they couldn't keep up.

She groaned and leaned her forehead on her fingertips. Where could she turn for help?

The door jingled and Ash came whistling in.

"Morning, beautiful," he called.

"Oh, hi, Ash." At last, a friendly face. A sliver of happiness worked its way through her despair. And she'd better make the most of it, before he suspected something was wrong and started to pry. She forced her lips into a smile.

He crossed the sunny, quiet room and stopped in front of her. "What gives?" he asked.

"Nothing." Unnerved, she frowned. "What a thing to say." She closed the big leather-bound book and tried for a change of subject. "How about, 'I missed you.' "

"All right, then. I missed you." He leaned over the counter for her kiss. Their lips had barely touched before he rocked back on his heels and said, "Now I know something's wrong. Give."

She feigned offense even as her tightly wound control began to unravel. "You're in a nosy mood this morning."

"I knew something was going on last night when I called to check in. You went from happy to grumpy in the space of a couple hours."

"Maybe I'm tired. It has been an active couple of days." She arched her brow to make sure he understood she was including *all* the activities.

"Everything okay with Lucy? Did she have a bad night?"

"No, she's bright and chipper as ever. The visiting nurse is really nice."

"But . . ." He pierced her with that x-ray cop vision of his, and Abby felt utterly transparent, as if he were melting through her defenses one patient question at a time.

Her nose began to itch.

"Stop interrogating me." She turned and pressed her hand over her mouth. No crying. She refused to cry. She'd held it together all morning.

Then Ash's strong, comforting hand slid over her shoulder, and she hiccupped.

"Abby?"

She broke away and honked her nose into a paper towel she ripped from the roll.

"Honey, what's the matter?"

"Don't honey me," she rasped. Any toughness she'd intended was ruined by her wavery voice and the watery eyes she could no longer fight. "Lucy is . . ." She made a jerky gesture with the damp paper towel. ". . . p-pushing me out of the nest."

"What?"

"She's selling the store." She put her hands on her hips and rolled an angry gaze to the ceiling. "Place has been losing money for years," she muttered. "No wonder. Look at it. Ancient old house, falling apart. Drafty in the winter and hot in the summer." She shook a finger at Ash. "I drove by the convenience store on my way here. They're open twenty-four hours and you know what? There were cars there. People lined up at the cash register at five o'clock."

He shrugged. "So your place doesn't open until six. People will come."

She dropped onto a stool. "I saw George Darcy there."

"Doing what?"

"Of course, getting his paper."

"Maybe he didn't think you'd be open today. Everyone knew Lucy came home last night."

She dismissed his words with a weary toss of her hand. "He's been missing days on and off for a while. I guess he can't wait long enough for us to open." She sniffled and glanced around again. "Other regulars have been trickling away for months. How can I compete with a chain store?"

"My poor girl. My poor Abby," Ash murmured in his low, lulling voice. He dragged another stool from the other side of the counter and sat knee to knee with her and held her hands. She gripped his hard, as if his strength might flow into her and stop this awful churning in the pit of her stomach.

"I'm sorry," he said softly. His silver gray eyes brimmed with sympathy, as if she'd suffered a death in the family. In a way, she had. "It seems like a sudden decision."

Abby stared at their linked hands. "She started talking about it before her accident. The stress of keeping the deli afloat has been affecting her health. I should have seen it." She recited the mental monologue she'd been telling herself all morning. "When I think of how thin she'd gotten, and all the pills she had to take for her blood pressure and heart. She never complained about money, and I assumed everything was under control. I was so stupid."

His thumbs made soothing circles over the backs of her hands. "No, honey, your aunt loves you. I'm sure she just wanted to protect you."

"I should have been protecting her."

A slim smile curved his lips. "She's too proud to admit she needed help. She had to do things her own way."

Abby sniffed. "That's what she said about me, too. That I'm like my m-mother. Stubborn." She bit the edge of her lip. "I'm not stubborn, am I?"

"Like a rock," he said.

"Oh. Well, actually, she said strong-willed."

"That, too."

"Ash." She pulled her hands from his grasp. "You're supposed to be cheering me up here. You're doing a pretty bad job." She blew her nose again. Over the edge of her paper towel, she watched his dark face. Lines formed between his drawn brows, and his lips thinned in concentration. Something occupied his thoughts, too. "What's wrong?"

"I'm sorry. It's just that I had something I wanted to discuss, and now I'm not sure if this is the best time."

"If it's an idea for how I can keep the store, I'm all ears."

He propped an elbow on his thigh. "I have a bad feeling you've already got a few of your own."

"I do." Maybe he'd cheer her up after all. At least he listened, even if he wouldn't lose the skeptical tone. Abby stood and paced the small space behind the counter. "I stayed up last night, thinking. You know how I always wanted to start a catering business."

"But there wasn't enough demand for one in Cranberry."

"Right. Well, I was thinking, this could be my base of operations, and I could advertise in the surrounding towns. If I bought a van and modified this back area into a decent kitchen, I might be able to do it."

He stretched his long legs out before him and crossed his arms over his chest. "You're talking a lot of money. Kitchen equipment, a car loan, to say nothing of buying out Lucy's half of the building."

Not to be dissuaded, she held up a finger. "I could get a loan. I don't have any collateral, but I have some bonds, and I'll sell Brian's engagement ring—"

Ash popped to his feet. He grasped her by her upper arms, putting a quick stop to her pacing. "Abby, slow down. The store isn't going to sell overnight. You have time to think about things. Lots of time."

Confused, she said, "Why wait?"

He stared into her face. Scowled. Ran his hand from her

arms to her wrists and picked up her hands again. "What if Lucy changes her mind?"

"She won't." A familiar frustration balled in her stomach. "In fact, she might not let me buy out the store, no matter what. She wants me to try something else."

His eyes lit. "Would that be so bad? Every ending is a new beginning, you know."

She tsked testily. "I guess I could buy another place in Cranberry, but I don't see the point when—"

His kiss caught her by surprise. His lips captured hers, took no prisoners, scattered all thoughts to the wind. He pulled her arms around his neck and crushed her breasts against his chest.

Had she been talking? Well . . . This was so much more interesting . . .

Beneath his tender assault, frustration melted away. Joy replaced it, an unwavering flame spreading warmth through her soul. Ash's embrace worked like magic. In his arms, she felt safe. Treasured. She savored the sensation.

Eyes closed, head tilted back, she sighed as he lifted his mouth from hers. She floated. Her fingers toyed with the short hair at his nape.

"You were saying?" he murmured, dropping light kisses on her nose and forehead.

"Uh?"

His low chuckle rumbled with self-satisfaction. It wasn't good to let a man get too pleased with himself. Although right now she was pretty pleased with him, too. Abby eyed him blearily. "You're trying to distract me."

"Did it work?"

"Mm. If only I could bottle that feeling, I'd make a fortune."

His silver eyes gleamed with healthy mischief. He curled a strand of hair from her temple and grew serious. "I might have a better idea for you. We can talk tonight."

She stiffened. "Tonight? Oh, God, you're leaving tonight!"

He shook his head. "In the morning."

Seized by panic, she gripped his biceps. "Oh, God. I blocked it." Tears blurred her vision and this time she couldn't stop them. "This has got to be the worst day of my life."

Her tears seemed to send him into his own personal angst. "Aw, no, don't cry, don't cry, I can handle anything but that." He pulled her close, stroked his hands over her shoulders and back.

But knowing she'd soon lose his strength and comfort forever only made Abby tremble harder. He murmured soothing sounds against her hair.

When she'd calmed to jerky sniffles, his chest rose and fell on a deep sigh. "Would it be so bad if you had to start over in some other place?"

His wary tone made her draw back enough to look at him. She'd never seen him so focused. Something stilled in her heart. "You mean like Buckland or Darrowby?"

One eye narrowed and his jaw tensed. "I meant like Florida."

# Chapter Nineteen

He expected her to laugh, or cry, or at least speak. He didn't expect her to stand gaping. Or to see her anger building like thunderheads.

She took another step back. "You must be out your mind."

He held up his hands, palms out. "I know that look, Abby. Calm down."

If anything, her brown eyes widened further. "I can't leave now. I've got a sick aunt, a struggling business—"

"I understand. I've considered all that. Lucy and I—"

"Lucy?" Her reddened stare ripped him up and down. "You talked to Lucy?"

Oh, man, he *so* should have waited until tonight. He tried a placating smile. "See, I had this all planned for later. Dinner. Flowers. Candlelight."

"What did you tell Lucy?"

He dropped his hands, stuffed them in his pockets. "I told her I want you to come with me."

"And?" Her voice cracked.

"She thinks it's a great idea." Although she, too, like his brother, had cautiously wished him luck.

Abby hugged her arms across her chest, as if guarding against a chill wind. "She doesn't want me to stay?"

"She wants you to have a life." He took a step toward her. "I know you couldn't leave now. Lucy needs you until she's well again. Then once you sell the place—"

She whirled on him. "So you knew she wanted to sell?"

"No!" Easy, easy. Things were getting out of hand. He took a deep breath. "She didn't tell me anything. I'm as surprised as you. I imagine she wants you to make a decision based on your, uh, feelings for me. Not on business."

Suspicion rolled off her like heat. "When did you talk to her?"

"Just before I came here today. I stopped by the house. I wanted to get her blessing before I, uh . . ." Blew it. Which was exactly what he was doing.

Her lower lip tucked out in a gloomy, thoughtful pout. The sudden silence scared him. What was going on behind those beautiful eyes? He fingered the ring deep in his pocket, but given her current mood, she'd probably embed it in his forehead if he showed it to her.

"We could have a life together," he ventured. Unfortunately, rattled as he was by her reaction, he sounded like a lame greeting card.

"In Miami." She raked her fingers through her hair and didn't look at him.

"Or outside. We don't have to live in the city. There are smaller towns. Not as small as Cranberry, but big enough that a new caterer could have an honest chance."

"I won't know anybody." Her voice grew weak, her anger's momentum dwindling.

He reached out to rub her back. "You'll know me. We'll have each other."

She paused, then lifted her chin. "We could be together here, too."

Uh-oh. "But my business is in Miami. And it's going to support us."

"If you stayed here, we could be partners. You've run the deli all week. Is it that intolerable?"

"Abby." His throat dried up. He rasped a chuckle. "I already have a partner. I've made a commitment—"

Her shoulders squared. "Commitment?" Her anger caught a second wind. Full sail ahead. "Six years ago, when the going got rough, you left. When being a cop didn't work out, you left. Now I need you, and you're leaving again. And you expect me to do the same, to my family, to my town and the people I love?" For all her brave words, her eyes glistened with pain. "You're so blind. Everything you could ever want is right here, but you won't see it because it's not good enough for you."

"That's not true," he started, but stopped when she held up her hand.

"What happens if your new job doesn't work out? Then you'll leave again, and this time, I'll have to go, too, after I've set down roots in some new town." She pressed her fingertips to her chest. "That's not what I want. That's not who I am, Ash. I need security, stability."

His own anger flared. "It's one thing to be stable, it's another to be stuck in a rut."

She gestured wildly. "Because I fight to save what I love? Because I won't give up on something worth saving?"

He ground his teeth. "Does it matter that I love you? That I want to spend the rest of my life with you?" Before he'd consciously thought out his actions, he snatched up her hand and slapped the ring down in the center of her palm.

Abby's gaze froze on it. She seemed to stop breathing.

Swift move, Ash scolded himself. He groaned, swiped his hand over his hair, jammed his hands back into his pockets. Into the vacuum, he said, "It was my mother's."

Her golden hair sweeping forward over her cheeks, Abby bent her head. She touched the ring as if it might shatter, or melt away like a snowflake. She took a long time to reply. "Your mother was never happy here. Was she?" Her lips softened.

"No."

She shifted the ring in her cupped palm. Cheerful sparkles bounced off the glass counter and danced in her sorrowful eyes.

"Oh, Ash." She returned the ring to him. Her voice lowered, but some inner courage kept it steady. "For the last few days, I admit, I had this little fantasy that you might change your mind and stay. The past week has been the best of my life." Her mouth lifted at one corner. "But it's not fair to ask you to change everything based on one week's togetherness." She touched his cheek. Love glowed in her smile, but sadness, too. Her warm fingers stroked his skin, and he leaned into them, aching for contact. Her hand fell away.

"It would never work out," she said. "One of us would always have an eye on the horizon."

He put the ring on the tip of his pinkie. It was warm from her, as if she'd imbued it with life. He fought not to yell, to beg. "So that's it, then? What now? I go, you stay. I come back to visit you and your Cranberrian husband?"

That dragged a dry groan from her. "Oh, no. I told you early on, no marriage for me."

Her gaze lifted, her eyes dark pools he could drown in. A sharp emptiness lanced him. The painful truth. There'd be no one else for him, either. He was almost thirty years old, and no woman had ever compared to his Abby. Wherever his travels took him, she would always be home to him.

He slipped the ring back into his pocket. "You can call me any time, for anything."

Her eyes closed, and she nodded.

"Be happy, Abby." He lowered his head for one last, sweet kiss. "Don't forget I love you."

Then, as if Fate had preordained it, he turned and walked out the door.

★　★　★　★　★

Abby pushed out with her bare foot. The old swing rocked her with a sleepy rhythm. The rim of the evening sky still bore the faint glow of the passing day. A night breeze danced with the loose ends of her hair. Crickets chirped, her favorite sound in all the world.

And none of it made her happy.

"Abby!" Doris, the visiting nurse, called her from Lucy's kitchen. Abby glanced over her shoulder and waved.

Haloed by the back door light, Doris said, "I'm leaving now. Your aunt is up from her nap."

"Thanks, Doris. I'll be right in."

Her toes skidded on the worn patch of grass beneath the swing as she brought it to a halt. Felt like an eternity since she and Ash had sat here, talking that night after she'd hit poor Peter. She remembered how she'd fought her emotions, battled her desire for him. Of course, she'd given in and gotten hurt. Well. With her thumb and ring finger, she scooped her hair away from her face. No regrets.

She gazed skyward to follow the blinking lights of a jet overhead. Tomorrow morning, that would be Ash, going on to his next adventure. She'd been right to let him go. This sadness would pass, this crushing grief. The best thing to do would be to get back to work. She'd find a way to talk Lucy into selling her the building, and she'd start restructuring the business. She'd be independent, as she'd always wanted.

But that didn't make her happy either.

Entering the kitchen's homey, golden glow, she found a smile for Lucy, who sat in her wheelchair at the old oak table. Doris had set out a bowl of soup and a sandwich for her dinner.

"Beautiful night," Lucy said. Her curious stare followed Abby, who wanted nothing more than to shrug it off and go hide somewhere.

"Yes. Fourth of July. Clear enough that we might see some of the fireworks if we sit out back around nine."

"Not going to the town picnic? You've never missed one since you were a little girl."

"I don't think so." Abby opened a loaf of bread and started to make a sandwich for herself. "I'm a little too old for fireworks."

Her aunt scoffed. "You're never too old. I'd go, if I could manage it."

Abby sat beside Lucy with her sandwich and a glass of milk.

Fiddling with her soupspoon, Lucy said, "I thought you might go with Ash. He paid a visit this morning."

Her aunt had slept away most of the afternoon, and Abby had dreaded this conversation. No avoiding it, though. She picked the crust off her white bread. "What did he have to say, exactly?"

"Well . . ." Lucy turned her spoon in the air. "What did he say to you?"

Nice try. "You first."

"Oh." Frowning, Lucy set down her silverware and folded her hands in her lap. "Ah, he told me he'd like to marry you. He asked for my blessing. He was concerned whether I'd be all right if you moved with him to Florida, and I assured him I'd be fine. After all, you've had your apartment for years, and I've managed." She peered through her silver-framed bifocals and carefully said, "Is that what he told you?"

"Did you tell him we were selling the store?"

Her aunt seemed appalled. "Why no, dear. That's between you and me. Besides, I knew how upset you were. I'd hoped his proposal might . . . show you there was . . . more to look forward to than an old run-down sandwich shop . . ."

Lucy's words stumbled to an uncomfortable silence. Abby stared down at her plate. Her aunt said, "He didn't ask you to marry him?"

Abby sucked in a deep breath. "No. He did." She let it out in a long sigh. "I'm afraid the old run-down sandwich shop won out."

"Oh, Abby." Her aunt slapped her hands on her thighs. Abby turned at the sharp sound. There was a new expression on her aunt's face. Anger. Shock stunned Abby. She couldn't remember ever seeing her aunt truly angry. "You turned down love for that dilapidated pile of sawdust?"

"That's . . . That's our business you're talking about."

"Our former business. I don't want it anymore." Lucy flicked her knobby fingers in a shooing motion. "I want to retire, Abby. I want you to go on to better things."

Abby's cheeks heated. Her tongue wouldn't work. She sputtered, "How is Florida better? It's so far away. I'd miss you, I'd miss Cranberry."

"I should have sent you away to college. It would have been good for you to leave home," Lucy muttered, almost talking to herself.

Abby looked on in horror. Maybe her aunt's pills were affecting her. "Have you never really wanted me?"

"Of course I wanted you." Lucy shook her head. Her hair might be gray, but her eyes were sharp and bright. "But loving someone means wanting the best for them. I saw how you pined after Ash when he left for California. You never talked about it. Kept it all inside. Then you met Brian, and you married him to try to forget. The only good that came out of that union was that you got an apartment and lived on your own."

Abby swallowed hard.

Lucy didn't relent. "You carry too much on your shoulders, Abby. Always trying to make things right for me. Blaming yourself when things go wrong." She reached to grasp Abby's wrist. "I understand it all boils down to your parents. You think because they left you, no one can be trusted." Her wise old eyes narrowed. "I tried to make it up to you by never pushing you to be more independent, and that was my mistake."

Stricken, Abby said, "But I really have been happy."

"As happy as you were this week, with Ash by your side?"

Abby thought about it. Thought some more. Then croaked, "No." Before Lucy could jump on her, she held up her finger. "But I've been happy in a different way. I've been . . ." What was the word? "Content."

Lucy groaned and sat back. "My darling, look at me. I'm sixty-eight years old. *I* should be content. You're twenty-six. You should be ecstatic, excited, looking forward to a future and a family."

"But I don't want a family. I want to be like you. You've never been married, and you've had a wonderful life."

Her aunt tapped her arm. "Go in my bedroom and get the black photo album from my book case."

Relieved to be out from under Lucy's all-knowing eye, Abby left to retrieve the book. She had to dig under piles of magazines and half-finished knitting to find it. When she returned to the kitchen, Lucy had cleared a spot on the table. She set the album down.

The worn binding creaked as Lucy parted the covers. Abby immediately recognized one face in the faded color photos, even though from much younger days: her aunt, and a handsome young man in a sailor's uniform.

"Auntie, who is that?"

A misty smile wreathed Lucy's lips. "I haven't looked at these pictures in years," she whispered. Her fingers lovingly touched the smiling man. "That was Roger, my steady."

Abby grinned. "Steady?"

"Oh, that's an old fashioned term. Nowadays, I suppose you'd call him my main man."

Maybe in the eighties. Abby bit her lip. "He's cute."

Lucy chuckled. "Yes, he was very cute. His only flaw was a crooked nose he'd gotten from boxing. He was the local middle heavy weight champion."

Abby didn't know what that meant, but the pride in her aunt's voice made it sound impressive.

Lucy turned another page. Roger held Lucy aloft like a human barbell while she stretched out on her side, her head propped in her hand. She wore a striped, one-piece bathing suit and a dazzling grin.

"Auntie," Abby exclaimed, "how risqué!"

Lucy laughed. "That was at Coney Island. We had so much fun." Her smile drifted as she turned another page. "We were engaged to be married."

Abby noticed her fading expression. "What happened?"

"He joined the navy. I begged him not to. I'd heard horror stories of Korea, and Vietnam lurked on the horizon. But he felt he had a duty to serve his country." She straightened a crooked photo. "He asked me to go with him. It would mean being stationed overseas, moving frequently around the globe. And, of course, never knowing if he would come home alive."

A knot tightened in Abby's throat. "So you refused."

"Of course." She closed the old album. Her age-spotted hands laced together on top of it. "Roger was killed, a year and a half after sailing out. You would think I'd be satisfied that I'd made the right decision to stay in Connecticut." She shook her head. "Instead, I've always regretted the time we might have had together. Months of happiness. Maybe a child to remember him by. A cousin for you to play with." She smiled and patted Abby's hand, then her gaze turned inward, to her distant memories.

What a perfectly dreadful story. A chill trickled down Abby's spine. Just like her and Ash. She stared at the shadows waltzing on the wall and tried to corral her galloping thoughts.

Then a sneaking suspicion nudged its way to the surface. She turned to her aunt, who gazed off and fingered the gold pendant she always wore.

"Lucy," Abby said.

"Hm?"

"Did that really happen, or are you just trying to get me out of your hair?"

One silver eyebrow rose in an affronted arch. She leveled a frosty stare through the upper levels of her bifocals and carefully removed the gold chain from around her neck. "Please."

Abby had to pick at the old locket with her thumbnail, but it finally opened. She squinted at the tiny faded photo. And shock rippled through her. "Roger."

Her aunt nodded sagely. "Do you want to be carrying a photo of Ash around your neck like an albatross for the next forty-five years?"

"God, no," she breathed.

Lucy leaned a wrinkled arm upon the table. "Then get off your rear end and do something about it."

Upstairs, kneeling on her bed, she phoned Peter's house. Merry answered.

"I'm sorry, he's gone, Abby."

Abby's stomach clenched. "Gone? But his flight isn't until morning."

"He packed up about two hours ago. I wish he hadn't left so abruptly, too. My children are heartbroken."

The acid disapproval in Merry's tone made even Abby cringe. "Do you know where he went?"

"No, but Pete might. Ash said he was stopping by the station to leave something with him. Don't know what."

Abby did. The ring. She cringed some more.

Merry said, "Try the station."

"I will." She didn't want to be rude, but she tried to rush Merry off the phone. "Thanks, good-bye."

"Well," Merry lingered, her vowels elongated by her soft Southern drawl, "I know you've always liked him, Abby, but I'm glad to have my household back in order. That man seems to cause trouble wherever he goes."

"Yes, he certainly is aggravating. Bye now. Thanks again."

She hung up before Merry's quizzical "you're welcome" finished. She dialed Pete.

He said, "He's on his way to the airport. Got an earlier flight out."

Her heart sank. "Oh, no."

"You can try his cell."

Hope sprang. "His cell! Great idea."

"Need the number?"

"No, I have it."

She hung up on Pete, too. She shuffled through her purse and found Ash's number. She closed her eyes and clutched the phone to her ear. Willed him to answer before she chickened out and changed her mind.

She got his voice mail.

She hung up. Maybe he was in one of those cell phone dead spots. She waited ten nail-biting minutes and tried again. Got the voice mail.

Just in case he was out of the car, she waited twenty minutes and tried a third time.

When his sexy, masculine voice requested she leave her name and number so he could get back to her, Abby's jaw worked but no words came out. Fear clamped cold, clammy fingers around her throat. He always carried his cell phone. Always had it turned on.

He must know she was calling. He didn't want to talk to her.

Oh hell. She hung up.

He was gone.

Would it be too pathetic if she called Merry and asked if she had his partner's number down in Miami? Should she wait until he called Pete with his permanent number? If he ever did. Ash had never been famous for staying in touch.

The excitement she'd generated while coming to her new decision sputtered, fizzled and died.

Ash had left.

Didn't give her another chance. Didn't leave a forwarding address. Cut his losses and took off.

If this was his idea of love, she'd be better off without it. Lucy's romantic story had clouded her heart. The pain she suffered now had an achingly familiar tinge to it. So similar to what she'd felt six years ago, when he'd taken off. Hadn't given her another chance. Not left a forwarding address.

Abby fell back on her mattress, threw her arms above her head and bunched her fists as tight as she could. Her fingernails dug into her palms. Her hands shook with the effort. Enough already. Enough.

She gritted her teeth rather than cried. Thumped the mattress rather than screamed.

Her albatross had flown.

Enough.

# CHAPTER TWENTY

Ash scooped up a handful of pebbles and stared at the lone, lit window. The heavy, humid darkness clung to him like a moist second skin. A lone mosquito buzzed by his ear and he swatted it away. He selected a stone. Been a long time since he'd done this. He prayed he didn't break the damned glass.

Still no lights on elsewhere in the house. That dog better not bark and ruin this for him.

Lower lip pinned between his teeth, he stretched back and threw the pebble.

Bingo! Right on target.

No reaction.

He threw another. And a third.

Too small. He tried a round, smooth river stone the size of his thumbnail. A shatter of glass broke the quiet.

He flinched. "Oh, sh—"

A moment later, the door leading to the widow's walk swung out. Luminous in her white night gown, Abby bent to examine the broken pane.

He aimed another pebble, bouncing it off the clapboard a few feet from where she stood.

She jumped and stared at the house. Ash dragged his hand down his cheek. For God's sake. "Psst!" he hissed. He waved his arms.

For some reason, she looked up toward the roof. Who was she expecting, Santa Claus? "Abby!"

Finally, her gaze jerked down to him. Her hand flew to her throat.

"Ash, is that you?"

"No, it's Jiminy Cricket."

She leaned over the railing. Her hair hung like Rapunzel's, gold laced with silver moonlight. "Go away, Jiminy. I have a restraining order."

He groaned and laughed. She couldn't hate him too much if she could still joke. The sheer strength of his relief staggered him back a step. "What are you doing?" he asked stupidly.

"Wondering if Lucy's home owner's insurance is going to cover this broken window."

"Sorry about that."

"You could have rung the doorbell."

"I'm trying to be nostalgic."

She backhanded her hair over her shoulder. It slipped down again. Her voice came softer. "Shouldn't you be in Florida right about now?"

"Probably."

She straightened, arms linked under her breasts. He appreciated the view. "Ash, are you drunk?"

"Nope." Just happy. Happy to see her again, to hear her. "Aren't you curious what I'm doing here?"

"Not particularly."

Liar. "You called me three times."

"Oh!" The hem of nightgown swayed gently about her ankles as her posture stiffened. "So you knew I was calling and didn't pick up?"

He bounced a pebble from one hand to the other. "You didn't leave a message."

"I was mad."

"So was I."

A lone cricket strummed in the field. Ash stuck the pebble in his pocket. "Why don't you get dressed and come down? Or better yet, get undressed and come down."

"Are you still mad?"

"No. You?"

"Yes." She wiped her cheek. He couldn't see her well enough to tell if she was crying. He hoped not. There'd been enough tears for one day.

"Don't make me come up there," he said, but his teasing tone faltered. He'd hurt her this afternoon. Hell, they'd hurt each other. But he wasn't running away, not this time.

He walked until he stood in the pale light puddled under the widow's walk and looked up into her frowning face. "I thought we had a date for the Fourth of July fireworks."

"You stood me up. It's midnight. They ended hours ago."

"Not all of them." He raised his eyebrows and sent a plea to Heaven.

After a pregnant pause, she said, "I don't know what you're talking about."

"Come and find out." He held out his arms. "Jump, I'll catch you."

She huffed. "I don't trust you."

Her words hung between them like smoke. He lowered his arms. "Trust me now, Abby."

The light traced the curve of her cheek, gathered in her glistening eye. Then she disappeared, and Ash heard the door close. His heart locked up in his chest.

Damn it, if he had to, he would climb the old trellis and bring her down like a princess from her tower. He appraised the rickety structure. The years hadn't been kind to the old wood. He patted his flat belly, calculating the weight of muscle he'd put on since he'd last scaled the latticework.

Fortunately for the trellis, the widow's walk flooded with illumination again, and Abby, dressed now in a light sweater and jeans, said, "Move, I'm rolling out the fire ladder."

He stepped back as a rope ladder cascaded over the railing. She came primly down. His open hands slid over her thighs and her lovely jeans-clad rear and closed on her waist to help her to the ground. He turned her to him, dying for her kiss.

She placed a firm hand on his chest.

Now he could see her face just fine. The scowl, the stormy brow and everything. She said, "Not so fast."

Should have known this wouldn't be easy. He hung a hand on a rung of the fire ladder. "This is nice. Why didn't we have it back in the olden days? I almost broke my neck on the trellis."

She brushed by him, fists on hips, head turning as she scanned the darkness. "So what is it you wanted to show me?"

He smiled at her brusque tone. Underneath it, curiosity burgeoned like spring grass under snow. "Something special. Got your shoes on?"

"Just socks."

He scooped her up in his arms. With a little screech, she clutched at his shoulders. He calmly explained, "The grass is dewy," and carried her toward the edge of the field.

"I get it." Her voice jolted with each step. "You're going to kill me and hide my body in the swamp."

"Oh, great, now you've ruined my surprise." He bent his head and kissed the tip of her nose, since she was so close now and couldn't escape. "Hush. I've been out here for an hour, preparing. Just glad Pawpaw didn't start barking and wake you guys up."

She glanced back at the house. "Lucy."

"We're not going far."

She relaxed against his chest. "She'll be asleep a few more hours."

"Plenty of time."

She gazed at him curiously. Her hair floated against his bare skin. Her sweet peach scent teased his senses. She said, "I could get used to this, being carried around."

They reached a small clearing and he grunted as he set her down. "Please don't. My back."

She tsked archly. Then surveyed his handiwork and gasped. "Ash, what have you been up to?"

Ah, so she liked it. Pride welled within him. Uncertainty rose along with it. Thin sweat broke out on his forehead. "I didn't get the opportunity to do what I'd planned. I thought maybe if you gave me another chance . . ."

"Dinner. Candlelight." Her voice held a note of disbelief.

At least she'd remembered, from the heated argument this morning. Her eyes gleamed in the glow of the candles he'd carefully set in a wide bowl in the center of the burgundy blanket. Beside the candles sat a picnic basket and a bottle of wine. His motorcycle leaned a yard away, and she nodded toward it.

"Red Betty."

"Well, I couldn't drive a car through the field."

She turned to him, brows furrowed. "Were you really on your way to the airport?"

He looked away and shuffled his feet. "Yeah. Then I got your call."

"Maybe I was calling to yell some more."

He smiled. "It wouldn't have mattered. I would have come back anyhow."

"Why, Ash?"

"I told you. I love you."

Her hair was a tousled mess around her pretty, stunned face, and he brushed it back off her cheek, tucked it behind her ear. "Is that all right?"

"Well." Wide-eyed, she looked at his picnic then back to him. "I don't know. What's changed?"

"Sit down. Let's do what you women like to do, and talk."

Her lips curved in a wry smile, the first of the night, and he caught it to his heart like a gold coin. She sat, and he poured wine into paper cups.

"What's in the basket?" she asked.

He wrinkled his nose. "Cheetos and Ring Dings. Sorry. Only had time to stop at a truck stop."

She laughed. "Is it red wine or white that goes with fake orange cheese?"

He tucked down cross-legged beside her. "If you drink enough, it doesn't matter."

"True." Her eyes assessed him over the rim of her cup as she lifted it to sip.

She hadn't said she loved him yet.

Ash gulped his wine and finished it off. "So, why did you call me?"

He noticed her hand trembled as she set her cup down. "I wanted to say I was sorry."

"For?"

"For accusing you of running out on things. I know you always have your reasons. I was upset, and I wasn't thinking." She toyed with a blade of grass on the blanket.

"Did you talk to Lucy about your ideas for the store?"

Her lips pursed. "A little. Now . . . I don't know. I'm back to square one." Her forehead furrowed and he wished she would look at him so he could see what emotions swam in her eyes. Then her chin came up and she faced him. "I want to go with you, Ash. I want to go to Florida."

A mosquito could have knocked him over with a brush of its tiny wings. His pulse pounded in his temples. "It's not a light decision, Abby. Are you sure?"

She nodded. "I don't want you to be a . . . an albatross."

"An alba-what?"

Her hand lifted and her mouth sloped up. "Never mind." Her smile spread, gloriously, across her face. "I want to be with you. I love you."

"Ah! I knew it!" He shook his finger. Hot damn. "I love you, too, and that's why I'm staying."

"You can't stay." Abby reeled back in shock. "What about your partner? And your business?"

"I got it all worked out. I called Ryan while I was driving. Explained everything." Excitement buoyed his words. "Ryan's a romantic, always has been. He thought it was hilarious. Apparently he's been listening to my rantings all week and anticipated this." He shrugged. "Anyhow, we worked out a deal, that I not withdraw my half of the investment, and he pays me back once he's got the business up and running."

"But his leg. I thought—"

"Turns out he's met someone, too. Our secretary. An ex-bodyguard. She's already been handling what were supposed to be my duties once I got settled." He chuckled dryly. "Leave it to Ryan."

It all seemed too easy. Abby shook her head. "What about Cranberry? You hate it here."

Ash pulled his lip, sobering. "Yeah, there is that."

Ah ha. She knew there was a rub.

He refilled his wine cup, then hers. She didn't even remember finishing her first cupful. He said, "I admit I've had some revelations this week. You opened my eyes, Abby. Now I see how people care about one another here. That there's a sense of all for one and one for all that I never felt part of when I was younger."

"You feel part of it now?"

His honest gray eyes met hers. "I think I could, in time."

She let out a long breath. "So . . . you wouldn't mind working at the deli?"

"Oh, well, that I don't know about." He lay back, angled toward her, propped on one elbow. "That might have to stay your domain."

"Then what will you do for work?"

He grimaced. "Excuse me for a moment. I have to go throw pebbles at Peter's window."

Abby surprised herself with a laugh. "You'll join the force? Oh, Ash, that's wonderful."

Staring into his cup, he shrugged modestly. "After all that's happened, I think maybe I could make a difference here."

She knew that was really all he'd ever wanted to do. She reached out and stroked her hand over his hair. He turned to her with a smile, his eyes full of love, and hope.

He sat up, catching her fingers before she could pull away. "I still have something for you." With his other hand, he dug in his pocket and produced a pebble.

She laughed. "Ooh, a new worry stone."

He sloped a grin and put the pebble on the blanket. "Hang on to it. You might need it." Then he dug again, and out came the ring. Did it sparkle even more now, or was that just her tears making it glitter and dance?

"Your mother's ring. I thought you'd given it back to Peter."

"No. Why'd you think that?"

"Merry said . . . Well, I called the house to see if you were still there, and she said you'd stopped by to leave something with him."

"Ah."

What a curious evasion. Even by candlelight, she could have sworn his cheeks colored. "What was it, Ash?"

He eased back on his palms and shook his head. "I guess it's yours now, anyhow. It was a passbook. I set up an account for you, to start your new business."

"But . . . that was before you'd decided to stay."

"Yup."

"I wouldn't have taken it."

"That would have been your choice. If you'd wanted to, you could have paid me back." He spoke calmly, but his eyes begged her to listen. "I knew you'd be angry at first. I believe in you, Abby. You've got a good head for business, and if you had a boost, you'd take the reins and run. Whatever you want to do, I'm behind you one hundred percent." He twined his fingers through hers. "You helped me find my heart's desire, and I want to help you do the same."

"My heart's desire," she murmured. "Lucy said I should look for it." And there he was, she realized. He'd been there all along. "Oh, you're so much better than a dilapidated pile of sawdust."

"Huh?"

Abby threw her arms around Ash's neck. He tumbled back, pulling her with him. They kissed through their laughter, until more than wine warmed her veins and the blanket of darkness began to give her ideas.

Lying on top of him, Abby crossed her arms over his muscled chest and rested her chin on her wrists. "We could still visit Florida. I've always wanted to travel."

He curved one leg over hers, trapping her comfortably. "You? I thought you had an electric shock collar that kept you within Cranberry town limits."

She pinched his side so he yelped. "I've been to New York, you know."

"That far?" His eyebrows raised, but he grinned and tipped back his head for her nibbling kisses across his throat. "Of course I'll take you to Florida. You can meet Ryan. We'll go fishing." His hands stroked her back and her bottom. "We'll bring the kids to Disney World."

"Kids?" She worked her hand under his shirt to the hot, sleek skin beneath. "Peter's?"

He shifted so she could tug his tee over his head. "Aren't we having any?"

She bit her lip. A vision of a little boy with Ash's gray eyes ran through her mind like a remembered dream. "Ash, you're going to make me cry again."

He combed her hair with his fingers, lifted his head to kiss her softly. "Aw, no, don't do that, honey. I've got a better idea. Marry me instead. Marry me, Abby McGuire, because I love you."

She touched his cheek and smiled. "Well, don't think this means I'm going to let you have your way every time, but just this once, I'll say yes."

"Ah, thank God," he groaned.

He rolled her over so the stars filled her vision and his love filled her heart. "Now, about those fireworks . . ."

# ABOUT THE AUTHOR

**Linda Ingmanson** lives with her husband, kids and many pets in the same small Connecticut town where she grew up. Originally (and still) a fan of sci-fi and fantasy, she discovered romance novels through a friend and got hooked. A freelance editor and long-time member of the Romance Writers of America, she enjoys corresponding with other readers and authors of all genres.